0 to 60

0 to 60

SUSAN SLATER

BASCOM
HILL BOOKS

Minneapolis, MN

Bascom Hill Books
212 3rd Avenue North, Suite 290
Minneapolis, MN 55401
612.455.2293
www.bascomhillpublishing.com

ISBN - 978-0-9820938-9-4
ISBN - 0-9820938-9-6
LCCN - 2009922384

Order Fulfilment Center:
Blu Sky Media Group, Inc.
P.O. Box 10069
Murfreesboro, TN 37129
Toll Free: 1.888.448.BSMG (2764)
Phone: 615.995.7072
Fax: 615.217.3088 E-Mail: info@bluskymediagroup.com

Cover Design by CGTechnicalgroup and Alan Pranke
Typeset by James Arneson

Printed in the United States of America

BASCOM
HILL BOOKS

"All right. But you have to get dressed." A note of concern thinned her voice. Time was slipping away. There would be five hundred people in the ballroom downstairs in less than an hour to celebrate Dr. Edward Sinclair's retirement. And their thirty-fifth wedding anniversary, not to mention her sixtieth birthday of last week. Milestones. Were they coming faster now? All bunched together in some ominous package? No, she couldn't think that way. This was another beginning—maybe the best one so far. Certainly one they had both looked forward to.

"Darling, are you feeling all right?" She leaned in, touched his cheek, and felt him tense. Now concern hovered in a line lightly etched, but no doubt permanently embedded, across her brow. Just more lines to match the faint tic-tac-toe grids at the corners of her eyes. And just another reason to think about surgery and lengthen her bangs in the meantime.

"God damn it, Shelly. Sit down."

"I forgot the sheeting on table six. It has a tear." She reached for the phone. His hand quickly covered the receiver.

"Don't. Leave it. Just listen to me."

"If you knew how much I have to do . . . " She let the sentence trail off. What was wrong? The air in the room seemed stale. She looked for a thermostat—prominent in most hotel rooms, but not this one. Would a window open?

"I won't be celebrating tonight. I won't be going downstairs. I won't be going on the cruise Monday morning. I thought I could go through with this but I can't . . . I'd just be prolonging the inevitable."

He sat staring at the floor. Shelly waited, almost afraid to breathe. What did he mean he wasn't going on the cruise? They'd had tickets for six months.

CHAPTER ONE

"I have a love child."

"Ed, I don't have time for games. OK, OK, give me a hint. Movie? Novel?" She continued to slip his tux from its protective covering, twist the hanger handle perpendicular, and stretch to secure it over the closet door. She smiled. They hadn't played a version of *What's That Line?* for years. But back when things were simple—before children, a demanding job with a six-figure salary—they'd open a bottle of wine and just be together. Would it be like that again now that he was retiring?

She glanced at the man sitting on the edge of the bed holding two socks under the dim light of the table lamp. Were they both black? It would matter to him. She distinctly remembered packing two black.

"Let me check them in natural light." She reached out, but he pulled away and dropped the socks on the floor.

"It doesn't matter." He put his face in his hands, then abruptly dropped them to his lap. "Shelly, I'm not playing a game. I'm not playing games any more."

"Shelly, I've asked someone to marry me."

"Marry? You . . . you have a wife." Her stomach fluttered and she swallowed twice. What was he talking about?

"You'll get pretty much what you ask for."

"Ask for?" She could hear her breath coming in labored spurts. Deep breaths. Breathe in, breathe out. This was a joke. Maybe if she moved . . . got air in the room . . . she walked toward the window.

"I won't cheat you. You can have the house—I suggest selling it and investing the money. I can't imagine you wanting to keep it up or even live there for that matter."

"It's our home. We built it." The window didn't budge. Locked down tight. Guess they didn't want you to jump —though it was beyond her how much damage you could do from the second floor. Still, at the moment . . . .

"Shelly, look at me. The house has outlived its usefulness."

She swung back around but kept a hand on the windowsill. Balance. She had to keep her balance. Her hands were suddenly so cold and numb she barely felt the metal. Maybe if she closed her eyes this would all go away. When she opened them Ed would be smiling, standing at her side, murmuring his appreciation for all she'd done in planning the party . . . .

She looked at him sitting on the edge of the bed, averting his gaze, not able to look her in the eye. Instantly, a flicker of anger squashed the queasiness and began to restore warmth to her fingers. This was not a dream; the bastard was dumping her—discarding her like used clothing. Choosing a night of celebration to do so. Well, he wouldn't see her fall apart. Somehow she wouldn't give him that satisfaction. She forced her shoulders back, her head up and willed her voice not to crack.

"A house is like a family member, Ed. The neighborhood . . . all our friends . . . it doesn't outlive its reason for being."

"I'm giving you two million dollars. You can go where you want, build or buy what you want. I suggest something modest and invest the rest—it has to last you for awhile."

"And you?" She was amazed at her steely, emotionless tone.

"I bought a house a few years back. It's in a good school district."

"What does a good school district have to do with anything?"

"I have a four-year-old daughter, Shel. I have a love child."

"You also have two sons, Ed." Maybe a reminder of family would bring him to his senses.

"At twenty-eight and thirty-three, I think they stopped needing me a long time ago."

"Is that what this is all about? Being needed?" Had she not been paying attention? Not noticed the possible hurt of an aging father when sons established their own lives?

"I don't need an armchair psych diagnosis. I fell in love; we've had a child together and we're going to establish a home for our daughter."

"Just like that? Out with the old, in with the new?" Anger again sparked from nowhere but worked to keep tears in check and her voice strong.

"We haven't had a relationship for a long time."

"How can you say that? You're my husband."

"A husband is not a relationship."

Silence. She swallowed, then, "Do I know her?"

"Yes."

She waited. "Well?"

"Shelly, I really think the less we talk about this, the better. Paul Green is handling the details. You can get your own lawyer, but I don't see why you'd want to waste the money. There won't be anything to contest."

"Nothing to contest?"

"I said earlier I'll be generous."

"Who is she?" Why was he dodging the question? Shelly was mentally running down a list of their friends—who was single, who had shown interest—but for the life of her, not one name popped out. Almost all their friends were married—and happily so. But, she thought ruefully, wouldn't they have said the same about the Sinclairs?

He looked away, then back, "Tiffany."

She choked back a laugh. "Oh, come on. This is a joke, isn't it? The receptionist? She's twenty-four? Twenty-five?" And an insult, but she bit back the words.

"Twenty-four."

"You're sixty-three."

"I don't have to be reminded."

"I thought men had midlife crises in their forties."

"I wouldn't call this a crisis—we're very much in love."

"My God, she's thirty-nine years younger."

"I don't think age matters."

"I never thought I'd wake up at sixty to realize the secret to happiness was perky boobs and elastic skin." Because that was the only thing the trailer-trash tart had that she didn't. What had happened to valuing a partner's years of support? Of growing old together with shared memories of family? This wasn't a level playing field.

She watched Ed shrug, "Whatever, Shel. I'm leaving now. Say what you want downstairs or have an announcement made, our friends will understand."

"What is there to understand? A sixty-three-year-old man gets his jollies with a twenty-four-year-old—is going to marry a twenty-four-year-old—and all should be forgiven."

"There's nothing to forgive."

"Then overlooked—maybe that's a better word. When you attend dinner parties with Miss Pop-Tart by your side, our friends will just pretend nothing has happened. Tell me, are you going to get her teeth fixed, or is she going to continue to look like trailer trash?"

"I won't listen to this. Tiffany has been disadvantaged—never had the breaks we've had. I intend to rectify that."

"I just bet you do. You don't see money as a motivator in all this?"

"Tiffany and I have been together for five years. We're confident of our love. I'm through discussing something you don't understand."

"Oh, I understand all right. You fucked a nineteen-year-old who had a baby at twenty. All when you were the ripe old age of fifty-eight and all behind the back of your wife." It was amazing how good the anger felt when it surfaced.

"I'm out of here, Shelly. I won't listen to that kind of language."

"Room service." A couple firm raps accentuated the young-sounding voice outside the door.

"Well, it must be the clowns. Right on cue. I'll just send them in." Shelly stepped forward, the anger bubbling like the bile riding up the back of her throat with no place to go.

"What are you talking about?"

"You wouldn't have a clue. Oh, shit. The champagne—. I'd wanted to toast the start of our new life."

"Not totally inappropriate."

"Fuck you."

She grabbed her purse, opened the door, pushed past the cart with a silver ice bucket, champagne flutes, and assorted canapés, then took the stairs to the parking garage. He'd parked next to her. The sleek black Porsche screamed midlife crisis. Her car, a station wagon overflowing with gifts and table decorations. Table decorations! Oh my God, she'd totally forgotten . . . fifty miniature love boats and scantily clad, plastic, bobble-headed natives in grass skirts. And the sprays of orchids . . . .

She dug in her purse for the spare set of keys to the Carrera. Somehow it just wasn't her problem anymore.

CHAPTER TWO

She prayed he wouldn't come home that night. She couldn't have stood it. But just in case, she sat in the driveway a long time in the fading light, making sure she could get away—back out and rush up the street before she had to see him again. *Him.* She wasn't even allowing herself to use his name. How could this be the end to a life together? Thirty-five years had to mean more. And then inertia set in. She couldn't have moved if she'd had to. Only her mind continued to grind away and entertain little voices that said, *You knew. You had to have known. Think of the trips . . . solo . . . reasons why you couldn't go, too.*

She looked at the house that sat on a slight upward slope above her. The entry was arched with pottery urns on either side. She'd nixed Tara-like columns. Too ostentatious—too un-New Mexico. Though now columns were everywhere. The edges of Corrales, an established township abutting Albuquerque on the northwest, were dotted with stuccoed monstrosities that sported the ever-popular Ionic, Doric, or Corinthian sentinels supporting fake balconies, narrow overhangs, or sweeping porches. No, she was pleased there were no columns. Still, the house was a monster with its three-stall garage and huge second story. A mixture of adobe look-alike flat-roofed construction with a quarry stone entrance. Not a house a single person would want to rattle around in. Not a house for someone alone.

The bigger questions—what would being alone mean? how would it define her life now?—didn't surface. Couldn't surface through the paralysis. She wallowed in the anger, let it take over—she was so afraid of the alternative. She was sixty and back to zero. There was something ominous about zero. But hadn't she gotten to where she was in record time? Zero to sixty in seconds, or so it seemed. So, what had happened to her life? Where had it gone? What was there to show for an investment of thirty-five years? Besides two children now well established and on their own. What had happened to her in that time—how had she lost touch with herself?

She shivered. The March evening had a touch of coolness—spring could come late 5000 feet above sea level. She watched the lights of Albuquerque twinkle on below her. Eventually she felt strong enough to get out of the car, but not strong enough to open the garage, park the car, and walk into the house. Lights on timers blinked on—upper hallway, a downstairs bathroom . . . the kitchen. For all the world, the house looked warm and inviting, like happy people lived there.

How could he do this to her? What gave him the right to start a new life? Leave her behind while he did it? And with someone thirty-nine years younger. She remembered when Tiffany applied for the job. A refugee from Oklahoma where her father did some ranching when he wasn't in jail for beating up her mother. A strange child with a hint of baby chubbiness under the oversized sweater, taffy-colored hair pulled severely into a bun—to look older? Or tame its wiriness? She hadn't graduated from high school but had a GED and begged for a chance. She wanted into the field of medicine. Receptionist/file clerk in a pathology lab hardly seemed to qualify, but she was adamant. Promised she would prove herself.

Shelly couldn't help but smile at the irony of that. So, when had it happened? When had Tiffany stopped being a lost kid and become her husband's lover? It had been Shelly's decision to hire her—at least, she gave the final nod. And that first week of November weather, with Tiffany wearing white fisherman sandals in the winter's first snow; it dawned on everyone that she didn't have another pair of shoes. Allison, the lab manager, remedied that with a pair of hand-me-down boots and sturdy brown loafers. Not the height of fashion, but warm and almost new. If Tiffany knew they had belonged to Allison's recently deceased mother, she didn't let on, but burst into tears at the largesse that was soon followed by hand-me-down skirts and blouses and a really stylish mauve peacoat. The last had been Shelly's contribution—one of those mail-order Bloomingdale's items that had been too small and somehow just never got returned.

Funny how she had always felt so sorry for Tiffany— the prominent, misshapen, stained front teeth with lips that couldn't quite close over them but formed a rosebud opening—sort of nature's Botox. Alluring? Maybe. But it was her eyes—huge, liquid ice-blue with lashes you wanted to tug on to insure they weren't glued in place. They were difficult to get past. Like God had given her one completely arresting feature in an otherwise nondescript, dumpy package. Sort of a "Here kid, the rest is up to you." If the stakes were different, Shelly would be applauding her success. But she was realizing that there were limits to sisterhood.

To be fair, Shelly couldn't fault her for not trying. Tiffany worked hard; she took direction and, once comfortable, offered to help others when paperwork in the lab got backed up. The pregnancy surprised everyone. The two-days-a-week bookkeeping stint in the back room kept the doctor's wife current on the gossip. No one had seen evidence of a boyfriend. There was a lot of speculation—everything from immaculate conception to the possibility that the greasy-haired boy who picked her up every night after work wasn't really her brother.

But then the baby came. Sweet, perfect Marissa. Tiffany ran home three times a day to breastfeed until Shelly put a stop to it and had her just bring the baby into the office. Her sons' baby sister, half sister. Almost a member of the family—and she had been clueless.

She thought of the night when Marissa was a toddler and she'd offered to babysit while Tiffany ran errands. Ed was furious that Shelly had brought her home. Said that the house wasn't childproof, there were too many dangers. He'd locked their twelve-year-old golden retriever in the garage—just in case. In case of what? The baby was enthralled with Sunny's long silken coat. And Sunny hadn't wanted to leave the child's side. Shelly'd laughed at Ed's protectiveness—just a male's reaction to the vulnerability of a tiny female. But she never brought her into the house again. Even then was there a flag on that entry in her brain's Rolodex? Something not quite right. Overreaction. Far too protective? Anger out of proportion with the deed?

This wasn't getting her through the front door, and standing in the middle of the drive was losing its appeal. The orange of the sky had turned a pale peach that outlined the underside of wispy gray clouds. A new moon had popped up between the two towering blue spruce that held court to her left. Didn't this beginning phase always herald starting with a clean slate? Not starting over to, perhaps, reinvent the past, but starting new—fresh, something uncharted— whether she wanted to or not?

The garage lay bathed in shadows. She made a mental note to check the motion sensors; the driveway should have been illuminated by her just pulling in. But she was certain that there would be a hundred small fix-it items— things that would have to be done before the house could be put on the market. Funny. She remembered standing on this spot thirty-five years ago—just six months before the wedding and Ed's graduation. The area later named Sandia Heights. Above the city nestled among chamisa and scrub brush at the base of the mountains. It took a Jeep to maneuver the roughed-out roads. The lot had been a little beyond their means with Ed still in school; so, his parents had stepped in and bought it for them as a wedding present.

The elder Sinclairs—moneyed, snobbish, controlling, and now dead. A car accident with Mame at eighty-three driving the wrong way up an off-ramp in heavy California traffic. Still amazing how she did it, how she could have reached 75 miles per hour in the Lincoln Town "boat" in such a short distance to careen off one car and projectile launch them at a semi. Ed had been devastated—because he lost a father who always had to have the last word, or because both their deaths boosted him to senior status within the family unit and heralded an impending end to his life, too? She suspected the latter. Interesting. It would have been about the time that he'd taken up with Tiffany.

What would his parents have thought of Tiffany? Would Ed be marrying her if they were still alive? Probably not. Shelly in her twenties had been crushed when she overheard Mame say that what Shelly lacked in breeding she'd make up for by being a solid mother. She almost laughed. It would have been worth it to see how Mame would have gotten past Tiffany's teeth. How many times had she heard Mame with her horse-perfect incisors say, "Teeth reflect breeding"? Could she have stood to have the Sinclair blood mixed with Oklahoma crude?

And her own parents. With a start she realized she'd have to call them. But not tell them anything. At ninety and ninety-two, they just wouldn't be able to comprehend. And Pam, the only sibling, twelve years younger and light-years different—she'd have to tell her. None of the telling would be easy. She knew she would very quickly tire of having to go over and over and over the story ad nauseum.

She left the Porsche in the driveway. There was no need to see Ed to exchange cars. He could just come by and trade. And she knew he would. The joke had been that he'd bring the car into the bedroom to sleep with it if he could. He loved the car that much.

She leaned back in its window, pushed the garage opener on the visor, and was appalled when the door's slow roll upward revealed, inch by inch, box after stacked box of . . . what? Did she even know anymore what packed the stall that held Ed's abandoned projects—a potter's wheel, woodworking tools, two sets of seldom-used golf clubs? Would she have to go through those boxes? Couldn't she just hire a backhoe and shovel them into a trash bin? How do you move from someplace that you've lived for thirty-five years?

But she knew she would move. The house felt more like a traitor than a friend, not a safe harbor anymore, just a reminder of what had ended. Was the house part of the two-million settlement? Or an addition? Just the beginning of a myriad of questions—that *her* lawyer could answer. Stephanie Brooks came to mind. She'd call her on Monday. But she'd call the boys over the weekend. And Patrice. Good friends could be as important as family.

She hit the button to lower the garage door and walked through the utility room to the kitchen. The house was so quiet. As she climbed the stairs, she didn't even glance at the chronologically placed photos in matching frames that stretched across the mantle. It wasn't time to face what had been.

At their bedroom door she caught her breath. Ties unknowingly dropped trailed between walk-in closet and bed. Underwear apparently deemed not up to snuff lay discarded in a heap on the floor, likewise, several "work" shirts, and a pair of chinos. Hangers were everywhere. She looked in the closet—the gun safe was empty. Shoes, other than throw-aways, gone. And the Wyeth watercolor above the bed, gone—only a faint outline where it had hung. Likewise, two others by lesser-knowns. She had spent the afternoon at the hotel overseeing preparations while her home was being ransacked.

But what had she expected? Did she think she'd be able to follow him from room to room, exclaiming over this piece or that, debating why she should keep it or give it to the boys? Maybe that would come, but she wasn't sure. A book closed, a door slammed. Ed had moved out. Just like that, he was gone. This felt so final—so carefully planned and so final.

The phone rang. She ignored it, even when it didn't stop but call after call started and, without a pause, linked to another in some unending jingle of bells. Her cell was off, but no doubt it was going through the same electronic gymnastics, storing far more messages than she was interested in retrieving. Their friends would have left the hotel by now, unanswered questions keeping them gathered here and there in the parking garage. How could she reiterate time after countless time what had happened? But starting tomorrow morning, that would be her litany. Fodder for the curious.

She switched off the bedroom light, then on again long enough to grab her pillow. Then grimaced. Patchouli. The scent Ed bathed in. Everything was steeped in it—bed sheets, pillowcases, duvet. She'd sleep on the couch tonight and get an apartment tomorrow. She could not—would not—stay in this house.

The couch was tolerable but smelled faintly of Sunny, now two years dead. She couldn't keep memories of the fat, funny, golden puppy from crowding her mind. A puppy for a teenage son left behind when his older brother went away to college. She wasn't sure when the tears started, but she sat and hugged her knees to her chest and rocked until she had no more energy, then slipped to her side and slept.

She heard Ed exchange the cars around two a.m. She roused and walked to the window to watch. He put the station wagon in the garage but not until after Tiffany had jumped out of the passenger side and slipped behind the wheel of the Porsche. Not a lot of twenty-four-year-olds had $85,000 cars. How could he know without a doubt that it wasn't about money?

Couldn't he recognize himself as Henry Higgins with another Eliza Doolittle? Creating his own child-wife with new teeth and a personal trainer? My, how the stakes for creating a "fair lady" had changed. But wasn't it really about growing old? Fearing the end and blindly needing to procreate and falsely buffer himself against the odds of dying alone? What price did taut young skin command?

To throw away a life with another person who had been your support, was mother to your children—but then, there was a new child. A new mother. The cycle renewed . . . youth revisited. The aging male lion "covering" the young lionesses once a day to assure his place as virile leader.

But a youthful bride wouldn't take the stiffness out of his stride or the hesitation when he stooped to sink into the Porsche's leather. Age couldn't be erased by Viagra—masked, perhaps, but not reversed. She waited until they were well gone before turning on the kitchen light and starting coffee.

She'd begin a list—one of many, probably—but it gave order to what she needed to do. She opened a drawer and dragged out paper and pencil. She placed a number one at the top of the page. What was first? What took priority?

She gathered pencil and paper and walked to the dining room, but stopped in the doorway. The table that would seat twenty comfortably loomed massively in front of her. What do you do with monstrosities? The table, the china cabinet, lighted and large enough to display three twelve-piece place settings of china with accompanying crystal . . . was there a market for these? She abruptly turned and went back to the kitchen and pulled out a stool from under the counter. She'd buy a townhouse, or at least a small house, compact with everything new. It was amazing, but there wasn't one thing she wanted from this house. Not one thing she could stand to live with. Wouldn't the memories finally fade if the reminders weren't in her face? She reached over the counter to pour a cup of coffee.

Sell house. That seemed a firm number one. Buy something smaller—number two. Auction contents? Consign some items? See if boys wanted anything. That stopped her. Of course, that would really be the place to start. But would the heavy walnut pieces really fit with Rachel's airy, pastel décor? Brian and Rachel, childless professionals— both lawyers. Funny how she could have given birth to someone as colorless as Brian. Did all mothers have a favorite? She used to fight it. Deny it. But the feelings of closeness to her youngest were always there. Jonathan. He'd love to have some of the furniture, but what would fit in his apartment? He was such a loner. Quiet. Reflective. Few girlfriends—years away from marriage, probably. An engineer who had chosen research for a career and buried himself in a lab. If there were things he wanted, she'd put them in storage for him.

She caught her reflection in the solid glass panel beside the French doors to the patio. She slipped off the stool to face the glass squarely. It had been a long time since she'd taken stock—looked at the plusses, evaluated the negatives. She would ignore the literally slept-in T-shirt and jeans.

She was medium height with wide shoulders, not enough neck for even the suggestion of elegance. Breasts that had started their pendulous, wayward trek south, lured downward by gravity. She cradled each in her palms, then pushed them upward and held them bunched within the tee's soft cotton and turned sideways. Still C-cups. Still hers. Would implants or lifting help?

The hair—never her crowning glory. Wispy, nondescript medium brown, pulled back and wadded into a ball anchored by bobby pins. Maybe a new color. She had been a redhead all those many years ago. Why not again? And a bob of some sort—modern, chin length, beveled across the back. And tighter jeans. She turned to one side and then the other. The butt was still pretty good—good enough to be defined by denim. And a tummy tuck. That would smooth a waist that was soft and dimpled. But a makeover, that would be first—hair and color.

But quick as a knife stab, she knew what she couldn't be. And that was twenty-four again. There were limits, even with surgery, as to what could be undone. She was sixty. It was beginning to sound like a mantra gone bad. She was sixty. She honestly had to repeat it to make it seem real.

How had it happened? Wasn't it just yesterday that she was pregnant, with one child already in elementary? And had she known the outcome, would she have done things differently? Could she have done things differently? Wasn't the American Dream of two-point-four children, the house in the suburbs, the adoring wife supporting the high-achieving husband a song of the sirens? Luring her to the rocks without warning? Who knew they were whistling Dixie?

What would she do? Not the to-do items on the list in front of her. Those would be completed in a matter of months. No, the "do" that came with the vacuum that was settling around her. The void supported by the empty closet upstairs, the vacant space next to her car in the garage. How much of her life had been defined by another person? Maybe 99.9 percent?

She had never been alone. There had always been someone who came home to her, provided for her and her children. Loved her, or so she thought. She put a hand out and turned in a circle. There were no boundaries, real or imagined. There was just her. She stared once more at her reflection.

At sixty, how much of "self" could be reclaimed . . . recreated? Was it too late for "Once upon a time"? And didn't "Once upon a time" lead to "happily ever after"?

Could she find another mate? Fall in love? Was sixty too late for a fairy-tale ending, let alone a fairy-tale beginning? Did they even make glass slippers in a size ten and a half?

CHAPTER THREE

She startled awake as a golden spear of light shot across her face. The sun had nudged the shadows to the side and burst into the room. She sat up and tried to orient herself—the living room, but why the couch? And then a feeling of incredible loss washed over her. Ed was gone. He'd left her. She closed her eyes, squeezed them closed, willing herself not to cry. Then when she felt that she could stand and actually make it to the kitchen, she fluffed the throw pillows and picked up the cup of cold coffee from the end table.

The kitchen faced the east. Something the two of them had planned—a huge room of warm wood vigas, an eight by ten butcher-block table in the center, black marble counters surrounding a deep garden sink. She wet a paper towel, draped it over her face, and pressed it to her eyes, breathing deeply and enjoying the coolness. Would she miss this? The Wolf ranges—two for entertaining—the Sub-Zero fridge, the warming ovens, the built-in griddles, fryer, and soup cauldron? Maybe. But she really doubted it.

She tossed the paper towel in the trash, dialed Jonathan, tucked the phone under her chin, and busied herself making a second pot of coffee. She assumed he was there last night. Brian and Rachel were in San Francisco, but Jonathan had planned on celebrating with them. He would be wondering what had happened. She was vaguely surprised that he hadn't come by the house to check. Six rings. Seven. She checked the kitchen clock. It was ten to six; surely he hadn't gone jogging this early on a Sunday.

"Hey, Mom, what's up? Sorry I missed the celebration, but I got called out before the fun started. Some lab screw-up that took half the night to figure out."

"Believe me, you didn't miss anything."

"Why are you up so early? Thought you and Dad would be dead until noon. Is anything wrong?"

Just hearing his voice was calming, gave meaning to her world. She took a deep breath and told him quickly what had happened.

"He's an asshole."

"He's your father, Jonathan."

"But God damn him, how can he do this to you?"

Jonathan's anger felt good. Let someone else give voice to her own outrage. She'd managed the entire conversation up to that point without a tear—just a matter-of-fact announcement, a reiteration of Ed's own proclamation of the night before.

"He doesn't see that he's doing anything to me. He thinks he's being generous and I shouldn't have complaints."

"Mom, you know, I think this will blow over. He'll be back."

"Jonathan, didn't I tell you he was getting married? That's not something you say if you're just planning a fling."

"Married? How can he get married?"

"I won't stand in his way. If the divorce isn't contested, it will be dissolved in a few months."

"He can't mean it. He won't marry Tiffany."

"Jonathan, he's Marissa's father."

She thought he started to say something, but stopped. Finally, "He told you that?"

"Yes."

"The fucking idiot."

"He's a balding man fighting an expanding waistline, at the end of his career and desperate to recreate his youth."

"I can't believe you're standing up for him—making excuses."

True. It surprised her, too—how she was quick to defend him. But if she didn't, it might mean that she'd made a terrible error. A thirty-five-year error. Wasn't her judgment on the line, too?

"I'm only trying to understand. Deflect blame. I don't think finger-pointing will make either of us feel better. He's your father; no one can change that."

"I won't have anything to do with him. He can't see what's right in front of him."

"We had a lot of good years."

"And why not more? I thought you two would sail off into the sunset together."

"Sweetie, I've got to run." Suddenly she wasn't so sure she could stay dry-eyed. "I need to look for a place to live."

"Is Dad making you move?"

"No, of course not. I just need something smaller. If you talk to Brian, tell him to call when he gets back."

She flipped the cell shut, then opened it and entered her overfull voicemail. Without listening to any of them, she deleted every message.

"OK. You can't hide forever." Patrice had knocked once before sliding the glass patio door open.

"I'm not hiding."

"Not answering is hiding." Patrice waggled her cell in Shelly's direction. "I left messages until it wouldn't let me anymore."

Shelly shrugged. "I don't think I'm ready to meet the public." It wasn't even seven and Patrice was color-coordinated perfect, blond hair cascading from a tortoise hair clip to brush the shoulders of her pink velour hoodie. In contrast, Shelly acutely felt the lack of a shower.

"Can't be that bad. Speculation has it the two of you got carried away with a little pre-celebration and one of you was just too drunk to meet your guests. Sorry, but the nod went to you. Ed would have been too shy to go it alone, but you wouldn't have been." Patrice poured herself a cup of coffee and pulled a stool out from under the counter. "So, guess we were wrong. Ed must be the one sleeping it off." She gestured upstairs.

"Ed doesn't live here anymore. He's moved in with his fiancée and their child." The silence was deafening and the stunned look on her friend's face was somehow reassuring. What had happened was shocking.

"I know you well enough to know you're not joking. But you and Ed? You've been a couple forever. I can't believe this is happening."

Shelly blinked back the beginning of tears. "Believe it."

"Oh, my God. Just like that. The bastard tells you before the party? What a sweetheart." Patrice took a couple sips of coffee. "Shelly, it isn't the end of the world. Have you thought about counseling? Maybe get the boys together and have a 'come to Jesus'?"

"Too late for that."

"You can't be sure. Oh, hon, I just feel terrible." Patrice hopped down from the stool.

"No." Shelly waved her off. She wasn't ready for "poor you" hugs and pats of condolence. She grabbed a paper towel and blew her nose. Patrice just watched. One test of a good friend was knowing when to shut up.

"Can you talk about it?" Patrice sat back down.

Shelly nodded. Maybe it would do her good. It would be a warm-up for the countless times she'd be repeating the story.

"Do I dare ask who she is?"

"Tiffany."

"You know, I'm not even going to comment. Well, maybe one—is Marissa Ed's child?"

Shelly nodded.

"My God, he must have been fifty-eight when she was conceived."

"I'm not sure the penis stops working even at death."

A laugh, "That's good—you need to show a little humor."

"I need to feel a little humor."

"What do the boys think?"

"I've only talked to Jonathan. He's upset, of course."

"Do you think Ed'll come back?"

"Jonathan thinks so. But what makes everyone assume I'd want him back? I'd even take him back?"

"Habit. Love. Thirty-five years of both."

"Maybe it's time for a change."

"You talk brave now, but it's tough living alone. You've never done it."

"Then I'll just find someone new." The minute the words left her mouth Shelly couldn't believe she'd said them out loud. Did she really want to start over? A man? Now? Maybe.

"That's the spirit. Not the only fish in the sea. You know what they say about falling off a horse."

Shelly couldn't help but think the ground was looking pretty good. And the vision of climbing back on with all its sexual connotations wasn't pretty.

"I know this sounds so selfish, but I'll love having someone to cruise with."

"Cruise?" Had Shelly heard correctly? Yes, and she was pretty certain it didn't pertain to a caper on the high seas.

"Well, you know, follow the pursuit of cute fifty-somethings."

Wouldn't tripping a cute fifty-something to the floor be considered robbing the cradle if one were sixty? Oh my God, how had fifty-year-old men become some sort of geriatric jailbait? San Quentin Quail in Depends. The image wasn't pretty.

"I don't know, Patrice . . . Some things would be just too difficult."

"Let bygones be bygones. This is a chance at a whole new life."

"OK, enough, Miss Pollyanna. You know, just twenty-four hours ago I was happily married."

"Twenty-four hours ago you were deceived into thinking that. Shelly, isn't that Ed?" Patrice was pointing through the glass doors. They could just make out a figure in madras shorts and deck shoes hunched over a riding lawnmower. Both watched as Ed rode the shoulder of the half-acre back and forth over the lip of the rise that dipped sharply where lawn met desert.

"It's barely six thirty. Why is he doing this?"

"Probably came by to talk and is just waiting until I leave. I'm sure you two have things to discuss. Give me a call later—sooner if you need anything. You're two of my favorite people—I just can't believe that this has happened. But I can't wait to see what the future holds." Patrice winked, then blew a kiss and walked out onto the patio. "I mean that, you know, about calling. Don't let things pile up before you talk about them." And then she was gone, around the corner of the house.

Shelly watched Ed park the mower and walk toward her. She remained polite and tried to inject a neutral note into her voice when she called out, "Want a cup of coffee?"

Ed nodded.

She busied herself with getting a mug out of the dishwasher and setting the carton of half-and-half on the counter.

"Why are you mowing the lawn?"

"One less thing for you to do." He took a long time administering to his coffee and didn't meet her eye. "Have you talked to the boys, yet?"

"Just Jonathan."

"Shelly, I don't want you to poison them against me."

"They're adults. They can draw their own conclusions."

"Yeah, but you know what I mean—don't let your bitterness rub off on them."

"Oh, so I'm bitter?"

"Tiffany says—." Too late he realized what he'd said.

"Is she the expert now?"

"I know you don't give her credit but she's wise beyond her years. I think people who have to grow up quickly and take on a lot of responsibility are that way."

"You could have told me your plans—not tell me when you did and let me come home to an empty house."

"The time just never seemed to be right."

"Yes, I'm sure in five years, there wouldn't have been a moment that could've worked."

"Don't be sarcastic, Shelly."

"Who the fuck are you to say what I can or cannot be? Jonathan's right—you're an asshole."

"See? That's exactly what I'm afraid of. I don't want our boys taking sides."

"They'll make up their own minds, Ed. They're adults. They know right from wrong."

"Right from wrong," Ed sighed. "There's never been any gray area for you, has there, Shel? Everything is just one extreme or the other. You refuse to see how I feel—see what I need."

"And me? What do I feel? What do I need?"

"You won't need for anything. I've told you that."

"Money will keep me warm at night? Make love to me?"

"Shel, there hasn't been much of that for a very long time."

"Servicing two of us just a bit too much for the aging?"

She wanted to draw a hash mark on the wall when she saw him grimace. One for her side. How could he be this unfeeling? Had he always been? Hadn't there been a slightly bashful boy-man who had wooed her, promised to honor and obey until death, slipped a band on her finger in front of two hundred people? Oh, God. What would she do with the wedding pictures? A celebration that had become a sham? A ring that had no meaning?

She absently twisted the band, then pulled the ring off. The stark white indentation underneath seemed to scream "newly divorced—on the market again." Maybe if she rubbed in a little self-tanning lotion. She placed the ring on the counter.

"You know, I had counted on the two of us being friends." Ed poured a healthy dollop of cream into his coffee before looking up.

"What gave you that idea?"

"I think that's what you have left after thirty-five years."

"No, I think what you have left after thirty-five years of living together, raising children together is a solid understanding of one another, a history of helping one another . . . loving one another. A time to look forward to living out the last part of your lives together."

"It's no one's fault, Shel. I'm not blaming you."

"Not blaming me?" She hated the elevated screechy quality to her voice. No tears. No screaming. No throwing. Those would be her rules. No matter how difficult to follow.

"Discussing our relationship isn't going to change anything. We had some good years—I don't deny that—but it's time to move on."

"Some . . . good years? A handful out of the thirty-five? What would that be . . . four or five? Maybe nine or ten? Looking back, I'm not sure which ones those were, Ed. Could you help me here?"

"When you look at it, if you really don't know, that could be a major part of your problem."

"My problem?" No screaming, no screaming, no screaming.

"I can't believe that you didn't see this coming. Our friends aren't surprised."

Their friends? Had he talked to people, shared his plans? Apparently. She didn't think she'd ever hated anyone in her life, but right at that moment she did.

"You need to take what you want out of this house and leave."

"What I need to do is finish the lawn."

"No. The lawn is my responsibility. This is my house. I will decide what it needs and when."

"Don't be ridiculous, Shelly. This house is an asset; you have to keep it up. You need to get top dollar for it. I have painters coming tomorrow to do the trim around the garage."

"Cancel. Take what you want this morning or this afternoon and don't come back."

"You're being unreasonable. You're not thinking. I'll just—"

"I will get a restraining order—you can and will be removed from the premises if I say so."

"You're crazy."

"I don't care what label you put on it. You're history."

"Paul Green will—"

"Threats don't become you, Ed. What you leave, I'll dispose of. You might want to call the boys and go through things together."

"This is absurd. These are your things, too. This house is your life—filled with all the moments—"

"I only want to be free—free of you, free of everything that reminds me of you."

"You'll change your mind. You're just saying this in the heat of the moment. You're sixty, Shel. Isn't that just a little late for freedom? Some latent flower-child escapism?"

She ignored the barb. "I'm taking what clothes I want now—I won't be back to live here. What you don't take, I'll put into storage or sell."

After all, the antiques and leather furniture had been Mame and Ed Senior's. What wasn't divvied up she would auction. She didn't want the Persian rugs or crystal from Germany or a hundred other memory-inducing *objets d'art*. What she needed to do was reclaim herself. But she wasn't even certain that she'd recognize that self if she flushed her out in the open.

Ed gave one of those "whatever" shrugs, expansively lifting his hands in the air, and turned back to the riding lawn mower. She didn't say anything. Had he ever listened to her? Had they always just gone their own ways after a perfunctory sharing of opinions that had no meaning? Odd. Her life as a mime.

She watched him bounce away from her, maneuvering the mower back toward the edge of the lot. When had he gotten old? The slope of his shoulders, the skin once taut across elbows and knees now puckered and rolled. And when had he stopped loving her? But maybe more importantly—when had she stopped loving him? What a thought, she chided herself. Of course, she loved him— had loved him. He was her husband, the father of her children, a terrific provider . . . yet not one of those terms said love. Not one. Was the emotion that she seemed so afraid to let surface one of relief?

She took a deep breath. She was hurt. She felt discarded—tossed aside for someone so very much younger. Her self-worth—pride in who she was—had suffered. But these were ego-governed losses. Why couldn't she conjure up the caring, the emotion-laden need and wanting for another human being? The tingle of excitement that would emanate from her very core making them inseparable, linking her with this soul mate in that bond of never needing to even define what was between them?

Because it was dead. It didn't exist. And it was relief that she felt. Pure and simple. Letting go of something that she assumed was there—never questioned, just assumed. Thought somehow it was her right to love and be loved— the mother, the supporter, the unflagging cheerleader for the team. How could she have been so blind?

But would she know love? Recognize it, not perhaps on a white charger, but dragging its feet from a Shetland pony? Was Patrice onto something? Would Shelly be happy riding with the hounds running some fox to ground? But what would it feel like to be loved? Again. Because she had been once upon a time, if not by Ed then by Max, the Korean War vet, twenty-eight to her eighteen, who was so afraid of her getting pregnant that he taught her everything there was to know about oral sex ,or so he said—how to give pleasure and to receive. And just short of carrying her knee pads in her backpack that freshman year of college so many years ago, she became a woman under his tutelage. Someone who loved to touch and be touched and could offer her body in a spirit of abandonment and enjoy—truly enjoy—being a sensual, sexual being. Could she go there again? Or was there some kind of roadside marker that said she'd passed "Go"? And couldn't return. Was being sixty such a marker?

Yet, a smile caught at the corners of her mouth. It was exciting to think of making love. Ed was right; there had been precious little of that recently. Precious little of that ever. With a start, she repeated that thought. Theirs had not been a sexual marriage—not one driven by the excitement of two bodies coming together, the crash of cymbals, stallions pawing the air, waves hitting the shore.

They had waited the perfunctory two years before presenting the world with Brian—conceived in the basement of the elder Sinclairs' home, a cheap, safe haven while Ed finished medical school before they took on the debt of building a new house. She remembered closing the furnace vents if she even thought that Ed might get amorous, not something his parents would want to listen to, their frolicking naked, sprawling across the feather bed of his grandparents. No, there was something inhibiting about screwing literally underneath his parents. There had been far too many discussions of "duty" always ending in a long-suffering stance by Mame that indicated "it" was not something that would ever be done for fun. So typical for her generation. And explained Ed's being an only child?

Shelly remembered the night the two families had rented *Pretty Woman*. At the infamous piano scene, Mame had made gagging sounds and rushed from the room. When Shelly had followed, thinking Mame was ill, she found her busily preparing a new round of drinks in the kitchen. "I knew you wouldn't be able to watch either. There's no word for that. Not even depravity." Shelly didn't contradict but silently toasted ol' Max.

Shelly's first sexual "problem" with Ed was who could initiate. He wanted, no, demanded that sex be only at his bidding. The rigors of school and the internship forced sex to take a back seat—and killed all spontaneity. He didn't feel "right" about his wife asking for "it." And "going down" on him? Well, that was something "good" girls didn't do. A few times when he was drunk, he'd asked for it. So, she opted for the life of a doctor's wife—money, prestige . . . security. Had these been enough? Was it normal for a newlywed wife to curl up next to her husband in bed and pleasure herself—careful that her husband was breathing evenly? Probably not.

CHAPTER FOUR

She sacked up the wilted orchids and dumped them in the large roll-away garbage bin at the edge of the drive. The grass-skirted dolls and thatched huts went next. She didn't even flinch. She had to stop having second thoughts—she couldn't go back, undo something that had been set in motion. Even her best friend was telling her to start fresh. Her marriage was over. She was not going on some extended cruise with a husband. She was starting out on her own. At sixty. There it was again, the mantra—she added "get a grip."

A quick shower, a change of clothes . . . she threw cosmetics in a bag, a hairdryer and five days worth of underwear. Then gathered an armload of jeans and tops, slipped into a pair of denim-colored clogs, and loaded the car. She'd run the station wagon through a car wash and get rid of the stale flower smell. Today would be a good day to look at houses. She might look near downtown. Some of the houses near Old Town were great buys. And small. She was finished with rambling five bedroom/four bath monstrosities. The house had always been a little too big for them—in the beginning there had been the hope of another couple children; but it simply wasn't meant to be. She slipped behind the wheel, and started the car. Anything to get away from the house . . . and Ed . . . and memories.

She hadn't backed all the way to the end of the driveway before her cell went off. She dug in her purse and checked the number. She was more than a little tempted to just not answer. Was she up to rehashing everything for Pam? No, not yet. But still, family was family. She flipped it open.

"You have to do something." Shelly moved the phone away from her ear.

"Well, hello to you, too, Pam." With Pam there was always a note of hysteria—just something a bit below the surface roiling away, ready to erupt.

"Shelly, listen to me. I just left Mom and Dad's. You won't believe it. Dad's put newspapers on all the furniture—the chairs, even across the foot of the bed."

"Calm down. Is he painting the house again?"

"Shelly, I'm not talking about painting. I think someone's incontinent."

"Come on, Pam. Someone's wetting on the furniture?"

"It smells worse than urine."

"What did you do?"

"Nothing. What could I do? I'm calling you."

She hoped the groan was inaudible. Of course, Pam's idea of taking action would be to call someone. Usually, she was the someone of choice. But not now. How could she handle one more catastrophe? "This is not a very good time, Pam."

"Well, I don't think things are just going to wait until they're convenient for you. I'm telling you, he's put newspaper on all the furniture. And the smell—you won't be able to stand it."

"I'm sure it's just musty from being closed up."

"Shel, you're not listening—the house stinks! Somebody's incontinent. Maybe both of them. And Mom . . . all she did was repeat the same old thing."

"Which was?"

"'It's a good life, if you don't weaken.'"

"Some truth to that."

"She must have said it twenty times in a half hour. And I know she didn't remember. Then she started in on 'I'm crazy as a loon.' She'd stop and ask me, 'What's a loon?' I'd tell it was a bird that looked like a duck—I even drew her a picture—but two minutes later, it was the same question. Shelly, she didn't know my name."

"Did she know who you were? That you were her daughter?"

"No."

"She masks so much when I call them. It never dawned on me, but she must mimic Dad. If he says Shelly, then she just repeats it."

"Shel, I haven't told you the worst part, but you need to see for yourself."

Shelly absently wondered how much worse it got. Was this just melodramatic Pam or had their parents slipped—maybe to the point of needing permanent care?

"Where are you now?"

"On my way back to Tulsa."

Shelly made herself count to five. Dump and run. Typical Pam. "How did you leave things?"

"Like I found them. I didn't say anything. They won't listen to me anyway."

That was probably true. Not that Shelly could do better, but she would be more forceful.

"And you know Dad's still driving. I don't think he has a license anymore, and the registration sticker wasn't on the tag. I think it's expired."

"What do you want me to do?"

"Go back there. Maybe it's not as bad as I think. Shelly, they're so pitiful. Mom . . . Shelly, she hasn't taken a bath in six months."

"How do you know that?"

"Oh, Shelly, you have to go back. You can do something. How long has it been since you've seen them?" There was muffled crying, and Shelly waited while Pam blew her nose.

"Five months, no, maybe six or seven." The twice-a-year visit to see her parents had fallen to Shelly the last few years. Ed had been too busy. With a little jolt, she realized just how busy he'd been. And what had kept him in Albuquerque. The months in between Shelly's visits were Pam's obligation. Neither child enjoyed the scrutinizing of their cantankerous father. They were never quite good enough. But had she had blinders on? Had she missed these ominous signs of lives declining? Very possibly. "OK, Pam. I have a few things here that I need to do first." Understatement. Where would she find the time? But if things were that bad . . . "I'll try to get a flight before the weekend."

"This is so much easier for you to handle—you're the one married to a doctor. Be sure Ed knows what to expect."

"Ed won't be able to go with me."

"Shel, I think if you told him what's going on, he'll make sure he's there."

"I'll see." Somehow, this wasn't the time to go into the last twenty-four hours of her life.

"And Shel, in case you don't know, Costco sells caskets and urns now."

"What?"

"They are way cheaper than the local mortuary. I checked. You can get an urn for under a hundred. And they have overnight delivery."

"Pam, Mom and Dad aren't dead yet."

"I think it's best to plan ahead, don't you?"

Shelly had nothing to say to that. They said their goodbyes and she sat at the end of the drive before turning toward the city. Costco? Could Pam be right? And overnight delivery? At the same time you purchased six months' worth of toilet tissue, and a year's supply of mayo, you could add a coffin to your bill? Simply too bizarre.

But home . . . newspapers on the furniture? Could it be that bad? Yes, she supposed it could. Perhaps her father had had a stroke. And her poor demented mother . . . If she was as bad as Pam made out, then the challenge of taking care of her would be too much for her father. She took a deep breath. Of course, she should have seen this coming—but now? The timing was rotten.

It was just one more thing to add to the list. She'd try to get a flight into Wichita on Thursday. And in the next four days, she'd call nursing homes. If things were desperate, then that was the only way to go. But she'd have a fight on her hands. At best, her father was obstinate. And proud. She'd suggested Meals on Wheels and he'd thrown a fit, saying he'd always refuse charity. No explanation could change his mind.

She had had the discussion with him a hundred times about what he wanted to do once he was unable to care for himself or care for her mother. Fleetingly, she thought of asking Ed—out of habit? Because he would be able to take charge? Well, she'd have to get used to taking charge, now. There was no backup . . . unless she called Pam to meet her there. That might be best. Present a united front.

She turned onto I-25 and kept pace with the early-morning Sunday traffic. She'd lived in Albuquerque long enough to see it bloom to half a million people, its freeways having to be overhauled twice to meet the burgeoning growth. She took the I-40 loop west and exited at Sixth Street. She'd look around downtown just to see what was on the market and then get a room at the Doubletree. Patrice would have offered her spare room, but that wouldn't give Shelly the alone time that she needed. A time to plan . . . examine where she was, where she wanted to go. No, she was not going home. In fact, the sooner there was a replacement for "home," the better.

CHAPTER FIVE

Did she believe in things happening that were just plain meant to be? Of course. It drove Ed nuts. Poor, practical Ed with his "A leads to B" thinking. She wasn't the black/white thinker—her life was Technicolor compared to his. When she turned a block too soon and ended up on a short half street of tile-embellished cottages and saw the real estate agent pounding an open house sign into the yard of the one on the corner, she stopped. It was perfect. A Frank Lloyd Wright wannabe with original glass, a Rose of Sharon bush beside the enclosed front porch just sprouting leaves, blue tile above the stoop to match the denim and violet trim around the windows . . . she was in love.

"Come take a look." The agent, a woman with big hair and a too short skirt—the mark of the real estate maven—smiled brightly. Like the ones that beamed selling prowess from news racks filled with brochures hawking the latest subdivision. Women of fifty using photos from thirty.

Shelly parked at the curb. She could see a garage behind and a short red-brick driveway. Blue-gray plank fencing ran along the sidewalk and circled the back. The house was compact, nestled under an apricot tree and a desert Cyprus. Several flowering shrubs hugged the sidewalk. The house had been well loved. The wrought-iron fence cut the corner at a diagonal, flanked by half a dozen mature yuccas. Everything was green and budding and inviting.

"Are you working with an agent?"

"No. I hadn't thought that far ahead." Shelly followed the woman into the house. Gleaming hardwood floors echoed the click of the Realtor's heels.

"Charming, no?"

Shelly was speechless. Two floor-to-ceiling double doors opened off the dining room onto a deck that circled the back and side of the house. If the place was small, this invitation to extend the living area beyond mere walls opened the entire house, magnifying its size.

"I'll take it."

"You haven't seen the rest. The kitchen floor needs to be replaced. Ditto, the bathroom. There's a basement—"

"I don't need to see any more."

"Well, I'm not the listing agent. I'm only holding the open house. Let's write it up." The woman beamed her approval.

"What are the chances that we could close in three weeks?"

"Excellent. The sellers live in Santa Fe but will be moving to California in a month. I think that time frame would suit their plans nicely."

Before Shelly left she had inspected the basement, the garage, the two bedrooms—both with floor-to-ceiling French doors—and the bathroom with a deep, straight-sided tub that called out for long, soaky baths. And she'd called Patrice, then wished she hadn't. Yes, there could be hidden problems. Yes, it was a quick decision—no, not exactly "snap," but a bit sooner than she'd expected. Didn't one have to "strike while the iron was hot?" Oh my God, she heard her mother's voice. Yes, she'd be careful. Yes, she'd pay for inspections. She promised to call Patrice in the morning and hung up. So, what was her reasoning? Quite simply, the house felt good. And she was going to trust her intuition.

She'd written it up for cash—she'd borrow against the divorce settlement—but already the sense of freedom was invigorating. This house was hers. All hers. It was ready for her to make memories, not bury them.

The week started like a whirlwind. She'd discovered that keeping busy was the best antidote for depression. The loneliness could be almost palatable at times. So, first there had been the hair appointment—color and cut. She still couldn't walk past a plate-glass window or mirror without tossing her head just to watch the red gold sleekness fan out, then swirl back to lie perfectly along her chin line. The bangs were left a half inch below her eyebrows. She'd have to learn to not bat at them and to put her mascara on before she fixed her hair. And color? Warm bronzes with copper eye shadow and a blush of sienna. She looked great and she felt alive!

Maybe if she had done this before now . . . but when the "maybe" meant that she might still be with Ed, she was learning to squash those thoughts before they even drifted full blown to the surface. She wasn't with Ed. She would never be again and new hair and makeup wouldn't have kept him. There were things that she had to let go of . . . she hadn't awakened last night at two or three to cry herself back to sleep. Life was getting better.

After a quick trip to her favorite Scandinavian shop, she picked out couches, chairs, tables, rugs, and beds to be delivered the day of closing and hired an artist to paint the interior. Her bedroom would be salsa; the study, pumpkin; the kitchen, wheat with warm brown, and brick red Italian tile on floor and counters. Tuscany tile accents of fields of sunflowers and lavender and poppies would ring the sink on one side of the room and the stove and counters on the other. A butcher-block island with hanging cobalt blue glass lights swinging above, two Mexican thatched-seat stools snugged up against the blocky table, and the room would be complete. There were no Wolf ranges, or walk-in freezers, and she didn't even care.

She met with Stephanie Brooks on Tuesday. After the first round of condolences, Stephanie sketched out what she thought Shelly should get—the house in addition to the two million, equal division of art work or compensation if Shelly decided not to take any pieces with her, the same for silver and china. And the car. The Porsche represented a substantial investment and it was paid off—Shelly was entitled to roughly forty thousand. Shelly's excuse of, "But that's Ed's car," brought a frown and an admonishing, "Get realistic. You're not his mother; stop taking care of him."

Shelly found herself tuning Stephanie out as she continued down the list. It wasn't that she didn't appreciate the gravity of the situation—she needed to be aware of her legal rights—but she also needed to establish a life. And sometimes just walking away had great appeal. She didn't want to fight. She didn't want the name-calling, the belittling, the blame. She needed to have her memories intact, not smeared, or hinted at that she'd seen the thirty-five years through rose-tinted glasses. Stephanie was finally finished. She would talk with Paul Green and get back. More condolences and Shelly was on her way to the dry cleaners.

By Thursday she hadn't talked to Ed, but had filled Brian in on Wednesday. Ever so slightly, he had seemed to support his father—to take his side while being stiltedly polite. The conversation had been brief. By Friday morning her cell had stopped its incessant ringing. There must be a new, more exciting topic for discussion out there than the demise of the Sinclairs' marriage. So, in a mere five days there was nothing left to do but make the reservation and go home—the home where she was raised. The "home" that Thomas Wolfe so aptly pointed out you couldn't go to again. Shelly knew he told the truth.

CHAPTER SIX

Everyone had to be from somewhere. That wasn't original with her or even her father, but it's what she heard every time she groused about her birthplace. She supposed that if that somewhere just happened to be Kansas, you were roll-of-the-dice lucky or unlucky, entirely depending upon your point of view and whether or not your name was Dorothy. Going home never got easier. It astounded her that at sixty she still was reluctant to face her parents, face the inevitable criticism. She still could feel a rush of quiet desperation by the second night in a town that probably gave birth to the term "one-horse."

Her birthplace had been the bloodiest town in the West for one year back in the 1890s. Then cattle drives were diverted to Dodge and the frontier continued west. The town rejoiced when the Carnegie folks bought the corner property just off the main street tracks and built a library. The town's red-light district lost its center. And, perhaps, its heart. She didn't remember hearing any stories from her grandmother about men gone wrong after the whorehouse was torn down. Building a library was an investment in the community—an investment in goodwill.

But railroad men always got in trouble. They were the civilized vagabonds, the travelers with a sweetheart at every stop . . . the romancers of Harvey Girls. The precursors of airline stewardesses, these young and pretty girls worked the restaurants along the Santa Fe line, promised not to marry for up to a year, and then took off, mated, and peopled the West. Young women above reproach in stiff crinoline and wrap-around white aprons. Her grandmother had been a Harvey Girl before she married a railroad man.

But it was the other side of the family—the people who adopted her mother—that could boast of wildness running through their veins. Womanizers, daredevils. Men who spent money faster than it was made. A grandfather who divorced his wife to be with his lover. And this in 1929. Only to die a year later, the year his only child was graduating from high school, already a married woman herself—a secret well kept. It was, perhaps, the only daring thing Shelly's mother ever did . . . something that smacked of deceit and double-dealing. She ran off and got married. At seventeen. Without telling her mother or another living soul.

There were three women in her family who had defined her life: Shelly's grandmother and the woman's two sisters, born in the latter 1800s, who would share only one natural child among them. Shelly's mother had come from the elite, albeit stigmatized, home for the wealthy unwed called The Willows. A Kansas City fixture until 1969.

Her grandmother had taken the train to Kansas City in March of 1913, having signed papers to adopt a red-haired boy, only to be captivated by a five-day-old, dark-haired girl. The child, who would resent her ignoble beginnings all of her life, refused her papers when offered at The Willow's closing. "If they didn't want me, then I don't want them." The imbedded anger and bitterness defined her mother's life. Or did. Shelly wondered how she would find her now.

Small town stories. As a child, she'd sneak into the bathroom and press her ear against the heat register that was shared with the kitchen. The "women"—her grandmother, her grandmother's sisters, and her mother—would shell peas or stem strawberries and discuss local current events.

It was the stories of Marie, her grandfather's sister, that fascinated Shelly the most. Even more than the hushed discussions of how the local priest had run off with the Quilty girl. Surely, double damnation leading to a spit-roasting of both in hell. That image had bothered Shelly as a child. Would sharp stakes really be run through their bodies to be crank-turned by an attendant with a forked tail?

But Marie—a little girl's answer to the princess search, that need to find someone in one's lineage who had been beautiful—was worthy of a child's imagination. It was darkly hinted that Marie had gypsy in her. The one picture that Shelly'd ever seen seemed to attest to this. Wild black hair erupted from her head in a tangle of unmanaged curls, and the lace-up boots showed much shapely leg between their tops and the bottom of a white petticoat. She was a big woman, five feet eleven, and favored off-the-shoulder peasant blouses and floor-sweeping skirts of dark prints with red sashes—tied at the waist or around the forehead.

Marie's problems started when her fiancé didn't

return from WWI. "Didn't return" and "got killed" were not the same. Shelly learned this when as a child she innocently asked if he were buried in the cemetery at the end of First Street. There were hints that he didn't return to this town. Not that the war caused his demise. But it did seem to be the demise of Marie.

The "trolley jumped the tracks after that," as her grandmother would say. An early euphemism for just plain crazy. Marie developed a fondness for dancing naked down Main Street. "Damned good dancer," Shelly's uncle had once chimed in when the sisters were discussing yet another episode. He was, of course, instantly tsked into silence. In the spirit of a Zelda Fitzgerald skinny-dip in a fountain, Marie would bare all and waltz the one-mile length of the town's center unless the local sheriff picked her up first. Which was often. Harry Goodman, swarthy and brusque, boasted that he served the best food within fifty miles—given that it was in jail and prepared by his wife, Lottie. It still helped him win election after election on the fact that he didn't just lock people up; he took care of them. For many of the local ne'er-do-wells, those three squares were lifesavers.

Marie, on the other hand, had family. Family that had a reputation to protect. So, they started locking her up at home. The result wasn't exactly what had been antici-pated. She began tearing her hair out in clumps until finally she was found with a belt around her neck, feet swinging free, one end secured to a willow branch. Dead at thirty-seven. For love? Shelly always wondered about that. Could a man be worth hanging yourself over? Or was it ego? He hadn't returned to her. Whichever, the story always brought an unbearable sadness.

A hometown always had stories, tales that lived on in

the telling. Would it have been different if she had been born in Dubuque, or Omaha or Lincoln? She thought not.

The plane landed late. She had just enough time to grab a rental car, find one auto-parts store open, buy a Club to lock the steering wheel of her father's car, and drive the thirty-five miles north to a motel. She would face her parents in the morning, in the light and after a night's rest. The bed with its tilted, lumpy mattress felt like heaven. She didn't remember closing her eyes until the bouncy tune from her cell brought her upright.

"Shelly, why didn't you tell me what was going on?"

"Ed?" A quick look at the bedside clock read 11:25. She'd probably been asleep for forty minutes.

"I'm catching a flight out there in the morning. This isn't something that you should face alone."

"Why would you come here?"

"Because you need help. I can talk 'doctorese' and help you get all this sorted out."

"Ed, it's sorted."

"Pam—"

"You talked to Pam?" Of course, or how would he have known? She was beginning to wake up, to think clearly. She sat up and hugged her knees to her chest, then leaned against the headboard, the cell squished between ear and shoulder.

"Yes, she called. Couldn't believe that I didn't know."

"I suppose you told her about us?"

"Of course. I don't understand why you hadn't."

You wouldn't, Shelly thought to herself. How could he be so obtuse? It was more than just a male thing.He really didn't understand feelings. He didn't see pain or its causes. But had she ever expected a pathologist to have a bedside manner? Not something a cadaver demanded.

"I also want to talk with you about the house."

"What house?"

"Our house—former house."

"And?" Instinct made Shelly pay attention. Did she trust him? Not really. His allegiance was placed elsewhere. She shifted the phone to her right hand.

"Tiffany and I want to buy it. We'll meet the appraised value. It will make things easier for all of us. You can move things out at your leisure. You won't have to put any money into it upfront. We'll take it as is."

"What happened to the house in the perfect school district?"

"I'm not sure that's the house that Tiffany sees us in—sees us expanding in. We both hope there will be more children."

"What if I don't want to sell it to you?"

"That is the most asinine, childish comment—I'm not even going to acknowledge it with a reply."

"Whatever."

"Shelly, stop it. Do I have to remind you that at the moment the house is in both our names? I'm bending over backwards to save you time and money and this is the thanks I get. I'm dismayed at your behavior. I counted on you for more."

"And may I say the same to you."

She snapped the phone shut and sat up straight. Did she really care if Tiffany and Ed had the house? It rankled. But how much was spite? Fighting Ed's superiority? Wanting at some primal level to screw Tiffany and her "expanding family"? The expanding family comment hurt. If the ovaries weren't kicking out eggs once a month, did that lessen Shelly's worth? Apparently, yes. It wasn't quite time for the ice floe. Not yet. There was a lot of life in front of her—even at sixty. But she needed to get over base reactions. Not becoming. Still, it was tough to overcome the anger. Ed had to get out of her life. She needed to heal, establish her own life, find her identity and have the time alone, unencumbered, to begin that search.

Tomorrow would be a long day. After she went to her parents' house, she'd call Pam—insist that she drive back up from Tulsa if things were bad. Shelly dreaded what she might find. She could only hope that Pam had exaggerated.

CHAPTER SEVEN

But she hadn't. The minute Shelly stepped inside her parents' house, she barely kept from gagging. Hugging her mother meant taking a deep breath first and holding it. She almost cried out when she saw the scarf on her mother's head—with two inches of hair growing through the loose cotton weave. No wonder Pam had said their mother wasn't taking baths. Her mother could not have removed that scarf in over four months.

There were newspapers everywhere—even on the piano bench. Shelly chose an overstuffed chair and started to remove the papers, but when she saw the stains, she remained standing.

"We need to get someone in here to help you clean, Dad."

"Clean? Everything is just fine. Mom and I don't need you coming back here telling us what to do."

"I'm talking about steam-cleaning—have the carpets done, the furniture and drapes. The type of cleaning that needs to be done once a year. The kind that you or I can't do—don't have the equipment to do."

"That's a lot of nonsense. Just who's going to pay for this cleaning?"

"I imagine you can, Dad."

"I don't throw money away like others I know."

Shelly didn't take the bait. She always thought her father resented the discretionary income that she and Ed had later in life.

"I'm going to take Mom into the clinic Monday morning for a checkup."

"No, you're not. I won't allow it."

"Dad, how long has it been since Mom's had a physical?"

"Don't need one. They just poke around until they find something wrong. Have to, to justify the prices they charge. Sent her home two years ago with a quart of cranberry juice. Said she had a urinary tract infection. That cost me over four hundred dollars."

"Year before last? Mom, did you have a physical this year? You used to always see Dr. Allen in January."

"Oh, I'm sure I did."

"But you don't remember?"

"Remember what?"

"If you had a physical."

"It's a great life if you don't weaken."

"I know, Mother, but we're talking about your getting a physical."

"A what?"

"Your annual examination by a doctor."

"She don't need to be seen by any doctor. I'm telling you, it's a waste of good money."

This was getting her nowhere. "Dad, I am going to take Mom to get her hair done."

"Thelma Reese is dead."

"I'm sure there are other hairdressers in town." Shelly had no idea how she would get her mother bathed and dressed to go out.

"Well, you're not going to do it. We don't want meddlers. You just take yourself and your concerns and march right on out of here, Missy."

Maybe if she changed the subject. "When Pam was here, she was afraid that your car registration had expired. Is everything up to date, Dad?"

"Of course. Why would she say such a thing?"

"Don't know, Dad. But I think I'll check." Shelly walked into the hall, then through the kitchen and into the garage. The ten-year-old red Pontiac had a new-looking crease down the passenger side door and a dent on the driver's side rear bumper. And no current registration sticker on the plate. She'd have to call and check insurance.

"See. Everything's just like it should be." Her father stood in the doorway to the kitchen.

"No, Dad, it isn't."

"I don't understand why you're lying."

"Come look. There's no registration sticker."

"I don't have to listen to this. I think it's high time you go home. Your mother and I don't need you around here trying to cause trouble."

"Dad, you're going to be in trouble if you don't take care of things like your car registration. Did you renew your driver's license in January?"

"Of course I did."

"If it has expired, you'll have to take a test to renew it."

"I'm telling you everything's just fine."

"No, Dad, this is less than 'fine.'" She pointed at the plate.

"You're a liar. You just come snooping around here where you're not wanted."

"It's a good life if you don't weaken." Her mother stood on tiptoe to peer into the garage from behind her father. "Now, who used to say that?"

"You did, Mom."

"No, I never said that."

"Dad, I'll check on your auto insurance tomorrow. You have to have your license, the registration, and the insurance current. You can't drive without all three up-to-date."

"Oh? And just who says so? Who's going to take away my car?"

"The police will, Dad. They'll stop you, ask to check the paperwork, and impound the car if it's not current. You'll be treated to a ride home by the police."

"Well, I can treat people to a little surprise all my own."

"What do you mean by that?"

"Nobody's going to come in here if they're looking down the barrel of a .410."

The childish bravado would be funny if it were someone else's father. It was time to leave and call Pam. There was nothing more to do here unless she wanted to become confrontational, and that wouldn't get her anywhere. They needed to act, and they would need help to do it.

"I'm going to go now, Dad." She pressed the button to raise the garage door.

"When you come back, you bring Ed with you. Women shouldn't travel by themselves. Too many things can happen. I'm surprised he lets you come here by yourself."

"It's a good life if you don't weaken." Her mother blew a kiss in her direction.

Shelly waved to her parents and climbed into the rental car. Everything Pam said was true—but would she have been prepared for the two inches of hair protruding through the scarf on her mother's head even if Pam had told her? Could she have believed it without seeing it? And Pam hadn't mentioned the dime-sized growth on the side of their mother's nose. Things had gone wrong—terribly wrong. The tears rolled down her cheeks and Shelly didn't try to hold them back.

At first she didn't see him leaning against a pale cream Impala parked squarely in front of her room. Ed. Shelly fought back the urge to ram his rental car or try to hit him. It steadied her to give into the ludicrous at least in thought, then make a rational decision to just pull in alongside, get out of the car, and walk to her room.

"Where have you been? I've tried to reach you ten times on your cell."

"I had it turned off."

"That's obvious. But why?"

"I wasn't expecting any calls and I didn't want to be interrupted."

"Have you talked with Pam?"

"Exactly what I'm going to do right now."

Shelly ran the card-key through the reader, opened the door, and closed it behind her. She didn't care what Ed did. She would look at nursing homes while waiting for Pam. She heard Ed's car start and fought an urge to peek through the curtains. Would he go home? Somehow, she didn't think so.

"It was awful, wasn't it?" Pam answered on the first ring.

"Yes. We need to put them in a home. They just can't take care of themselves."

"Dad's going to be impossible."

"We'll have to work around that."

"How?"

"I don't know yet. We need to get Mom in to see a doctor—there's a growth on the side of her nose that could be a carcinoma."

"Didn't I tell you about that?"

"No. Or I missed it."

They talked for a few minutes longer and Pam promised to be there by late afternoon. Shelly would not have believed that the thought of having her sister with her could be so comforting. But it was.

Homes seemed to escalate in price in direct proportion to the absence of urine smell. The more antiseptic, lemon-Pledge fresh the foyer, the more one would pay to live there. And "live" was a questionable term. Largesse also seemed to be measured in the number of pianos that crowded dining areas, sitting rooms, chapels, and the ends of hallways. When Shelly questioned her tour guide, he exclaimed that they had had to put a moratorium on gifts of pianos. The Baldwins, Steinways, and Kimballs interspersed with Yamahas cluttered passageways and were becoming safety hazards. Of course, he had hurried to add that the home had recently accepted a lovely Steinway Baby Grand for the front chapel, and looked at her expectantly, no doubt hedging his bets that she might also have a several-thousand-dollar piano to offer. He looked disappointed when she didn't follow up with a comment. Her mother's Baldwin Acrosonic spinet would, no doubt, be turned down.

Yet, maybe all the pianos would encourage her mother to play. There had been a time when her mother had given lessons. Surely it would be good for her memory. But Shelly had no idea if her mother could still read music. So many things were different—irretrievably so. At the end of the tour, she wrote a check for one thousand dollars to hold a double-occupancy room near the lounge and made a list of what would be needed to furnish it. There would be no bringing furniture from her parents' home—a bonfire came to mind.

By late afternoon Shelly had exhausted the limited offerings of the small town, but come Monday morning, two adjustable twin beds would be delivered, along with a bureau, two night stands, and two recliners. A lifetime of accumulation reduced to half a dozen pieces of furniture—all to be squashed together in one room with one closet and one bath. The fifteen-by-fifteen-foot room a mere nine thousand dollars a month. What a bargain. Things could have been so different if her parents had only planned. She wasn't sure she'd be able to pick the things they'd want or need, and her father was likely going to be too upset to help. If faced with fight or flight, she knew the one she'd choose.

But when she turned into the motel, there was Pam's car in front of the office. Reinforcements. Not the whole cavalry—she hoped Ed had gone home—but someone to help. Pam got an adjoining room and soon came over to Shelly's with a tall glass half full of something over ice. A little too urine-sample-yellow to look inviting, Shelly thought. And the fact that Pam was drinking at all didn't bode well.

"Moscow Mule."

"What?" Shelly wasn't following.

"This." Pam clinked the ice against the side of the glass as she held it out. "I can go make another one."

"Thanks, no. Maybe later."

"So, what's the plan of action?" Pam slouched into the one overstuffed chair in the room and stretched perfectly tanned legs out in front of her. "Great hair, by the way, and the color is perfect."

"Thanks." Shelly was mildly surprised that Pam noticed, and more surprised that she had commented— positively. Pam, at forty-eight, had already had everything sucked or tucked—whether it needed it or not. And she looked good. The lime green cropped cargo pants and matching multi-pocketed jacket over a turquoise cami perfectly set off the short blond Sharon Stone haircut. As Pam would say, she was between husbands. That put more emphasis upon buying only Neiman Marcus, or at least that had been her rebounding technique in the past. Shelly thought that she could still count the number of husbands on one hand, but she'd given up trying to keep up with Pam's love life a long time ago. This was a woman who divorced her third husband because he sat down to urinate. Shelly always suspected there was something else, but knowing Pam, she guessed there didn't have to be.

"I think the first thing is to get Mom seen by a doctor." Shelly couldn't get the thick, brown growth on her mother's nose out of her head.

"Dad is going to protest."

"He already has."

"We can't just abduct her." Pam made a show of digging

an ice cube out of her near-empty glass and popping it into her mouth.

"We can involve the cops."

"What?"

"If Dad refuses, we won't have much of a choice. He already threatened to meet anyone at the door with the .410."

"What are you saying? We should tell the cops what he said? That he's threatening us? That was just childishness, senility. He wouldn't do anything."

"Do you know that?"

Pam took a deep breath. "No."

"So, what options do we have? Do you have a better idea?"

"No, but if I did, it wouldn't involve cops. I grew up in this town."

"And I didn't have that pleasure?"

"It just seems way too drastic. These are our parents."

"A demented, cantankerous old man who can no longer keep a house and take care of his wife. Pam, we're not talking Ma and Pa Kettle skipping off into the sunset blowing kisses. We have to intervene. Mom needs to see a doctor." Shelly mentally admonished herself to cool it. Nothing would be gained if she alienated Pam.

"I need another drink." Pam got up, then turned and picked up her glass from the end table, wiping the ring of condensation with a tissue. "Don't go away."

Like where was there to go? She had never felt so cornered, so backed against the proverbial wall. Shelly propped two pillows against the headboard, kicked off her shoes, and leaned back. She was exhausted from the day and it wasn't over. How were they going to gain entry, as the saying went? Would their father really threaten them if he felt threatened? Maybe. The suggestion of cops just came out, but in retrospect, it wasn't a bad idea. Distract her father while she and Pam guided her mother out of the house and into the car. A clinic appointment probably wasn't necessary. With the concerns that they had for her health, the emergency room would work just fine. But their father. Would he act like nothing had been said and go with them? And after they put their mother in a home, would he follow and live with his wife? Surely, he wouldn't insist on living without her. And what would they do if he did?

"OK. I'm ready again." Pam pushed the door shut behind her and placed another glass of amber liquid on the end table. "Were you serious about using cops?"

"It's an option."

"You don't think Dad will come to his senses?"

"Pam, coming to his senses isn't in his vocabulary."

"He has to go with Mom."

"I agree. You know if he refuses to go, we'd have to prove him incompetent, get a court order to commit him. If he insists on living at home, I suppose we could have someone come in and check on him every day."

"That would be ugly."

"Pam, there isn't one thing 'pretty' about any of this. Maybe we should encourage the option of having him live on his own for a while. There are various services that provide transportation to the elderly. A housekeeper and a cook and he'd survive."

"But how expensive would that be?"

"I don't think we have a cheap option."

Shelly thought she heard the muted "ching" of a cash register. Her sister would be ever mindful of her inheritance or lack thereof. And it would be a drain on her parents' nest egg to support the two of them in a home or one at home.

She hadn't thought about it before, but Pam was probably planning on a sizeable inheritance. Shelly was never certain where Pam's money came from. Some alimony, probably. In the past there had been a lot of help from her parents. And then there were Pam's stints as a women's apparel consultant. As closely as Shelly could figure out, that meant stores hired Pam to make suggestions to patrons as to color and style and get them to buy far more than they had anticipated. She would be good at it.

"I hope you're going to let Ed help us."

"I think we can handle it."

"I don't. Ed said you'd probably let your anger with him get in the way."

"My anger with him?"

"You know, your decision to divorce him just because of a little indiscretion."

"It was because he had asked the 'little indiscretion' to marry him that I thought it might be prudent to make other plans."

"You're kidding. I don't think he mentioned that. Who's he marrying?"

"You know, Pam, I'd rather not talk about it. I frankly think we have enough on our plates right here in front of us without going into the Sinclairs' love life."

"It would still be easier if Ed helped us—you know, Dad would listen to him."

"Pam, I don't think we're going to have the luxury of doing things the easy way."

"So, that means calling the cops?"

"I don't know what else to do—one, how will we get Mom out of the house; and two, who could put the fear of God into Dad about not driving without a current registration? Yes, I think involving law enforcement is the best way to go."

"I wasn't thinking of that, Dad's driving. I wonder if his license is up-to-date?"

"I doubt it. He dodged the question when I asked him. I'll ask the officers to check it."

"When does all this happen?"

"The sooner, the better. The home is holding a room and I don't see putting off the inevitable."

"I suppose you're right. But it just seems so final."

"Pam, the end of life is final—death is final. I just wish Mom and Dad had planned for it. Let us know what they wanted done when they couldn't live by themselves anymore."

"They're very private people, Shel."

"Private is not an excuse for letting others guess at how to take care of you."

"Do you have everything spelled out somewhere? A will or something?"

"Not any more. Ed and I did have. We drew up wills stating exactly what we wanted done. One more thing I need to do." Shelly mentally added it to her to-do list.

"Do you think any confrontation could wait until the morning? My head is splitting. I thought I'd grab some fast food and sleep it off."

Could you sleep off cheeseburgers? With Shelly, they always found her thighs in the dead of night and attached themselves for posterity—but this wasn't the time to comment on faulty pronoun reference. "Morning will work. Do I have your blessing to talk with law enforcement?"

A pause, then, "If that's the only way."

⁜

"So? What do you think?" Shelly took another sip of coffee and watched Pam pick at her Denver omelet.

Breakfast was at Newell's—a truck stop of some renown in the area. Once ensconced on old Highway 81 at five-mile corner, the restaurant's bad coffee and good pie reputation survived the moving of commerce by new interstate arteries, because it relocated. The food was good Kansas fare, but neither one of them was hungry. There had been no sign of Ed—had he gone home?

"Let me see if I understand this. You talked with the cops and because this can be listed as a domestic incident, they can intervene? You actually intimated that Dad would use the shotgun? On us? Himself?" Pam emptied half a juice glass of skim milk into her coffee.

"Doesn't matter. He's threatened harm. Because of that, they can help us enter, remove Mom, find the guns, confiscate all of them, and check Dad's driver's license to boot."

"God, I don't want to be there. What if the neighbors see?"

For just a second, Shelly heard her mother. The parameters of growing up were always defined by what the ubiquitous neighbors would think. Holding hands verboten, kissing in public a straight path to hell—all because of those neighbors. She had been grounded for a week when her father had seen her kiss a boy on the front steps of the high school. Yep, even across town those neighbors must have gotten wind of her indiscretion bordering on a felony.

"Will you understand it if I say screw the neighbors? We are faced with a crisis. Our mother needs medical attention—the sooner, the better. Agree?"

Pam finally nodded. "It's just that this is so drastic."

"We've covered this. There's no need to rehash." Shelly took a breath—she had probably mastered counting to large denominations trying not to yell at Pam. "We're meeting the cops at the house at 10:30. I bought gowns, underwear, a robe, slippers, elastic-waist slip-on slacks, and blouses. We're not taking clothing out of that house. I don't know if there will be a hospital stay, but this will meet Mom's immediate needs. Oh yes, I bought two boxes of Depends."

"You seem to have thought of everything."

Sarcasm? Shelly waited, but Pam didn't seem to want to follow up. "We can pick up anything I've overlooked later—when we know the situation."

"How long will you stay?"

Shelly hesitated. She had wondered this herself. She had a hundred things to do at home—the last place she wanted to be was Kansas. "As long as it takes to get things settled. And you?"

"Well, I was thinking. Things haven't really been . . . well, easy since Darren left."

Darren was number four, Shelly thought, the pharmaceutical salesman. And things not being easy was only a euphemism for Pam's being out of money.

"What would you say to my staying at the house? Oversee a thorough cleaning, tear up the carpet, redo the floors, gut the bathroom, replace everything, dump the furniture . . . ."

"With or without Dad being there?"

"Without. We both agree that Mom has to be in a home, and I think he has to go, too. If you thought it was a good idea, I'd let my car go back and use the Pontiac."

In true Pam-style, her baby sister had just set herself up to get a house and a car—free! But wasn't that a small price to pay for someone to be here? To just watch over her parents. Something in all honesty she wasn't willing to do. Not now and maybe not ever.

"I think it's a great idea. I'll help when I can, but now isn't the best time for me to get away."

"Thanks. This means a lot to me. Have you thought more about having Dad proved incompetent?"

"I'll see a lawyer while I'm here. It should go smoothly. I'm sure the courts are beginning to see a lot of this. I'll stay 'til Wednesday, but I really need to get back."

"So? Now that you're single, what's it going to be? Real estate? Volunteer work? Maybe lend your expertise to Albuquerque's botanical gardens once a week? Buy a B&B?" Pam ate the orange pulp from the rind on the garnish.

"Massage."

"Massage what?"

"Massage therapy—I'm going to become a massage therapist. I've been giving it a lot of thought and I think that's what I want to do."

"Shelly, you have to touch people to do that."

"Yeah, and your point?"

"No, I mean it takes a special person to do that sort of work. The first case of smelly feet or advanced crotch rot and you'll be out of there. I know you."

"I don't think so. I think I'll be good at it."

"You can't make a living at it."

"I don't have to make a living." It was out of her mouth before she knew it. The truth, but still nothing she wanted to flaunt in front of Pam. "I just need something to do. Something that I like—that I feel has some importance. I thought I could volunteer at hospices."

"Yes, but you have to study anatomy, take a test—"

"Careful. You're about to step off into deep water, sister dearest."

"No, no, you can do it, of course—but it's a lot of

work. Do you want to work that hard at sixty? Especially since you don't have to?"

Shelly didn't catch even a hint of sarcasm. But she needed to watch the money comments. "Maybe that's what I need right now—something to get my mind off of things. Something totally different that I can immerse myself in."

"What you need is a love interest."

"You sound like Patrice, but I just don't think I'm ready." What was that Shakespearean line about the funeral meats not yet being cold?

"You'll never be ready if you're waiting for a sign."

"I'm not certain I'd recognize a sign. I mean, it's not like an earring in the left ear . . . or is it the right?"

"See? That's what I mean. You're not letting yourself go. You've always gotten too wound up in minutiae."

"Minutiae?" Pam was trying to be nice, so why did Shelly feel the faintest prickle of irritation? But didn't this sound like something Ed would say?

"What I'm trying to say is open your eyes, look around you. You're a great-looking woman."

"Thanks . . . but I'm thinking of getting a little work done."

"Really? Cosmetic surgery? Like what?" Pam seemed genuinely surprised at the mention of surgery. But wasn't she the pro?

"Well, I really don't think one needs more than one chin."

"Shelly, you have a little fullness under the jawline—"

"Called chins. If I were a turkey, I think it would be called a wattle."

"It's just the Walters' look."

"Not a part of my inheritance that I intend to keep." Shelly didn't mention that lucky Pam had seemed to miss that bit of inheritance, or had ditched it.

"If you're really serious, there's a good surgeon in Albuquerque. Neil Chen."

"Chins by Chen?"

"You can laugh, but you need to interview him. Are you going to stop with just your face?"

Shelly counted to five. "What else would you suggest?" And was really pleased there wasn't a bit of pique in her voice.

"You could hit the trail again as a totally new you. I mean, the tummy, inner thighs—"

"Stop right there. I wouldn't be doing this to 'hit the trail'; I just don't like looking in the mirror. That woman is tired and haggard. I'm not that woman."

"Whatever your reason, a man would be a fool not to see what a super catch you are. Your inner self absolutely glows."

Shelly chose to ignore whatever was glowing. "You don't think he'd see the fact that I'm comfortable, own my own house? I wouldn't be a sitting target for every ne'er-do-well?"

"You can't use money as a shield."

"Pam, I haven't dated in thirty-five years. I think about going out. I'd like to, but I don't think I'd know what to do."

"I'm sure your instincts would kick in."

My instinct to run, probably, Shelly thought; she had reflected more than once on her outburst to Patrice about replacing Ed. Could she do that? Was companionship that important? But Pam was trying to be helpful and supportive. This was beginning to qualify as the best sister-to-sister discussion they had had in years.

"Do you want to marry again?" Shelly was curious.

"I don't know. Maybe. I'm not sure moving back to a small town ups my chances, though." The smile was rueful. "I think I need to take a break from matrimony."

"See? My sentiments exactly!"

"I'm a couple trips to the altar ahead of you. And if you'll excuse me, there's nothing like getting dumped to put the competitive edge back in place. Get those chins done and get on out there." Pam couldn't have looked perkier if she were holding pom-poms.

Shelly checked her watch and hoped "those chins" weren't resting on her chest. She felt Pam's scrutiny. Once the left eye of the camel had been pointed out, it was impossible not to stare. "You know, like it or not, I think we better head to the house."

"I'm dreading this. I just want it over."

Shelly nodded in agreement.

Two police cars blocked the drive, so Shelly parked across the street. They had left Pam's rental at the hotel knowing space would be at a premium. She took a deep breath and got out of the car. She'd leave it unlocked—just one less thing to worry about as they hustled their mother out.

"Are you ready?" The young cop met them at the curb.

"As ready as we can be, I suppose." Shelly turned to Pam. "This is Officer Wilson. My sister, Pam." Shelly realized that she didn't know what last name Pam was using. Oh well, under the circumstances, she could be excused a lapse in manners.

"I want the two of you to stay out of line of fire. Officer Roberts will knock on the door. Who usually answers the door? Your mom or dad?"

"I'd guess Dad." She'd winced at 'line of fire'—could things really turn that ugly? Precaution was necessary, she guessed. And Shelly honestly had no idea of her mother's level of activity. Did she still go out and get the paper? Did she pick flowers? Bring in the mail? She guessed not.

"Just to be certain we have the right person, nod if it's your Dad who answers. I keep forgetting to ask—do you know where your father keeps his guns?"

"There's a gun cabinet in the basement—rifles and shotguns. He has two pistols upstairs. Unless he's moved them, one is in the hall closet, second shelf and the other is in the bed stand on the right side." Shelly knew her father was a creature of habit—she'd bet the guns were still there.

"That will make things easier. Now, why don't the two of you stand behind the cruiser?"

They all turned at the screech of tires as a car swerved into the alley alongside the house and stopped in a shower of gravel and dust. Ed. Shelly started to explain to the young cop next to her but hadn't gotten past "My former husband" when Ed slammed out of the car and exploded.

"What are you doing, for Christ's sake? Do you know how this looks?"

"Excuse me, sir, if you'll just step over here."

"You've totally lost it, Shelly. *Lost it*. Do you hear me? Storming your parents' house behind men with drawn guns. What if your father is looking out the window at this very second?"

"You don't understand what's been going on. You don't understand the shape things are in."

"You really don't." Pam chimed in.

"There is nothing that would suggest this kind of aggression. Nothing. The people in that house are elderly and infirm, not a danger to themselves or to others."

"Excuse me, sir, stay behind me."

"This is an outrage. I can't believe that the two of you set this up. Just what do you hope to gain?"

"Ed, you're out of the loop. Don't you realize that you chose to leave this family? You have no reason to be here."

"I have every reason to be here. As a friend if nothing else . . . a friend of thirty-five years."

"Funny how important the years seem to be to you—when you're using them to make a point."

Ed turned to the three cops. "Gentlemen, I'm Dr. Sinclair. I think it would be in everyone's best interests if you all go now. I assure you everything's under control. Mr. Walters is not a threat to himself or his family. This is just a misunderstanding."

"Sir, with all due respect, we're working with Ms. Sinclair. We believe we have a reason to be here."

"Well, I'm telling you that you don't. I want you off of this property now. I appreciate how you could be taken in by a hysterical woman who has over-dramatized every aspect of her life—all her life. But it stops here. Now."

"It's our understanding that Mr. Walters is driving on an expired license, in an unregistered car that has no insurance. While we're here, we'll check it out."

"Since when has checking a license involved breaking into someone's house with drawn guns?"

"That's not what's happening, Ed." Shelly stepped between the young cop and her soon-to-be-former husband. "You haven't heard the threats, seen the problems. I suggest you leave. This truly doesn't involve you. This is my family and I'll always do what's best for them. But things are out of their control. Decisions have to be made for them."

"Oh, Shelly, always the melodramatic. Just give it a rest. I am sick and tired of your control fetishes."

"What?" No screaming, no screaming, no screaming.

"Oh, what's the surprise? You have to have everything your way. Overkill. Yes, how's that? That's the word I think of. Over the top, always over the top. Do you know what it's been like living with you for a lifetime?"

"I don't think a discussion of our life is of interest to the people here. We have a reason to be here and it's not our marriage."

"Oh, that's big of you, Shelly. Everything for appearances. Sometimes I can't believe that we lived together for thirty-five years."

"Nor can I."

"I think the two of you need to finish your discussion elsewhere. We need to confront Mr. Walters and get Mrs. Walters to treatment." The young officer was clearly losing patience. "Mr. Sinclair, you need to leave now."

"If you continue on this course, I will personally see that the Walters sue you and the city for false—"

"Rick, radio for backup."

"I'm leaving, but you haven't heard the end of this." Everyone stood mute as Ed got in the car, slammed the door, and gunned it down the ally.

"I'm sorry—"

"No need to apologize, Mrs. Sinclair. I just went through an ugly divorce myself."

My God, Shelly thought, how "ugly" could divorce be if you were in your early twenties? Would the pain and problems run as deep after only two years or three? She guessed amount of time probably didn't have anything to do with it.

"Are we ready?" The cop named Rick was already standing on the porch. "Remember, just nod if your dad answers the door. If it's your mom, I'll motion for you to come up here with me and we can go in together." He checked everyone's position and rang the doorbell.

It was her mother who opened the door, and Shelly

stepped up quickly to go inside. Pam was on her heels and the two of them gently—one on each side—took their mother by the elbows, waited until the last cop had entered, and then propelled their mother between them, out of the house, down the steps, and across the street to the car.

"I don't want to go anywhere." This accompanied by the dragging of feet and a little girl's petulant voice.

"We're just going for a ride. You'll like that." Shelly opened the passenger-side door.

"I don't want a ride. I don't want to go. Don't make me. You can't. No, no, no." Her mother was pulling away, stamping her feet and twisting to the side. One of her crepe-soled canvas slip-ons flopped to the curb. The putrid stench of body odor wafted between them. Shelly thought she heard Pam gag. But Pam was right there when their mother tried to sit down. The two of them then leveraged her frail body onto the car's front seat. Pam squeezed into the back and reached forward to anchor their mother, keeping her arms out of harm while Shelly closed the door.

The short mile to the clinic seemed like a hundred. Shelly pulled into the emergency entrance and left Pam long enough to brief a couple orderlies who grabbed a wheelchair and headed back to the car. The doctor on call met Pam and her mother at the door and directed the orderlies to an empty exam room. Shelly crossed the lobby to admissions. She'd fill out the necessary paperwork in case the doctor admitted her. But that didn't remain a question for long.

"They've taken her downstairs for lab work and then they're going to clean her up and admit her. I gave them the OK to cut the scarf off of her head." Pam stood beside her.

"Oh, Pam." Shelly embraced her sister. There didn't seem to be anything else to say.

Cleanup took almost two hours, but when they visited their mother, she smelled good, sported a pixie haircut, and was finishing a cup of chocolate pudding. She looked up, dwarfed by the sparkling white-sheeted bed, and Shelly wondered with a pang how long it had been since she'd been tucked between such cleanliness. Her mother seemed intent on her pudding. Had there been these little extras at the house? Had her father been doing all the cooking? Grocery shopping? There were so many unanswered questions. Shelly and Pam slipped into the hall when the doctor arrived.

When the doctor rejoined them, she explained what would happen. "I'd like to keep her here a week for observation. I'll go ahead and schedule a consult concerning what appears to be a carcinoma on her nose. It would be good if the two of you sneak off now; she's obviously content. Never knew chocolate pudding had such a sedative effect."

"That kind of euphoria should be reserved for Twinkies." Shelly added.

"About your dad. Try to bring him out to visit your mother in the morning and I'll do an impromptu test for cognizance. I'll fill out the paperwork and have it ready. The fact that he cannot or will not take care of his wife will be enough with my diagnosis to put him in a home with her. Do you think you could get him here by eleven?"

Shelly and Pam nodded, then expressed their thank-yous.

"We need to tell Dad." Pam was clearly not looking forward to this.

"I never got the Club on the car—gotta do that."

Charles Walters opened the door before either daughter had knocked. "Those boys took my guns."

"Yes, Dad, I'm sure they did."

"What'd they think I was going to do?"

"They wanted to make sure you didn't do anything, Dad."

"And this here. Look at this."

Shelly took the warning ticket he held out. "Says that they are citing you for an expired license, registration, and insurance policy. I'll get you signed up tomorrow for senior services."

"I'm not going to get on a bus with a lot of old people."

"Those oldsters go to the bank, the pharmacy, the grocery store just like you need to."

"Well, you listen to me, Missy, I'm not a gonna do it." Suddenly, he turned to Pam. "Where'd you take Mom?"

"She's in the hospital, Dad. We'll take you to see her tomorrow."

"I hope you two girls are paying for it. I don't have that kind of money."

"Dad, I'm sure you want to see Mom get the best care."

"She can get good care right here at home."

"Why hadn't you taken her to have the growth on her nose checked?" Shelly was surprised at Pam's straightforward approach. She'd never been one for confrontation.

"There's nothing on her nose."

"No, Dad, there is—a rather nasty carcinoma. Shelly and I met with the doctor just before we came back here. It will require surgery."

"You expect me to believe that?"

"No, that's why you'll go with us in the morning to see Mom and talk to the doctor yourself."

"You going to take me there?"

"Yes, Shelly and I both have rental cars."

"Well, I think I'd rather drive myself. What time do I have to be there?"

"I'm afraid that can't happen. Remember what the policemen said." Pam looked at Shelly.

"Dad, I'm going to put what they call a Club on the steering wheel of the Pontiac. It's what the police suggested. You won't be able to drive until you've been tested—a written exam, an eye test, and a road test. If you pass these, you will be able to apply for a new license and bring the other paperwork up to date."

"This is all your doing. You're liars. There's nothing wrong with my license or the registration."

"The police thought otherwise or they wouldn't have written this up." Shelly held out the ticket. "I'll be right back." She headed toward the garage and half expected him to follow, and hoped Pam would deter him. But he didn't follow. She assumed the Pontiac was unlocked, and it was. The Club slipped neatly in place and she pocketed the keys. She didn't allow herself a moment of sadness over the situation. This was just something that had to be. If she stopped to sort through her emotions, she might not be able to make the decisions that were necessary. She walked back into the house.

"Done. Dad, I want you to get a good night's rest. Pam and I will pick you up in the morning at 10:30. Is there anything we can get you before we go?"

Her father shook his head.

"We can bring you something warm for dinner. What would you like?" Shelly noticed Pam wasn't inviting him to go with them. Out of olfactory concerns in a small space, no doubt. This time her father waved them away and didn't even get up when they left.

"So? What do you think? Will he go with us to see Mom in the morning?" Pam asked as they walked back to the car.

"Don't know. We're just going to have to face that when the time comes. I don't think I have the energy to visit Mom this afternoon. I may catch a nap and finish up the shopping for Dad, then get to bed early."

CHAPTER EIGHT

Dusk shrouded the room in tones of gray when Shelly woke. Quarter of seven. Still time to buy the necessities that her father would need in the home, get gas in the car, and go to dinner. She dialed Pam's room but there was no answer. Just as well. She was weary of family . . . and then instantly had pangs of conscience. But it was true. She needed a break. She splashed her face with water and pulled a baseball cap over her mussed hair, tucking errant wisps behind her ears. A little mascara, eyeliner, shadow, and she was out the door.

Being in this town of her birth always brought back memories. Not an unpleasant childhood, but not a happy one either. Dreams had kept her going as a child—with Cinderella simplicity. Yet, somewhere around the age of ten, she looked in the mirror and realized she wasn't on the Miss America track. Sometimes like tonight she just wanted to revisit those memories, revel in the nostalgia. So many things that had shaped her life had sprung from this beginning. Her role models were here; the remnants of her dreams . . . the specters of her conscience.

The women she remembered were all gone now, but for the memories of holidays celebrated to the smells of cookies and pies and candies filling baskets to be delivered around town. The gifts of food from the Humphrey sisters were always well received.

Good cooks were a given in her family. A great aunt who had to be driven to the country farm to check the poultry on the hoof. Then would poke the live goose to determine the fat layer and demand to purchase it at Thanksgiving and have it finished on corn for the Christmas holidays. Those holidays that also produced English plum pudding—the festive staple meticulously steamed every year from a two-hundred-year-old recipe that required kidney suet. Did anyone ever really know that the bag of tallow-yellow fat had been trimmed from the calf's kidneys?

She was taught the way to a man's heart was through his stomach—by eighth grade she'd figured out a circuitous route. Sex wasn't easy to figure when your parents had never done it and mentioning it would get you grounded. Being "boy crazy" was a disease that one seldom recovered from. So-and-so was boy crazy, and that always seemed to explain so-and-so's fatherless child—a really huge no-no guaranteed to damn one to hell. The priest. The Quilty girl. And all those unwed mothers—hell was crowded. But the message? Sex was the one thing guaranteed to put you there.

It was the ol' left eye of the camel again. If you're told not to look, what becomes the obsession? Of course, the left eye of the camel or, in this case, the one-eyed wand of life. In the sixth grade she'd paid Rosalie Bottleneck (a nickname for McKinley Grade School's tough) two Zero candy bars and her entire week's allowance of fifty cents to explain the difference between boys and girls. She'd never felt so taken in her life when the answer was, "Boys have a pencil in their pants." It would be two more years before a #2 Eberhard would enter her life—and forty years before "got lead in your pencil?" would take on any special meaning.

Shelly pulled to the curb in front of a used car lot at First Street and Kansas Avenue. As a child, Charleston's Market and Cold Storage reigned supreme on this very corner with frontage on both streets. The market always smelled slightly like Brie cheese tastes. The cement floor rinsed with a hose after a once-a-week dousing of Clorox, vegetables limp before they were removed from shipping crates. A red Coke cooler in back where a nickel placed in the slot released the bars holding the necks of little bluish green bottles so cold the liquid inside stung her tongue with icy slush.

But across the street—the Missouri Pacific tracks—the Moppy. Not the Atchison, Topeka and the Santa Fe railroad that kept a quarter of the town employed, but a spur, a feeder line that carried freight and met up with the community benefactor some ways out of town. Here in a field alongside was an area to play baseball. Lighted in the evenings because of the nearby intersection, twelve to fourteen pubescent boys would gather for an impromptu game. A dozen or so boys and one girl.

Shelly was twelve that summer—one year into wearing a bulky cotton bra that chafed her nipples, teased them erect and kept pointy indentations outlined in her T-shirts. It would never have dawned on her mother to provide something feminine, soft cloth against softer skin—that would have been too expensive.

In gym class that first year in junior high, she saw what caring mothers provided—in shades of ochre, rose, and white satin—wispy nothings with narrow straps that didn't bite into young flesh across the shoulders. She wished with all her heart that she could fold her bra and slip and leave them on the bench in front of her locker—not wad and stuff them into the pockets of her shorts so no one would see. Only to put them on after a shower, limp and reeking with sweat.

But that July afternoon with her own mitt oiled to perfection and her own bat tied to the basket on the front of her bike, the game took precedence. She was a short-stop—and a good one. The first game had been close and the second saw the other team win. But it was all in fun. There was laughing and the usual farting contests—lighting these emissions hadn't captured the imagination yet. She unfastened the wrist strap on her mitt and rebuck-led it, threading the strap through the wire weave of the basket on her bike. She didn't want to lose what just might be her most prized possession. A possession begrudgingly purchased by her father for her tenth birthday.

She backed her bike out from the cluster left leaning against the fence at the end of the makeshift field. Home was only a matter of blocks away, but she hadn't been watching the time. It was late.

The first blow caught her off guard and staggered her. Struck from behind, she fell forward, straddling the bicycle, wincing as the sharp edge of the pedal raked her inner thigh. The palms of her hands burned where she'd smacked the ground. She half-turned to see what had happened, but strong arms on either side of her dragged her backwards and turned her on her back.

"You go first."

She gagged on the stench of sweaty adolescent male underarms hovering above her nose—unlike her own Arrid Extra Dry pits, white and gummy from overgener-ous application. The button on the band of her shorts was the first to cave—pull through the cloth and separate. Then grubby hands fought for the side-placket zipper. Twisting only made them grab onto her arms tighter. But as a hand raked her panties aside and fingers pushed into her vagina, she kicked—doubled up both legs and kicked, connecting smartly with the groin of an unsuspecting twelve-year-old.

The satisfaction of hearing him yelp was short-lived. The slap that followed almost knocked her out. Hands now had pulled her T-shirt up and tore at her bra. Pairs of hands—three or four—squeezed and pummeled, bruising her nipples.

"Hey, you want me to show you how it's done?"

The oldest of the boys, some thirteen plus years, stood between her legs. And there it was. The sacred pencil. Shorts to his knees, a slender, fleshy protrusion with a rounded button-top stiffly pointing upward, and she could almost hear the "ohs" and "ahs" of admiration from the group of younger boys. Obviously, pencil-penis was leader by default. But he was not going to be leader because he got his pencil anywhere near her.

Catching the worshippers off guard, she twisted to the side and then back again, jerking her legs upward and outward. And then she started screaming. But what was amazing—someone else was screaming, screaming and riding toward them on his bicycle.

"I'll tell. Leave her alone. If you've hurt her—"

Was there air in the pencil? Suddenly it just sort of dangled to the side, deflated. Its owner stepped back and quickly tucked it from view.

"Hey, ease off, nobody got hurt." This from the leader as he picked up his bike and, followed by the others, quickly rode off the field.

Her savior was a boy her own age, Terry. He helped her up and didn't look when she adjusted her underwear, pulling the bra back down into place, tucking very tender breasts into wadded cups. She would have to think up a story to tell her parents—she guessed she would just say she wrecked her bike. Already she could see faint black-and-blue bruises rising like welts on her thighs. And her clothes . . . maybe if she tore her shorts.

But the one thing she could never do was tell the truth. She could just hear her father berating her for "asking" for it. What young girl played with boys, and baseball at that? No, it was her fault. And it came to her in a single crushing blow—she would never be able to play baseball with boys again. Never. Breasts and that thing between her legs had seen to that.

Shelly pondered the fact that the incident was not about losing virginity but all about losing equality and power. Forty-eight years later, she still marveled at her coming-of-age story. Was there a woman alive who didn't have one?

CHAPTER NINE

The morning was overcast and muggy with intermittent showers. Shelly and Pam filled the trunk with the evening's purchases—socks, underwear, slippers, easy-on slacks, pajamas. The only thing missing was Depends. Did he need them? Shelly guessed that the home would provide if he did. The question was would he go to the hospital at all? There was no second-guessing. With the doctor set up to determine his competence, it would be so much easier to get everything over with all at once.

"Look!" Pam excitedly leaned forward as Shelly pulled into the drive. "The door's open. I was so afraid he'd still be in bed."

"Or worse, just not open the door."

"Do you think Mom would like these?" He met them at the door with a package of glazed doughnuts.

"I don't know, Dad. I think they have her on a special diet." Shelly looked at Pam for backup.

"Yeah, lots of vegetables and fruit."

"Oh, well, these are her favorite. I guess she can have them when she comes home."

Shelly held her breath to see what would follow, but her father just pulled his sweater on and prepared to lock the front door. So far, so good.

The walk across the parking lot at the hospital took forever. She had no idea how frail her father had become. In a twenty-yard stretch he stopped three times to catch his breath and regain balance. And, it was apparent, he couldn't see. Standing directly in front of the lighted entrance sign, he asked twice if this door was the one to use. It alleviated all guilt over the Club.

Their mother was sitting up in bed, sipping on a straw placed in a plastic glass of ice water. Her first words were devastating.

"Do I know you?" Her mother looked expectantly from one to the other. "There's room to sit if you want." She pointed to two chairs next to the bed. "Do I work with you?" This directed to Shelly.

"No, mother, you don't work. I'm Shelly, your oldest daughter."

"Oh my, I don't work? I thought I did. I have money." She reached into the nightstand and pulled a dollar bill out.

"Nancy, stop talking nonsense." Her father stepped up to the bedside. "We're getting you out of here."

Shelly caught a panicked look from Pam. This was not going well. Should she call the doctor? Probably a good idea.

"Pam, why don't you let Dr. Sylvan know we're here?" Pam nodded and disappeared into the hall.

"Did you have a good breakfast?" Shelly asked.

"Oh, I haven't eaten. Is there a restaurant here?"

"They bring meals to your room."

"This is a lovely motel."

"Nancy, you're in the hospital."

"Who are you?"

"You know who I am. I'm your husband."

"I don't work. Do you think I'm lazy? Did I ever work?"

"Mother, you're not lazy. You used to give piano lessons."

"I don't think so. You must think I'm lazy. If I don't work, I must be lazy."

"Nancy, just shut up." Her father's face was red as a beet and he was gripping the bed's footboard.

Shelly was startled. She had never known her father to speak roughly to her mother.

"Are you my cousin? Are you Harold?"

"Harold's dead. *I'm your husband.*" Spittle sprayed across the coverlet.

"My, but you're a loud old man. Do you work here? I don't work. I must be lazy."

Shelly stifled a smile. If this entire exchange wasn't so pathetic, it would be funny.

"She just ain't no good anymore." Shelly's father, the anger gone, sat heavily in a chair behind him. "Just no good."

"She needs special care, Dad." Shelly took it as a positive when he didn't answer.

"Well, looks like everyone is here. Nancy, how do you feel this morning?"

Dr. Sylvan swept into the room. She was a solid woman, more given to pulling a fetus calf from its mother if trouble arose than treating mere ill humans. She oozed action and take-charge technique. Shelly silently said a prayer. This wasn't a woman to cross, but it was someone to put their trust in.

"I don't think I can complain. I'm not sick; I'm just lazy."

"Well, I don't have a cure for that. And you? Mr. Walters, I presume? How are you this morning?" Dr. Sylvan shook her father's hand.

"I guess OK, but my wife's crazy."

"I'm crazy as a loon. But then I ask myself what is a loon? Do you know?" Her mother sat up straight in bed and turned toward Shelly.

"Mother, a loon is a kind of duck."

"Does it quack?"

"I don't think I've ever heard one." Where was Pam, the expert, when she needed her?

"Oh, I guess they're just crazy. I'm crazy, you know, crazy like a loon."

"Shelly, there might be less distraction when I interview your father if you step outside. There's a gift shop and snack bar downstairs; I'll meet you and Pam there when I'm finished—probably in about an hour. I've asked Dr. Taylor to join me. He heads up the case workers and will help us all make the right decisions." Dr. Sylvan smiled. "I want this to be as painless as you do."

One hour and ten minutes plus two cups of tepid, tasteless coffee later, Dr. Sylvan pulled up a chair.

"First, let me say that I'm admitting your father. There's evidence of a recent stroke—possibly several. His cognitive abilities are severely diminished. This is not a man who can live on his own, cook his own meals, pay bills, attend to personal hygiene, let alone take care of someone as limited as your mother. I believe you told me you've reserved a double at the Manor?"

Shelly nodded. A series of strokes would explain everything—dropping the ball on the car registration, his license . . . she idly wondered what other surprises there might be. She needed to check his bank accounts. At least she was listed as a cosigner and wouldn't have to have a court order.

"We may have to keep him sedated or at least in a locked ward while he's here—and I'll make the same recommendation to the home. He's not going to want to do any of this. But I suggest that he not go to his own house again. In fact, he'll probably react better with hospital personnel directing him. I know this will be difficult but I'm going to suggest that you don't visit until we get him set up at the Manor. I anticipate we'll move him Thursday morning."

Shelly left a bag of clothes at the front desk—just things he would need in the next five days. The rest she'd drop off at the Manor later—tomorrow or Monday, whatever time permitted. She and Pam needed to at least get the valuables out of the house and begin to box the extensive sets of china and glass. They could start that this afternoon. With Pam staying, there wasn't as much urgency. But Shelly had no idea when she could get back. It was a godsend that Pam was taking over this part of the ordeal.

Shelly would also try to hire some muscle. A couple guys to haul furniture out—maybe rent a dumpster to put in the driveway. All the carpet would have to go, the drapes, bedding, clothing . . . a dumpster was a good idea.

The two of them worked until 1 a.m. on Monday morning, then met again at ten and continued through the day. They saturated the house with air fresheners and hooked up three ozone machines, but still wore masks.

Pam took care of having a dumpster moved in and hiring day labor. She also contacted several contractors to get bids on a total refurbish. Shelly, in the meantime, picked up Dr. Sylvan's diagnosis and saw a lawyer. By Monday afternoon there was a feeling of calmness, if not finality.

"I think I'll head back in the morning. I'll look in on Mom but I don't really see a reason to wait until Thursday just to see Dad for ten minutes. You're in good shape here. I close on a house next week and still don't have anyone set up to tile the kitchen and bathroom floors."

"Don't worry about Dad. I'll look in on him. You know, if the circumstances had been different, this would have been fun—I mean working together, getting to know each other again."

Shelly hugged her sister. In spite of everything, it had been fun. A reuniting of kindred spirits that she wouldn't have thought possible just a few days ago.

"I'll continue to get Dad's affairs in order. I'll check on due dates, but I'll cash out and reinvest annuities and CDs as quickly as I can. I'll draw on their capital to pay the hospital bills and the home—I'm having all those bills sent to me. I figured you had enough to do with the house. Let me know what you need. I've set up a personal house account in your name—use it. Oops. Almost forgot—here are the keys to the Club."

CHAPTER TEN

Normalcy. Or, at least, what masqueraded as such, had settled around her. The bungalow simply sparkled—new tile floors, new paint, new furniture. All new appliances gleamed in the kitchen. Her parents were doing as well as could be expected and Pam had sent pictures of progress on the house. She hadn't heard from Ed since the Kansas debacle. She guessed it was time to take a deep breath and just enjoy life—and get ready for school. "What do you think?" Patrice was the first to see her darling.

"It's perfect. It's so you. How did you ever rattle around in that monstrosity of a house for so many years after the boys left?"

"You forget, we did a lot of entertaining. Come look at the deck."

Shelly opened the floor-to-ceiling doors off the dining room and walked out onto the wooden decking that surrounded the back of the house. Ten feet deep and four feet high, covered with a tile overhang, and protected from view by eight-foot wooden fencing that ran along the sidewalk to the south and defined the short driveway beside the garage to the west—the space was both private and inviting. Shelly pulled two metal lawn chairs away from the house and flipped over their rain-stained seat cushions. "This is my favorite place to be—morning or night. Is it too early for a beer?"

"Never, if it's handy."

Shelly walked the half dozen steps to the kitchen and returned with two Dos Equis, each with a quarter lime.

"Do I dare ask if you've seen Ed lately?"

"No. I keep holding my breath, but he seems to have cooled down after the confrontation over my parents."

"Did you decide to let him have the old house?"

"Yes. I just want done with it."

"Come on, Shel, I never thought I'd say this, but I don't trust Ed Sinclair. I don't think that your state of mind is conducive to your driving a fair bargain."

"I'm not going to fight him on it. If the price is even halfway fair, I'll accept. He's supposed to send an offer to Stephanie."

"Think this through. I know you don't need the money now, but what about the future? One market blip and you could be wishing you'd handled things differently. And I just don't want you to let him get away with anything."

"I just want to get on with my life—I need to move on. I start school tomorrow."

"You're really going to go through with it? Actually massage people?"

"You're beginning to sound like Pam—she thinks the first case of crotch rot and I'll be out of there."

"Well?"

"Oh, come on, give me more credit than that."

"Shelly, I just can't imagine you doing this—enjoying this."

She packed and repacked her tote before taking off for the first night's class. Two sheets, a bottle of oil, textbook, two towels, large bath-size—everything white. Oh yes, a robe for her. Two pencils, a pen and notebook . . . she felt like someone should take a first-day-at-school picture.

She was the oldest in the class by an easy ten years and one of six women. Four men, boys really, not one over twenty-five, lined up against the opposite wall. Quakerized. Men and women separate. Shy? Or an age thing? Only one of the women, barefoot, gauze skirt, no bra, honey-golden braid to her waist, got any attention. Rapunzel had worked at a spa and seemed light-years ahead in terms of general knowledge. Rapunzel or Eve, as her name turned out to be, seemed also to be the darling of the instructor.

They were starting out with anatomy, then would segue into technique, including a month's introduction to various schools of thought. Ethics, accounting, product, and starting one's own business rounded out the curriculum. The national-level proficiency test after they graduated would be grueling. Twenty points application; eighty points general anatomy. Six months from today. Whew! Did she really know what she'd gotten herself into?

"Let's start with introductions. Why don't you share why you're here, what you do now, and your goal—how does massage therapy fit into your future?" The instructor, Greg, was thirty-five or thereabouts, black, bald, and wore an earring. Handsome, she thought, by most standards, but a little brusque.

The first woman to speak gave complete credit for her school decision to a palm reader. She had been at a crossroads and someone suggested seeking a reading and here she was. No one seemed to doubt her story or even think it strange. Maybe if Shelly admitted to having her tea leaves read . . . .

Shelly was really glad there were four before it would be her turn. She needed to replace Junior League with something more in keeping with this audience, but what had she done since college? Housewife, mother, supporter of highly successful husband—she was really a generation or two or three apart. She listened quietly to how an MT license would enhance an RN degree, how massage would allow one woman to reach her lifelong dream of owning her own business, another to add a part-time job to an already full schedule as an HR manager, and finally to Eve, who had been practicing without a license but wanted to become an onboard therapist for the Carnival line of cruise ships.

Shelly's turn. A deep breath. "Well, in retrospect, I don't think I've done the things in life that truly have meaning—aside from raising a family. I'm sixty and have a chance to make decisions for me now. I want to work in hospices—not just as a hand-holder, but someone who can contribute comfort. Touch is healing. I want to be the person to lighten someone's pain." Polite applause. Was she hearing, seeing correctly? The quick but genuinely warm hug from Eve sealed it—she was going to fit in!

Two of the guys were decidedly a couple, Donovan and Vincent. Twenty-somethings. They let everyone know right up front that it wasn't Donny and Vince—no nicknames, puh-lease. They were kind of cute, openly holding hands. First stages of puppy love, Shelly guessed. The closest to her in age was fifty, the HR manager, a somewhat sour woman, blond pageboy, achingly thin and prematurely wrinkled, probably from running marathons unprotected in New Mexico's sun. Strangely enough, it was Eve that she felt most drawn to. Age difference be damned.

Greg lectured for two hours, and just when Shelly thought her head would burst, he changed gears.

"Let's end the evening by evaluating skeletal balance or lack thereof. Everyone strip to underwear. I want to say now that modesty will go out the window very quickly in this class. I don't want to be unfeeling, but evaluation of problem areas on the human body are better done without clothing getting in the way."

Specter of Ann Landers . . . was her underwear presentable? Thank god she'd worn the sports bra—she wouldn't be embarrassed by gravity. The ten of them lined up against the wall and Greg pulled Eve from the group. Big surprise. Using her as a model, he pointed out how slightly rounded shoulders were pulling her hands to the front of her body. Arms relaxed and loose, the thumbs should point straight forward and palms face thighs. Everyone had to imagine a string dropping straight from earlobe to elbow—unbroken, no twists or turns. Shelly got called to step forward because her imaginary line was perfect. Thanks to a mother who really did make her walk with a book on her head.

Bad posture was rampant—their assignment in addition to fifty pages of anatomy was to observe people and make notes on what they saw. There would be a discussion hour on Thursday evening. The end of the first evening, and Shelly knew she'd made the right decision. She stuffed everything into the tote and headed for the parking lot.

"Shelly, wait up. Do you want to go for coffee?" Eve rushed up, a little breathless.

"Sure. What's close?"

"A Starbucks, of course. Follow me."

Any place that smelled of coffee was welcome to Shelly. Anytime. She sank into an overstuffed chair by the fireplace after ordering a latte.

"So, what do you think? Was it what you expected?"

"I think so. I like the class size. Ten seems really manageable."

"Will it bother you to be nude in front of strangers?"

"Maybe, at first. And you?"

"I've done it so often; I don't care anymore."

Shelly toyed with asking what the circumstances had been. She was acutely aware of the unveiling of a thirty-ish body versus one twice that old. As if she could read thoughts, Eve added, "There's no way you're sixty."

"I'm afraid so. But, thanks." She still hadn't made those appointments to interview cosmetic surgeons. Was she really serious? Only when she saw herself in the mirror.

"I had my boobs done."

"Really?"

"Graduation present after high school."

"That's a great gift." Did she really believe that? Children barely out of puberty having adjustments—that had serious, long-term implications. Thank God she'd given birth to male children.

"I guess boob jobs weren't really popular in your day."

Shelly was quickly trying to calculate when her "day" had been. "No, absolutely unheard of." Undoubtedly, mounds of Kleenex had been wasted on going from an A to a B cup, but no surgery. Silicone was gaining popularity in California her senior year of high school, but "older" women in their twenties were doing it, not teens. Thinking what her father would have said if the subject had come up made her smile. You lived with what God gave you. She stole a look in the plate-glass window beside her. Could be better. Maybe after the face life . . . no one ever said God couldn't use a little help.

"If you're really serious about getting some work done, I could give you a name or two."

"Sure." Shelly needed to feel better about herself, and giving up those chins was a place to start.

"I think the best in town is Neil Chen."

"Funny, my sister who lives in Tulsa had heard of him."

"When you're in the business, you'll see the results of lots of tucks and sucks—not all of them stellar."

"I can't imagine anything worse than a goof-up that everyone can see."

"It can be pretty bad. Most mistakes can be fixed. Still, it's best to first go with the best doc."

Shelly agreed. At the end of school she'd go for it. Celebrate her new career, her new life. "Need anything? I'm going to get a slice of pumpkin bread." Shelly pushed up from the overstuffed cushions and went to the back of the ever-present line. She idly wondered what the take was on a weekly basis.

"Tiffany!" Shelly probably wouldn't have called out her name if she hadn't been so surprised to see her. But there she was, four ahead of her in line. The fringed suede jacket in powder blue with boots to match was less than slimming. But the outfit matched her eyes. Had Ed picked it out? Did it matter? Well, there was no excuse for having bad manners. Shelly stepped forward.

"Don't think you have to say hello to me. I've heard how ugly you're being."

"Ugly? How?"

"Ed and I both agree that you're being childish about the house. It was Ed's money that built that house. It wasn't like you contributed. And just because we live in this state, half of it is yours. I don't think that's fair."

Ed's parents' money to be exact, Shelly noted, and the house was all hers, according to the mutual decision of both parties in the divorce. And when did running a house, taking care of children, and supporting a husband's career become non-contributory?

"I think there are a lot of things you don't understand." Shelly bit back any smart-ass comment about the fairness, or lack thereof, of life.

"I think you don't understand how you drove your husband away with your demands, your better-than-anyone attitude."

"My what?" No screaming, no screaming, no screaming.

"No man wants to stay with a woman who's frigid. And flaunts her supposed superiority."

"Frigid?"

"You're obstructing our lives all out of selfishness. Just because you can't have what you want."

Shelly was tempted to ask what it was she wanted, but thought she might find out anyway—and wasn't disappointed.

"It's always been the money and the kind of life that Ed could give you, and now that it's gone, you don't want anyone else to have it."

Shelly stole a look around. Even Eve was staring. Not the kind of floor show that Starbucks would have chosen, given the chance.

"I don't think we need to be parading our lives in front of others."

"No, of course you wouldn't. Always so important to keep up pretenses."

If Shelly had thought Tiffany was just getting warmed up, she was surprised when she turned on the heel of her baby blue, pointy-toed suede boots and walked out. Somehow the pumpkin bread had lost its appeal.

"I want the Porsche." It was ten after ten when Shelly got home, but she'd made some decisions. Decisions that Stephanie needed to act on.

"Shelly? What changed your mind?"

"If I'm getting such bad press, I want to live up to it." She briefly filled her in on the Tiffany encounter.

"I would think that Ed and Tiffany would want the station wagon, with a child and all that entails."

"Especially since the family will be expanding—once Ed finds his dick."

"This has really upset you, hasn't it? I'm sorry, Shelly; I tried to tell you things would be nasty."

"I still can't believe it."

"Believe it. I go through just this scenario five times a day, and I was the one who couldn't stand the violence of criminal law."

"I also need to make some decisions on the house."

"I'm still looking into that. I've ordered an appraisal, which should be completed in the next couple days. I'll get back by the end of the week."

Shelly felt vindicated. Forty thousand of the car was hers. It was a large investment. The car was in both their names. Would Ed be surprised at her demands? Did she care? It had not been discussed, just assumed that the Porsche would go with Ed. Well, there would be more discussion from now on and a lot less assuming.

She found the Porsche sitting in her driveway, keys taped to the windshield (stupid move) three days later. No note. And when she opened the garage door, no station wagon. She slipped behind the wheel of the Porsche only to choke on patchouli. Had Ed soaked the steering wheel in the scent? There was a stain on the passenger-side seat and three tubes of cheap, very red lipstick in the cup holder. And a pair of pantyhose, worn, behind the visor. Disgusting. A hollow victory. But she could always have the car detailed and then trade it. Why not? There was absolutely nothing that said she had to hang onto memories—material ones.

When she picked up the car, the kid who had worked on it that afternoon handed her a plastic sack of more goodies harvested from under mats, between seat cushions, and in the glove box: a child's small plastic action figure, two pair of bikini underwear (adult sized), a child's sock, a child's pink barrette, a plastic water bottle, a package of Trojans . . . rubbers? She stood staring.

"Looks like you have a teenager."

"Former husband in his second or third childhood."

"Oh. Sorry, but we're not supposed to throw anything away." The kid gestured toward the Trojans. "I threw the used ones out."

"Oh my God. That's disgusting. I'm so sorry."

The kid looked embarrassed, then added, "I got the stain out. Uh," he turned crimson, "the one on the front seat. Looked like kid's watercolor paint. I dyed, actually refurbished, with a leather tint on that seat and the driver's. I think it's hard to tell where the stain was. It'd be best to park this baby in a garage tonight and leave the windows down."

Shelly paid the three hundred and fifty dollars and

added a fifty-dollar tip. It had to be worth something to pull dirty underwear and other playground items out from under seats. And she didn't feel like telling him that it wouldn't be in her garage tonight or any other night. She had called the BMW dealership earlier and a silver 640Ci convertible was sitting in the lot with her name on it. No more patchouli, lipstick, errant pantyhose, or . . . rubbers.

Coffee after class became a staple. Eve and Shelly expanded the group to include others—Donovan, Vincent, and Lori, the HR maven. Saturdays were study sessions—long study sessions with few breaks. Shelly knew she was ignoring Patrice; a couple phone calls now and then but no heart-to-hearts, shopping, or afternoon movies. Well, she was taking the weekend off. Two months of the grindstone and only one more before she would have real clients. She needed to come up for air. Yet, it had been a productive spring.

Life revolved around fixing up the bungalow, school, and intermittent trips to her lawyer. Calls exchanged with Pam gave her updates on the refurbishing and her parents. Nothing out of the ordinary. Late spring and all the new plantings of shrubs and flowers needed daily attention. She watered in the early morning before class and sometimes when she returned in the evening. And the yard was beautiful! Sunflowers—some Kansas holdover, no doubt—lined the back wall. It would be a few months until they bloomed, but the result would be breathtaking. She'd even planted roses along the front to gain the east morning sun. She loved her house—she was beginning to love her life. Predictability was a good thing. And being in control of one's own destiny even better!

CHAPTER ELEVEN

"Now, all you need is a man." Patrice dipped a peeled shrimp into Papadeaux's crab and artichoke bisque. To make up for being preoccupied, Shelly had suggested drinks and an early dinner at their favorite haunt. Plus a ride in the Beemer.

"I'll admit there are moments . . . but I just don't have time."

"That's your choice. You've packed your life so as not to have time."

"It's given me distance. I seldom think about Ed and what was. I'm really in a different space."

"That sounds a little too New Age for me. You can't tell me there aren't nights you turn over in bed and pray there's someone to snuggle into."

"Well, yes. I want companionship." Shelly paused. "To be really truthful, I wouldn't mind just getting laid."

"Hallelujah, the truth at last."

"Don't look so smug. I'm only human. Sometimes I think I'd really enjoy having someone in my life. I miss hopping in the car and just taking off for the weekend.

Years ago Ed and I used to do things on a whim—California wine country, Cabo, New Year's Eve in London."

"Then, do it again. All work and no play—"

"Careful, I'll reserve the room next to my mother."

"You know what I mean. Your house is adorable. You'll graduate in three months. You found the balls to take that car back and get something you wanted. The divorce will be final soon. What's there to wait for? And don't give me that baloney about having your face done first."

"I did make an appointment with Dr. Chen for next month."

"I'm so jealous. I'd go for the tummy tuck first, I think."

"That's my second choice, but we'll see how the face goes."

"Well, in the meantime, I think you need a diversion."

"I'm not sure I like the sound of this."

"I look at it like I'm saving you from yourself."

"And just what is this little diversion?"

"A blind date . . . sort of. Charles has an associate coming into town from Dallas next Thursday. The sister firm of Walsh & Benson is located there. His name is Arthur Conley, recently widowed, loaded, multitalented . . . of course, it would have to look like a business meeting for Charles and me."

"Of course." Patrice's penchant for dating only married men—this time her boss—had stopped being a thing of mystery. If you don't want to marry and are willing to accept the warm body in bed every other weekend or sometimes month, then it would work. Would that work for her? Shelly didn't want a part-time relationship—but did she want marriage? She honestly didn't know.

"So, is it a go?"

"I'm reluctant, but count me in." There was something sweet about Patrice's concern. It made no sense to turn her down. And, just maybe, someone out of town wouldn't crowd her. Make too many demands on her time. Part-time could be a good thing.

Arthur, it turned out, was ten in dog years, which could have been all right, but wasn't. A thick head of white hair and only a slight paunch resting above the All-American Bull Rider buckle (1972)—a gift from a client, he'd owned up to later—made him not altogether unattractive. But mentioning his dead wife twelve times in thirty minutes—Shelly counted—left her ready to bolt long before dessert. But maybe she was being unfeeling; after all, he'd lost a life's partner.

"Arthur is thinking of retiring to New Mexico," Patrice offered over a second round of pre-dinner cocktails.

"Retire, hell. We'd finally get some work out of him if we could keep an eye on him." Polite laughter, then Charles continued, "Here's to retirement, Art. You deserve it."

"Dora and I always thought we'd end up oceanside, you know, some little cabana in Costa Rica. But I guess that wasn't meant to be. I'll be honest, I don't know what retirement's going to look like now."

"I suppose the most important thing is not to rush your decision," Shelly said.

"I've heard that before. Dora was big on not just pulling up stakes and moving before we'd spent a year in the place we thought we wanted to be. You know, test it out all three seasons."

Shelly absently wondered what had happened to the fourth and might have commented, but she caught

Patrice's eye. This was going to be one long dinner. They were called to their table before Dora could be mentioned again, and the Rancher's Club didn't disappoint—the steaks were as big as some people's belt buckles.

"Great steak. Rivals anything in Dallas. And that's saying something! I didn't even know that Albuquerque had a good steakhouse." The slab of moo-raw meat had been disappearing from his plate at an alarming rate, Shelly noticed. If there was truth to the warning that beef took over twenty-four hours to digest, someone's stomach juices would be working overtime tonight. She and Patrice passed on another round of drinks but watched the "boys" knock back a Chivas and a single malt. She was glad she wasn't picking up the tab on this one.

"Shelly has been doing the most interesting things. She just finished renovating an absolutely adorable bungalow and will graduate in three months as a massage therapist." Absolute silence followed this outburst. Would she ever forget Art looking at her, down at her, with that slightly quizzical expression? Patrice wasn't close enough to kick.

"Does that mean you're going to have your hands on some naked men?"

"I hope so." Now it was Patrice's turn to want to kick someone under the table. Shelly deftly tucked her feet under her chair.

"You know, Dora and I lasted forty-eight years because we never tempted ourselves. Never put ourselves in harm's way. Can't say I've ever met a woman who was a masseuse. I mean talked about it in public." He acted like this was the funniest thing he'd ever heard. Charlie followed suit, guffawing right along.

"Really? You seem a bit behind the times. By the way, the correct term is therapist . . . massage therapist. I'll be specializing in neuromuscular therapy." Her instructors were encouraging her; they said she truly had the touch. And it would give her credibility in health-care circles. But there was a distinct lack of credibility here.

"Honey, I don't care what you call it, you're gonna get a whole lot of ponies to rear up and say 'howdy.' Up to you to ride 'em down, I guess." This time the laughter was so raucous that two tables of diners paused to stare.

"Excuse me." Shelly pushed back from the table and reached for her purse. "Thank you for dinner." Patrice followed her to the door.

"It was the booze. I've met Art before. He's really not like this."

"Only takes one time." She turned and embraced Patrice. "I'm not blaming you. I even agree it's good to get out. I'm just not ready for fifth-grade humor."

Shelly made a pact with herself on the way home to not get sidetracked with dating until she'd graduated, and then she'd be in control of the search for Mr. Right. If she even wanted to search. He was probably out there; it was just a matter of turning over the right rock. And that would take more time than she had right now.

CHAPTER TWELVE

"Shel, I'm so sorry for the other night. I never saw that coming."

"It's all right. I consider it a sign."

"I was afraid of that. One wrong encounter and you apply that experience to everything." Patrice was lounging on Shelly's new flowered settee, feet in four-inch wedgies dangling over the side. How she could even "lounge" in a suit, silk blouse, and hair extensions was a wonder to Shelly. And, look great!

"I really do think it's time you started dating again. Keeps you from dwelling on what might have been. You know, the best place to start is online."

"You've got to be kidding. Only losers advertise online."

"I'm not sure I'd call it advertising. But how do you know? Have you tried it?"

"Of course not."

"Well, don't knock it. I met Larry online last year. And Sam."

"And where are they now?"

"That's not the point. The point is to get you out there—circulate. Do more than mope around here."

"Mope?" Shelly certainly didn't think that was an apt description.

"You've buried yourself. Maybe barricaded is a better word. You've put everything between you and having a good time."

"Patrice, I can't."

"How do you know unless you've tried?"

"It's so impersonal . . . so anonymous. So meat marketish."

"And the problem with that? Just look, Shelly, most services give you access to their database whether you join or not."

Patrice sat down at the computer, opened Internet Explorer, Googled adult dating services, and bookmarked the first one to Favorites.

"I can't believe I'm doing this."

"Keep an open mind. Let's just read some of the subject lines—maybe something will capture your imagination. You sit here."

"Patrice, look at this one—Laprod7."

"Do you think that means—?"

"I don't think it's an automotive term."

"This is the worst . . . iliker4u."

"Oh my God, how does something like that get past the censors? They do have censors, don't they?"

"Supposed to. They say they check every profile."

"I think the pictures are the worst. Here's one that lists himself as fifty-four, above average in looks and intelligence. Baseball cap—that means bald; mouth recessed—probably false teeth; and look at the folds of skin around his neck. Above average? Maybe, if he was up for the Mr. Shar-pei of America title, *and* he's only interested in women eighteen to forty-five. Isn't that the height of conceit?"

"Let me see." Patrice leaned over her shoulder. "Your choices run something like this. Mr. Pitterpatter, eighty pounds, five foot one, or—oh, here you go: loveslargeladies."

"Thanks."

"Wait, how 'bout a Jamaicanjammer?"

"I doubt if the reference is to a fruit drink with a tiny umbrella."

"It's a little grim, but if you keep searching there are some gems. Here's one. Blueheeler. Isn't that a dog?"

"Look at the picture. And your point is?"

"Do you think we start looking like our pets as we get older?"

"Blue heelers are handsome—I would have said mutt."

"You're awful, Shelly."

"Just truthful. And, frankly, a little tired of the penis having such marketability. A lot of these guys are in their seventies."

"A little late in life for you to have penis envy, isn't it?"

"Probably. Or maybe I just haven't paid attention before."

'Here's a seventy-one-year-old, MrVyrl."

"Virile? He really said that?"

"Spelled differently but pronounced the same."

"What's the deal with the aviator shades and the shirt open to the waist?"

" Like hunkaburninluv there?"

"Yeah. Is that supposed to be sexy?"

"Check Luvdnunder. What do you think that means?"

"I'm hoping he's an Aussie."

"Oh. I think you're right. But this one—John Thomas—looking for Lady Jane. Isn't that a D. H. Lawrence, *Lady Chatterley's Lover* reference?"

"Yes. I don't think I could go to bed with someone who called my twat Lady Jane."

"OK, but he sounds literate . . . literary, even. And this gives you a place to start."

"Start what?"

"Shelly, if nothing else it's simply a diversion. Sign up to a couple services and see what happens. You never know. The laughs alone make it worth it."

"Based on what I've seen, I think that's all I'll get."

"So what are the alternatives? Are you going to join a church group? Start going to bars? How are you going to meet people? Get a life back? Get out of this house and start doing things . . . with people of the opposite sex?"

"And you really think that's the answer to life? Meet people? Men, that is."

"I think you need to move on. Establish new friends, date, go to dinner, movies, the opera. You used to be so active. Maybe I'm just not used to the new you."

Shelly knew Patrice was right, and she was intrigued. Long after Patrice had left, she looked through hundreds of photos and read profile upon profile. Some of the creative spelling was painful and relied upon creative interpretation. But it was a smorgasbord of opportunity. Or whatever. Finally, she plunged in: joined two different services, picked out a couple recent photos from some she'd saved online, and wrote a profile.

People refer to this particular time in life as "the last hurrah." My "hurrah" started recently but I don't see an end for awhile. Tomorrow is always my best day. Always. But, certainly, this time in life does put an interesting emphasis upon what type of mate/partner/companion one should look for—definitely not that adorable guy with the hot car . . . well, maybe I'll amend that—I'm still a sucker for a hot car! (Luckily, neither son seemed to mind that she had traded in Ed's Porsche.) *But the interesting thing is at this time in life, I can buy my own! I really think that finally I'm interested in a partner for all the right reasons—Someone to share things with, be a helpmate for, listen and support . . . in short, I could probably do "love" right . . . finally.*

So, I'm looking for someone who has many, many things left to do and wants someone to do them with. Someone who likes to travel or read a book by the fire, walk the beach or hike in the mountains. I thrive on good conversation, shared meals, and knock-your-socks-off chemistry. If you don't own a recliner or live in a van down by the river, write me.

She read it over a couple more times, then clicked submit. Now what happened? Was it a wait and see? Should she get aggressive and wink at men who caught her interest? E-mail them? Would anyone wink at her?

By Friday the winks had piled up. She invited Patrice over to help her sort. "There's got to be a hot one in all these."

"Doubt that. We have MrHorn, the leader of a mariachi band in San Diego; pedaltometal, retired from transportation—"

"Parentheses reads truck driver."

"Yeah, that's my take. Then, let's see . . . Oh yeah, Bozo1. I wonder how long he thought before he came up with that name?"

"You're kidding."

"No, look."

"What about BigHandle—think he's referring to his name?"

"Give me a break."

"Wait. You gotta wink at Slowhands."

"Actually, I'm tempted."

CHAPTER THIRTEEN

School suddenly got busy. Classes five nights a week were reduced to three so that everyone would have time to begin their student "practice." Dating would slide to the back burner . . . again. Shelly was so excited; this was what she'd been waiting for. The proving ground. She intuitively felt she was doing the right thing, but this was assurance. She'd accepted a late evening appointment, probably not using the best of judgment—she'd be at the clinic by herself—but because of work, this was the only time he had.

"I'll stay if you want me to, Shel."

"Don't worry. I'll be fine. I'll be out of here by nine." The school's receptionist, Patsy, was one of those Birkenstocked, sturdy sorts who never wore makeup and had probably been gray since middle school.

"Well, don't forget to leave the bathroom lights on and turn off the one in the west hallway when you leave. And, remember, you don't have to give a treatment if you are the least bit afraid. You stay in control."

"I know. Don't worry about me—seriously, I'll be fine. I have to start sometime." She hoped her smile didn't give away the butterflies in her stomach that were very close to swinging off her tonsils. Intern day—hadn't she been waiting an eternity?

When he called on the phone, he had sounded big. But when all six foot four and probably 280 pounds of him filled the doorway, he moved to the enormous category. She realized she was staring.

"You Shelly?"

"Yes."

"Brett."

"Butler?"

"Yeah."

"You know, I'm going to have a problem saying Brett Butler." She laughed.

"You and about a thousand others over the years—even considered changing my name."

She stepped forward. She had to do something. Shake his hand? He didn't seem like the type. The metallic blue Harley outside the door more than hinted at a less formal intro. He saved her any wrong move by stepping into the room and grabbing a magazine off the coffee table.

"You ready to go or do I get to leaf through this five year old *Field and Stream*?"

"Five years old?" Oh, my God, she'd have to buy current magazines. She'd never thought to check the waiting room's offering of reading material.

"Hey, don't go looking all worried, I'm just yanking on you." He smiled. "I didn't come here to catch up on my reading."

"I always wanted to do that."

"Catch up on your reading?"

She laughed. "Well, that, too. But no, fly-fish." She pointed at the cover of the magazine he still held.

"I've done a fair amount. Not good at it. Never tied a fly that didn't come apart."

"Could you teach me?"

"To tie shitty flies?"

"No, fish."

"They have classes for that at UNM. Try Continuing Ed."

She felt dismissed. But what a dumb thing to ask. And why? Why was she feeling so drawn to this lunk of a man? Had it been that long since . . . . Actually, she didn't want to go there. But she couldn't deny that the air felt electric. He was so alive and straightforward and honest and she was feeling something that had been buried for an awfully long time. She cleared her throat, but realized that he'd been watching her.

"Are you waiting on me? Am I supposed to follow you, or something?"

"Or something." She grinned. "Give me a minute to get set up." As if the room wasn't in perfect order—oil in a heating unit, rocks steaming in a Crock-Pot, sheets creaseless, pillows and towels stacked under the table. She ducked around the corner, gave the room a quick once-over, turned to go back to the waiting room, and almost ran into him in the doorway.

"Are you married?"

Did he really want to know? "Not in nine days, eleven hours and fifty-three seconds." She responded. "But who's counting, right?"

She liked his chuckle, deep, resonant—it seemed to start at his toes.

He stood looking down at her as she continued to stand in the doorway, blocking his entry. Move. She had to move, welcome him, turn down the top sheet, give him eight to ten minutes to undress . . . undress. Was that what was causing her paralysis?

"Last time I did this, I got to lie down on a table—like that one." He pointed over her shoulder.

"Yes, of course, I . . . ."

"Ah, come on baby, don't tell me I'm your first."

"You're my first." She tried not to grin sheepishly.

"Shit, I don't do virgins . . . but, you know, and excuse me when I say this—I wouldn't mind 'doing' you. You're a hell of a good-looking woman. But you're safe—as long as you're married." His wink was infectious and she burst out laughing. "So what do we do now? You want to go ahead with this?"

"I have to go ahead with this."

"No, you don't. You don't have to do anything you're not comfortable with—that includes 'doing' me."

"If I don't 'do' you, I'll never be able to do this." She half turned; her gesture included the room behind her.

"Probably some truth in that." He continued to look at her. He was close enough for her to feel the warmth of his body and catch just the faint whiff of cologne—something nice, not what she would have thought. This was expensive and understated and didn't fit with a Harley. "So, let me take you by the hand." He pulled her around and gently pushed her ahead of him into the room. "Now, the drill goes something like this, correct me if I'm wrong. You'll say, 'I'm going to step outside and let you get undressed. If you're comfortable removing all your clothes, it will make my job easier. Use the sheet to cover up with or this here towel—your choice. Take your time. I'll be back in five minutes . . . .' How am I doing?"

"Great. Perfect."

"Good. Then why don't you take five minutes an' go take a few deep breaths and then come back?" He gently turned her toward the door and patted her on the behind. "Just don't forget where I am. I'll be waiting."

When she returned and discreetly knocked before entering the room, she was amazed to see him sitting on the table with only his shirt off.

"I don't understand."

"I think half a body is enough to get started with. Besides, I didn't warn you that you'd be massaging a colored man." With that he turned, and Shelly almost gasped. The scene was vivid—stream, trees, female centaur, giant elk facing each other—all in glorious color and meticulous detail.

"There are a couple more." He pulled a pant leg up to reveal red-orange-yellow flames licking up the outside of his calf.

"This one ain't finished. Then there are these." He pointed to bicep and chest.

"Pretty impressive. I'm looking at a lot of money and a lot of time. Can I ask you a question?"

"Yeah."

"I saw a picture of a guy one time—one of those e-mailed photos that female office workers pass around ..."

"And?"

"Well . . . I'm not sure how to ask this."

"Just ask it."

"Does your penis form the head of a dragon?"

"What?"

"I think you heard me. In the picture the guy had a tattoo of this huge dragon. It's wings sort of folded up over his stomach, but his penis made up the head with a steel bar through the tip that formed the eyes."

"Nobody has ever asked me that before." He was shaking his head.

"Well?" She liked this banter. How long had it been—no, that wasn't the question—had she ever felt this comfortable this quickly, and been aroused this easily?

"No, no dragon. The artwork is pretty much contained above the waist."

"Pretty much?" She was grinning.

"Hey, don't believe me? I'll show you." He slipped off the table and started to unzip.

"No. That's OK." For just a second she wished he'd continue. With a jolt she realized she wanted to see him naked. Touch him. Maybe even . . . .

"Are you all right?"

"No, uh, yeah . . . sure, sorry . . . " Thank God the light was dim; she knew her face blended with her strawberry blond roots.

"You don't sound very all right."

"I think we need to get started. Are you still going to keep your pants on?"

"Probably should." He gave her a long look. "I can always give you the rest of me at some later time."

Later time. She would see him again. Was there a double meaning? The rest of him . . .

"Face up? Face down?"

"What?"

"Me . . . how do you want me? On my back? Stomach?"

"Stomach." And how did she want him? Any way. And realized with a jolt that this was probably the first time in twenty-five years that she'd had a lewd thought.

The rest of the massage was uneventful. His skin was warm and responded to her touch. She could feel his muscles relax, heard his steady breathing. He was easy to touch and she didn't want to stop. She wanted to climb on the table and just snuggle beside him, hold him, bury her face in his warmth. And if she did, she knew that he could make the world go away. This was the kind of man who could be an anchor. Suddenly, she knew just how much her life was missing. How much the good doctor didn't, couldn't, give her—maybe hadn't ever given her. This man was raw, yet oozed passion and, strangely enough, security—it was like she could feel it beneath his skin. It was the oddest sensation.

She waited for him to dress before turning off the lights in the hallway. It was already dusk. The waiting room was now in shadows.

"That was good, really good." He paused by the desk, dropped three twenties, and picked up one of her business cards. She wanted to grab it out of his hand and scribble her cell phone number on the back. But that would look a little too eager.

"I'm glad you liked it." She walked him to the door and stood looking at the bike.

"If you expect me to kiss you, I'm not going to."

"I'm not saying I expect it . . . but just out of curiosity, why wouldn't you?"

"Just gives you something to look forward to." He winked and laughed.

"I think that comes under the heading of teasing."

"Yeah, it's good for you. Don't want you to get the impression that I'm easy." More laughter. "Is there some better way to reach you than calling the office here?"

She took the card back, walked to the desk, found a pencil, and added her cell phone number.

Then he was gone. She stood for a moment, trying to figure out why she felt so empty. He was bigger than life . . . almost literally . . . and when he walked out the door, he seemed to take all the air in the room with him. Had she ever been so taken with someone so quickly? And the attraction seemed mutual. He would call. She was sure of it. She could still recall the feel of him. She shook her head. This wasn't getting the office locked up.

She literally slept with her cell phone. Four days and not a call. Why would he ask for her number if he hadn't planned on calling? She felt fourteen again—but not in a good way. This was all the pain of not being asked to dance—of hugging the wall attempting nonchalance. Of turning away so as not to appear eager, of keeping her arms ramrod straight and plastered to her sides lest maturing sweat glands suddenly became offensive.

She remembered too well the burning yearning of an awkward eighth grader—feeling trapped in a body that was leafing out in tune with the rites of spring. And virginity was heavy between her legs, a painful, throbbing lump that called out to be appeased but by what and how, she didn't have a clue. Even now, knowing the what and how didn't make things easier or the throbbing any less—so what had really changed in forty-seven years?

Patrice wasn't even sympathetic.

"Shelly, he's a biker. You know nothing about him. From what you've said, he knows nothing about you."

"You mean my age?"

"Well, that for one thing. How old do you think he is?"

"Probably older than he looks. But I'd guess somewhere in his fifties."

"So you could be eight to ten years older?"

"Maybe."

"Does he know you're comfortable?"

"I'm assuming that's a reference to the fact that I don't have to work?"

"Yes. Don't you think that might look attractive to him?"

"I don't know. He didn't seem the type."

"I think it would scare some, but really be enticing to others. I just want you to be careful. I don't want this to be some reaction to the Art debacle. There are good men out there, Shel."

The call came ten days later. As if no time had passed, she felt her pulse quicken at the familiar voice.

"Hey, baby, bet you thought I'd died."

"I did check the obits."

"Had to work out of town. Wasn't planning on it taking up a couple weekends."

"Where'd you go?"

"Arizona. Big project, but it's winding down now. That's probably my last trip for awhile. I gotta go back an' pick up my fifth wheel one of these days."

"Let me go with you. That could be fun."

"Naw . . . I'll take one of the guys. A five-or six-hour drive isn't my idea of fun."

There it was again. Did he think she was pushing? He could close her out as quickly as let her in. And didn't his cell phone work in Arizona? She felt peevish and more than a little let down.

"Hey, I called to ask if you'd have time to do a rub tomorrow night."

"Office is closed this weekend—owner's painting. I could do a treatment here."

"Now you're talking. You got any liquid refreshment in that house of yours?"

"I can make a mean pitcher of margaritas."

"Rubs and 'ritas . . . can't beat that with a stick. You tell me where all this is going to take place."

She gave him the address and they decided upon seven. She asked him to take a hot shower first and then instantly regretted it, but he didn't make anything of it.

"Hey, cute thing, you got twenty-four hours to decide how much of this ol' body you want to see this time." Raucous laughter and then a click.

She sat holding the phone—excited, perplexed, put off by his familiarity, drawn into it, remembering his warmth.

He called her from the corner for directions, but she could already hear the deep, throaty rattle of the diesel as the truck pulled to the curb in front of the house. He was here. One last look around. Table was up in front of the fireplace. A Crock-Pot of hot rocks simmered on the hearth. An assortment of oils and lotions lined up along the mantle. An oversized towel draped the table; sheets were pulled taut across a two-inch padding of Tempur-Pedic foam. Ready. Everything was ready . . . but was she? Deep breath, walk to the door, remind herself that even if this was her home, this was a business deal.

He smelled fresh, something cucumber and mint, and his hair was wet and curled down his neck and around his ears. She wanted to move into his body, just stop him there in the doorway to the living room and hold on, run her hands up his chest, pull his head down to her level, put her mouth on his. Instead, she moved around him and closed the door to the outside.

"I thought you'd ride the bike."

"Needed to put gas in that thing." He gestured at the Dodge one-ton. "You got any of those margaritas you promised?"

"It'll take me all of five minutes to mix some up."

"Well, let's get going."

He followed her to the kitchen and leaned against the counter as she poured mix and alcohol into a pitcher of crushed ice.

"You want a mango margarita?"

"Baby, I don't care, as long as it has booze in it. I'm not drinking 'em to get a vitamin C fix."

"Salt?"

"Yeah, if it's handy."

"Right here." She ran a lime quarter around the rim and turned the glass upside down on a plate of sea salt. A handful of ice, a stir of the pitcher, and she handed a glass to him. "Now, we're ready to go in there."

"Do I get a chance to finish this before we start?"

"Sure." She motioned toward the couch.

"Been a long week." He sank down, carefully balancing the glass in front of him.

He looked tired. She could have kicked herself, but she couldn't think of one interesting thing to say. She drew her legs up under her on the opposite end of the couch and waited. Without spilling a drop, he leaned back and soon began breathing evenly. He was asleep. She leaned over and slipped the glass from his hand. She watched him. He looked older in the half-light of the candles flickering from the mantle. Maybe there wasn't a big age difference. He was exhausted, but vaguely she was disappointed. Had she expected more? Yes. A kiss? A hug? Some kind of touching. She missed his poking fun at her.

She picked up her glass and walked to the kitchen. Oh well. She was scrubbing the sticky margarita mix off the counter when she heard him behind her.

"Hey, sorry about that." He stood in the doorway of the kitchen and finger-combed his hair away from his eyes. "Can't work them fourteen-hour days like I used to."

"Not a problem. Why don't you get undressed and get on the table?"

"We doing all of me tonight?"

"If you'd like."

"Yeah."

No banter. Was he just tired? Preoccupied? Not interested in her? Why had she suddenly become business only? But hadn't she been afraid just a few hours ago that she might not be? She was irritated that she seemed pulled in two directions.

"Let's start face up."

She waited until she heard him settle on the table before entering the room and dragging up a chair. She positioned herself behind his head. He was asleep before she even laid hands on him.

She took an hour to ease tight muscles, rousing him once to turn over. When she was finished, she let him sleep an extra half hour before waking him. She left the room while he was dressing, and after downing the watery remains of his margarita and a mumbled thanks, he left.

It was nine twenty. So much for a big Saturday night. She grabbed the margarita pitcher from the kitchen counter, filled her glass, and brought both into the living room. The letdown was so great, she burst into tears. Had she just expected too much? She just wanted to be held . . . kissed . . . touched. Angry that she'd let this man get to her, she jumped up, pulled the sheets from the table, and carried them into the utility room. It was obvious that they were attracted to each other . . . so, what had happened? Being tired didn't mean he couldn't have kissed her.

Suddenly, she didn't have the energy to take down the table and put away the rocks and Crock-Pot. She blew out the candles and went to bed.

It took her a minute to figure out the jingle of the phone. She turned over and eyed the clock. Four ten. Who would . . . ? Her parents. Oh my God. Something had happened.

"Hello."

"I forgot to pay you."

She laughed in spite of herself. "It's OK. We didn't have sex."

A short, explosive laugh on his side. "No, baby, I woulda remembered. And just in case you're wondering, I usually don't have to pay for it." Another laugh.

"Do you know what time it is?"

"Gotta go to work. Thought I told you. I'm going back up to Santa Fe for the day. Full crew's working."

"Do you ever get time off?"

"Not very often."

"Plays hell with your love life."

"Do I have one of those?"

"Would you like one of those?"

"I got this woman I'd like to see more of."

"How do you mean that?"

"Any way you want to take it, baby."

"I'm guessing that I know this woman."

"For all I know, you may be intimate with her."

"You're funny."

"Not very. I owe you an apology for tonight. I'm gonna make it up."

"How?"

"I'll think of something. Hey, I'm just pulling into the yard and I need two hands on the wheel. I'll be callin' ya."

He was gone before she said good-bye.

But he called the next night. And the next. And the next. The conversation was pretty much the same. His day. How had hers been? They slipped into an easy camaraderie far more comfortable than Shelly had imagined possible.

"Am I going to get to see you this weekend?"

"Don't know. I'm working on it."

"Working on it?"

"Yeah, might be out of town. Won't know 'til Friday."

"Do you think I'm ever going to get laid?"

"Shit, baby, I don't remember kissing you."

"You haven't."

"Don't you think we need to do that first? Maybe kiss and a little fondle."

"Kiss and fondle?"

"Yeah, it used to be called foreplay."

"I remember that."

"Thought you might. Good stuff. Goes real well with 'ritas."

"And I should warn you, I don't do one-night stands."

"So, I gotta do it twice?" Feigned dismay.

"Yeah, but don't sound so pained."

"As long as I don't have to do it on consecutive nights."

"Shit, we'd be lucky if it were in consecutive years."

"Probably true." Deep, rumbling laughter.

"So how do I know I got something to look forward to?" Shelly was thinking of pinning him to a date—like when was this going to happen—but she loved his answer.

"I've been told I got the touch, baby. We'll see what you think."

She could still hear the echo of laughter after he'd hung up. Wow. She was going to get laid. Had she ever worked so hard all those years ago to spread her legs? Probably not.

Friday morning he told her he'd be by at 7:30 to pick her up on Saturday night.

"Where are we going?"

"To visit my mom."

"Does she live in Albuquerque?"

"Nursing home in the Heights."

The first time he had asked her out and they were going to a nursing home? There was either something really wrong with this picture or it was unbearably sweet—and she'd passed some sort of hurdle and was deemed worthy of being taken home to Mom—literally. Somehow she hadn't realized that the rituals were the same—at twenty or at sixty. It was just Mom who had moved.

He showed up on the bike and it only took Shelly two minutes to slip out of the demure skirt and cashmere henley and throw on jeans, a black T-shirt, and boots.

"Your butt's gonna look good on the back of the bike."

"Is that how you choose your girlfriends? Butt presentability doing eighty down the freeway?" She got the laugh she wanted.

"Yeah, it's as good as any."

Had she been on a bike before? Not for about forty years. But it felt good. Felt good to wrap her arms around him and just mold to his backside. The ride to the home was all too short. Mom, it turned out was only convalescing—two knee operations had left her hobbled. The tall, eightyish, recently widowed former beauty didn't mince her words and didn't fit the image of a tattooed biker's mother. What had happened to the overweight, chain-smoking floozy in a flowered muumuu spilling over the sides of a wheelchair that she'd imagined?

"So, is this the next missus?"

"Aw, Mom, you promised to be good."

"No, I didn't. Life is too short to be good. Wouldn't you agree?" This last was directed to Shelly.

"Absolutely." Shelly grinned as Brett looked toward the ceiling.

"If I'd had any sense when your father was alive, I wouldn't have been good. He didn't deserve a good woman."

"If you don't behave, I'm taking Shelly out of here."

"There's nothing I'd say that she hasn't heard before."

"I'm sure that's true." Shelly was enjoying this.

"His father liked women, you know." Carol Butler leaned back in her chair and played with the stack of gold bracelets that circled her arm.

Shelly didn't know, but vaguely wondered if the condition was hereditary.

"Come on, Mom. She ain't interested in family history."

"She might be." Carol looked at Shelly and winked, then addressed her son. "I thought you promised to bring me food. I'll never get well if I eat the pabulum they serve here."

"You didn't ask me to."

"Yes, I did."

"You know you're going to be hiding your own Easter eggs one of these days."

"I don't want any lip—I just want food."

"OK, Mom, let me guess. You want an order of wings from Hooters."

"Why, that would be perfect. How did you know?" A coquettish batting of eyelashes.

"Mom lives on those things. You up to a little food fetching?"

Shelly nodded. She hated wings and had never been to Hooters, but what the hell? Wasn't life all about expanding one's horizons?

It was apparent the minute they walked in that one of the waitresses, a twentysomething, probably had known Brett in a biblical sense. She sidled toward them, and Shelly wondered if she exhaled would she lose a cup size. Probably not, but hard to tell. The implants were grapefruit-half perfect.

"Hey, sweet thing, since when have you worked Saturdays?" Brett threw an arm around the waitress and drew her to him.

Shelly noticed that "sweet thing" seemed less than interested in striking up a conversation—probably because Shelly was there—and really wasn't interested in being hugged. Her interest and talent seemed relegated to maintaining full lungs of air.

"She the one currently riding the trailer hitch?"

Brett nodded. Shelly made a note to get clarification later. The waitress took the order for wings. The butt that was twitching its way to the back was adorable. Had that been enhanced, too? Coming and going, the package was perfect. And it was apparent that Brett thought so too. At this rate, she might not have his attention the rest of the evening. It was already nine and she had visions of being dropped off at the house—another disappointing evening.

"How old is she?"

"Twenty-two next month."

"Old girlfriend? And I use the term 'old' loosely."

"I told you about her."

"No, I would have remembered."

"Hey, don't go getting all pissed off just 'cause of your old man. Me an' her didn't have kids and I wasn't sneaking around on my old lady."

"Oh well, that makes all the difference." Shelly knew how she sounded, peevish and quarrelsome, but she didn't care. "So you're only thirty-three years older?"

"Thirty-two."

She'd found out his age, but it was a hollow victory. She was still six years older than he was.

"Hey, lady, look at me. I don't see anyone standing next to me right now but you. And that's the way I like it and that's the way I want it. You got that?" He'd taken her arm and squared her up to look at him. She didn't dare turn to see if sweet thing was watching. But she secretly hoped she was. "We're gonna drop off some wings for Mom and then we're gonna make a pitcher of 'ritas and see what happens. I owe you some lovin' and I plan to pay my debt."

She opened her mouth to remind him about her rule on one-night stands but he brushed her lips—a kiss? Not exactly, but not exactly not, either. And he was grinning. Ownership. She felt just like she'd been peed on, marked off like that Scottie her parents had had who staked out his territory by lifting his leg and watering her foot whenever another dog got too close. And she couldn't help but grin back and will her heart to stop pounding.

They sat on the couch facing the fireplace with a pitcher of margaritas between them on the coffee table. The first 'rita had slipped down smoothly and she realized she had a nice tequila buzz going.

"Before I forget, what was that trailer hitch comment about?"

"Biker talk. Don't need to put a seat behind the rider for his old lady, just weld a hitch to the fender."

"Nice picture."

"Hey, you asked."

"Thanks."

"I don't want to seem pushy but what's it gonna take to see some naked skin and nipples."

"Well, hey, why didn't you speak up before?" Shelly laughed and pulled the T-shirt over her head and turned toward him in a black lace cami.

"I don't think I gained any ground here."

"Maybe something more like this?" She rocked back, her legs beneath her, then pulled the camisole over her head, making certain her right nipple was about an inch from his mouth. And he didn't disappoint. Bracing her back with two hands, he pulled her closer.

"You're exquisite, Shelly."

Oh my God. Had he ever called her by name before? And exquisite? He could replace the boys in her will with far less. But all rational thought disappeared when he put the nipple in his mouth. No one had ever been as gentle. No one. Ed had always roughly "tuned in Tokyo," then headed south. Never this slow sucking, gently pulling outward, teasing a nipple to a point before circling it with his tongue. Were those aspirated animal sounds hers?

"I don't want to stop this for too long, but you got another piece of furniture in this house that we could stretch out on?"

She laughed, took him by the hand, and led him to the bedroom. No one said anything. She slipped out of her jeans, thought a nanosecond about leaving her underpants on, and then tossed them aside—all the time watching him undress—not even feeling embarrassed that he was devouring her body with his eyes. And it wasn't going to take any foreplay to get the other player to join them.

She pulled the blanket and sheet back, crawled into bed, turned on her side, and propped up on one elbow.

"See? No dragon." He was standing by the edge of the bed, inspecting his hard-on. She reached out and took his penis in her hand, running her thumb under the edge of the head, then over it.

"No hardware, either."

"Give you all night to stop that, baby."

He slipped into bed and took her in his arms. And she fit. Sweet and slow—the long kisses, strokes up her inner thighs until screaming was an honest-to-God option. Then he was between her legs, pausing with barely the head inside, letting her do the work, pull on him, hoping to hell all those years of Kegel exercises had paid off; then, arching upward, digging fingernails into his butt, she brought him fully into her. And got lost. Legs around his neck.

"Yeah, baby, oh yeah."

His excitement was her excitement. The rhythm was perfect. She was lulled by the reaction of her body—the wanton wanting. And suddenly the world turned tingly warm and liquid with ripples of breath-catching intensity that rolled upward and outward. At the same time? Close, she knew that. It was plain vanilla, but definitely Häagen-Dazs. The sex was hauntingly beautiful in its simplicity. He had made love to her.

He rolled to the side, traced a line from below her belly button to her chin, and turned her head toward him. The kiss was sweet—playful pulling on her lower lip, then tracing the outline of her upper lip with his tongue.

"You OK?" He pulled back to look at her.

"I don't think 'OK' quite captures it. How 'bout you?"

"Probably coulda lasted longer. Been too long. Almost forgot how good that stuff is. Give me a minute. I'll be back."

He pushed up and away from her after one more soft, teasing kiss, which stirred something that should have been satiated. The moan gave her away.

"Hey, I know we got a contract, but no seconds in the same night. I gotta give this ol' body a little rest."

She watched him walk down the hall to the bathroom and was pleasantly surprised when he returned with a warm, damp washcloth and hand towel.

"Do I get to do the honors or think you can handle it?"

"I probably have it covered—so to speak."

He took both back to the bathroom when she'd finished, then came back to sit on the edge of the bed.

"You know, my best friend defines chivalry as a guy's willingness to sleep in the wet spot."

A chuckle. "She's got a point there. But I'm not going impress you with chivalry tonight. I hafta get going, baby. Gotta be at the yard at ten."

She roused and started to get up.

"Hey, I don't want you to move. I'll lock up." Then he leaned down and kissed her on the forehead and tucked the covers under her chin. "Talk to you later."

She didn't need someone to tell her not to move. The bed felt too good—she felt too good. She heard the click of the front door lock and the throb of the Harley. She turned over and dragged a pillow closer—bathed in his scent—and just buried her head. When she woke, it was to the room starkly outlined by a flash of lightning. Then the rain began. Soft, steady . . . the desert's elixir. Five a.m. She pulled on a tee and underpants, went to the bathroom, opened the window, and let the mist float in. The palest of peach light streaked the sky to the east. The rain wouldn't last long; already she could see faint patches of blue bordering the gray.

She breathed deeply and leaned into the window, cheek pressed against the screen. The dust and lime-sweet smell of rain on cement, pungent yet the teaser of a hundred memories, made her take comfort in feeling so alive. It had been a long time. She couldn't stop smiling, but stood there and hugged herself in the rain-chilled morning. There was something bittersweet about offering herself now at this time of life. Beginning anew yet knowing it was the last fifteen or twenty good years. It put such emphasis upon knowing what she wanted—no time for mistakes, trying something out and then starting over. A biker? Did he fit? She had always been thankful large puzzles came with a picture on the cover of the box. But there wasn't any picture now. And if she didn't even know the plan, how could she put the pieces together?

He called at six, just as she was carrying a second cup of coffee to the living room.

"Can't talk long. Just wanted to make sure you were among the living."

"Barely. Sex has always been my drug of choice."

"Yeah, I probably shoulda stuck with it way-back-when myself—fewer side effects."

"You sure about that?"

"As long as you don't go falling in love with me."

"You think that's a possibility?"

"Stranger things have happened."

"I don't think you have to worry." For just one perverse second, she felt like hanging up. Talk about being slammed to the floor. But wasn't he good at doing that? Just when she felt a connection, she was reminded there wasn't one. Was there any danger of her falling in love? If she wanted to be truthful? Yes.

"Well, just checking. I'll call you later."

With a third cup of coffee, she moved out onto the deck with breakfast—a croissant that she didn't need with butter and raspberry honey that she really didn't need; the handful of grapes was the only healthy thing on the plate.

The air was fresh and the slight breeze cooling. Drops of water still glistened on the dark red leaves of an ornamental plum. Her world. Peaceful. Relaxing. Conducive to muddling through whatever it was she thought she wanted to do with her life. And whom she wanted to do it with.

The doorbell startled her. She hadn't heard a car, but she leaned over the fence and saw the station wagon parked across the street and two houses down. Ed was standing on the front steps, simply staring up at the house, taking in the Rose of Sharon and the tile overhang. It would be interesting to know what he was thinking. But there was no reason not to be cordial.

"Hi."

"Do you have time to talk?"

"About?"

"I contacted Stephanie and put in a house offer a month or so back. I haven't heard anything."

"OK. Just a minute." She gathered the breakfast things and placed them in the kitchen sink on her way to the front door. Stephanie had called her, ranting about the offer—some fifty thousand below market—and said Ed had cited numerous repairs, which Stephanie listed and pointed out were mostly cosmetic. Shelly had really not felt like confronting the issue before—had it been one month? Two? Probably. Guess now was as good a time as any.

"Tiffany and I are anxious to reach a mutual understanding on this. Time's getting away. There's lots to be done before we can move in." Ed perched on the overstuffed arm of the loveseat. "Have you even gone back to start sorting? It doesn't look like anything's been taken."

It rankled that he'd been in the house. He'd supposedly given her all the keys and the two garage door openers. But, no, she hadn't been back.

"I was hoping that one or both of the boys might go through things with me. It's their things, too. Somehow coordinating everyone's time has just been impossible."

"Of course, the offer still stands—if you want to wait until after we move in, that's OK, too."

"I'm surprised you're so certain that we have a deal."

"Of course, we have a deal. Why wouldn't we? You aren't moving back."

"When Stephanie presented your offer, there was some question as to whether it was fair. I've contacted two Realtors who specialize in the area and I agree with Stephanie. The offer is easily fifty thousand below market." A white lie, but if she could believe Stephanie, true.

"That's ridiculous. I itemized all the repairs—did Stephanie share those figures?"

"She did. I thought several were more cosmetic than necessary."

"Such as?"

"Bricking the front entry to replace weathered cement, putting double-pane wood windows in the utility room, changing out all ceiling fans—"

"Three don't work."

"Then you get them repaired."

"What are you saying, Shelly?"

"That I want fair market price."

"You are so out of touch. You have no idea what it's going to cost us to just make that house safe for children. The swimming pool alone—"

"Those are expenses that you will incur with a growing family. Fencing and gating the pool was not a requirement for us."

"It's meeting the subdivision's code."

"Code now—not then. Why should I be penalized for changes beyond my control? Beyond my needs? I'm not going to pay for making your family comfortable or safe, Ed."

"No, and I'm sure it's too much to ask to have you stop embarrassing us, too."

"Embarrassing you?" Where had that come from?

"Paul Green saw you riding on the back of a motorcycle last night—behind a man with tattoos. You pulled in front of him to go into Hooters." Ed's smugness was suddenly unbearable. His arms were crossed over his chest and for all the world it looked like he'd just delivered a scolding to a small child.

"Can't help it if the new boyfriend has a few tats."

"Shelly, I want you to take your maiden name back."

"What?"

"I think you understand me. As long as you are going to be irrational, irresponsible, and run with scum, I want no ties to you."

"Sorry, Ed, no can do. My last name will match my children's last name unless I remarry. Shelly Walters no longer exists." The anger was vaulting to the surface. So this is why he came by. How dare him. What gave him the right to take everything—even her name?

"I will be raising children in this community—with the Sinclair name. I don't want my children linked to some crazy woman—"

"It's time for you to leave. This is my house. I won't listen to this."

"I wish you could see yourself, Shelly. How far you've slipped. It's pathetic. Brian is beside himself. I think they're rethinking even having children."

"What a shame. Surely Rachel's genes can overpower any weaknesses from our side. Now, out. I won't repeat myself before calling the cops."

And he left—without a fight, without another word. Shelly was surprised but relieved. Would she have the nerve to take out a restraining order? She wasn't sure.

Brett was working out of town but called every night and hinted that he could probably fulfill his two-night stand contract that weekend. She couldn't wait. She made sure she didn't have any massage appointments on Saturday. She wanted the day to do some running around and be fresh for giving Brett a massage that night. Was he costing her money? Yes. Somehow, when they'd moved from the office to her house, all compensation stopped. If it was a big problem, she guessed she could ask—but knew she wouldn't. She kept hoping that he'd at least bring a bottle of tequila, but he didn't. Cheap? Or just horribly strapped for money? He'd taken her out one time to visit his mother and wait in a restaurant for carryout. Even Patrice was giving her little lectures on how she was being treated. Still . . . the sex probably made it worthwhile.

He was late—pulling up about eight thirty. It probably wasn't a good thing that she was well into her second marg.

"What are my chances of putting this thing in the garage? I don't wanna leave it on the street."

Was he staying the night? She caught her breath.

"Good. I'll get the keys."

"If you give them to me, I'll do the do-si-do."

When he came in, she handed him a marg. He put it on the kitchen counter and pulled her into him.

"I've been thinking about you for days."

His touch was soft, teasing with promises. If she had to explain what made him the best kisser ever, it was his anticipation—his knowing her move before she even knew it herself. If she opened her mouth a little wider, his was open to match, his tongue, her tongue exploring at the same moment. Softly, tentatively. The pressure was perfect—she could feel his lips, follow his lead as he followed hers. Not like the boy in high school who should have worn a bib—saliva dripping out the side of his mouth as it was plastered to hers. Funny how so many men couldn't get something as simple as kissing right. Prolonged kissing and stroking were never a part of Ed's repertoire either—caused, no doubt, by coming home to grab three hours of sleep before going back on call, and not wanting to choose between sex and sleep.

This time she didn't leave the room as Brett undressed.

"You're getting pretty ballsy."

"Direct proportion to how much of this I've had." She held out the margarita glass.

"Which reminds me, I need another swig of that stuff." She brought the pitcher in from the kitchen and filled his glass. "You going to do me in the nude?"

"Hadn't thought about it."

"And don't give me any lip about needing to get tucked and sucked. I like your body, Shelly."

"Spoken like someone who's horny."

A chuckle. "Yeah, that, too. But I love your touch—love your softness. An' you've got about the most responsive nipples on the planet."

"Well, that's a plus."

"I think so."

"Let's start with you face down."

"An' when I start to levitate?"

"Guess we'll have to turn you over."

"I don't think that's going to be very long."

She laughed and pulled her T-shirt off, then added bra and jeans to the pile on the couch. Why did she feel so much better leaving underpants on? Some vestige of decorum, no doubt.

"So looks like you're just letting the sisters out tonight."

She hadn't realized that he was watching her. "Yeah. That OK?"

"Hey, I'll take what I can get."

"Then I need to get started."

She ran her thumbs down the long muscles on either side of his spine—the erector spinae. Tight. She leaned in with more muscle and felt her breasts brush the back of his head and top of his traps. Then she felt his fingers trace a line upward on the inside of her right thigh and his thumb push under the elastic at the leg of her panties. She caught her breath as his fingers began to explore and ever so gently tease.

"Not sure the therapist can hold up under those kinds of maneuvers."

"It's good for her. And me. You feel good, baby. I'm just thinking about where I want to be later."

"There's a lot of body I need to cover first."

"Nobody's stopping you. See? Hands above my head. Quit jawing and get a move on."

When he turned over, she abandoned her massage training and relied on Max's art. And from the sounds he was making, the choice was the right one.

"You're good at that, baby."

"I'm good at this, too."

She slipped out of her panties and kicked her sandals under the table. Would the table hold the two of them if she got on top? She remembered it held five hundred pounds, or thought she did. This was not the time to dig out the manual and look it up. She quickly calculated and for once didn't lie about her weight—even to herself. They should be fine. She had done pelvic adjustments on this very table before, which required her to straddle the client. Of course, her other clients were a lot smaller. Guess she wouldn't know 'til she tried.

Her mount would have gotten her perfect Olympic tens. She leaned across his chest and kissed him, then, guiding his penis, eased backwards until he was completely inside. Her moves were slow, deliberately arousing and getting the reaction she wanted.

Finally, "How 'bout we adjourn to that other room an' you let me back in the game? Don't want my evening to end too early." He got off the table and took her by the hand.

He started at her ankles and nipped and nibbled his way north. When she thought she couldn't stand it any longer, he entered her, and with long, rhythmic strokes took her over the top. Then he came himself, slipped beside her, and held her. There wasn't any conversation. He smoothed her hair back from her eyes and kissed her. Finally, she just cuddled into him and fell asleep. His soft snoring was soothing.

She wasn't sure what awakened her—a noise? Tree branch against the window? But she turned away from

Brett and looked. There was a figure in the window—someone looking in. She blinked, sat up, looked again, but saw nothing. Her heart was pounding. There had been someone. She wasn't imagining things. But there was no one there now. She clutched the sheet to her chin and tried to stop shaking.

"Hey, woman, my butt's freezing. Where'd you go?"

"Here." She slid down beside him again and turned away from the window—it could have been a dream. She'd been half asleep.

"You OK?"

"Just cold."

"Well, get over here." He took her arm and pulled her into him. And she gave into the feeling of safety and warmth. No one—no *thing*—could get her. She was protected.

In the morning there was time for coffee, and she followed him out to open the garage and move the Beemer that blocked the door. The bane of old houses—the garages were built for old cars, small cars more buggy-without-the-horse size. If the bike was in, her car was out.

He kissed her, then started the Harley.

"Call you later."

She watched him back out, turn, and take off up the street. She'd barely made it to the house when she heard her cell.

"Hey, your old man drive an older Benz station wagon?"

"Yes, why?"

"'Cause he's a madman, Shelly. He's stalking you. He was parked a block away. Pulled out like he was going to run me down. I ditched him by running a light."

She had seen Ed at the window. Oh, my God. She held the receiver with two hands to keep it from shaking and leaned against the kitchen sink.

"Baby, you still there?"

"Yeah."

"Call your lawyer. Get the restraining order. Do you own a gun?"

"No."

"Does he?"

"Yes."

"Then do the math on this one, baby—you need to protect yourself. You're already behind in the game plan."

"You think I should buy a gun?"

"Not if you won't use it. You own a gun, you're making the decision that you could kill someone."

"I don't know—"

"Ah, baby, you read it in the papers all the time—unsuspecting wife or girlfriend dies at the hand of someone they swore would never hurt them. And then all the neighbors say what a nice man he was."

"OK, I'll look into it."

"Do it for me, baby. I'd like you around for awhile."

That came as close to saying he liked her as anything he'd ever said.

The day rushed by. Another call from Brett reiterating her need for a gun. Again, she promised to look into it. She stayed busy and reveled in feeling sated and wanted. And knew she needed to be careful—with her heart. Being protected was a powerful incentive to establish emotional ties. She knew she'd end up with a broken heart if she did. It was one-sided, lop-sided. But the draw to be taken care of was almost too much to withstand—especially under the circumstances.

The last half of her day was filled with chores—laundry, paying bills, studying. She left grocery shopping go until late and then treated herself to a spree at one of the organic markets. She'd bought just enough groceries to warrant a couple of trips to the car. She got her keys out and grabbed the biggest sack. It would be easier to go in the front door and miss all the back steps up to the deck.

She moved the screen door aside and unlocked the front door. The bag of groceries hit the floor within a nanosecond of his turning on the light. She felt her knees turn to rubber. There Ed was on the couch in front of her.

"Get out of here."

"Shelly, I want to talk."

"There's nothing to talk about."

She fished her cell out of the back flap of her purse. 911. Domestic violence? Breaking and entering? Both?

"I can't blame you for being frightened, but you don't need to call for help." He crossed the room in two steps and twisted the phone out of her hand. "Just listen to me. I'm not here to hurt you."

"How did you get in?" Looking down, she realized that she was standing in a puddle of milk. Damn. The grocery bag had broken and so had the container of milk. She pulled the edge of the Persian carpet out of the way.

"You need to start locking the French doors." He gestured behind him toward the dining room.

"I need to clean this up." She willed her feet to carry her to the kitchen. Maybe if she didn't overreact, really did listen to him. Maybe if she could just stop shaking. Maybe if she bolted for the back door—but her keys to the gate were still in the car. She grabbed paper towels and went back to the living room.

"Let me help." He took the roll, pulled off half a dozen towels, wadded them, and knelt down to sop up the milk. "Take these." He handed her a jar of mayonnaise, a container of olives, the French bread, and a package of Feta cheese. She rinsed everything and put the olives and cheese in the fridge. Ed had returned twice to the kitchen to throw away the soaked paper sack and towels and finally to wet the sponge mop. When she returned to the living room, the floor sparkled. It crossed her mind that this was some kind of peace offering. In fact, curiosity was getting the better of her—what did he want?

He was sitting across from her staring at the floor and looked like hell—sallow skin, deep circles under his eyes. Had she noticed a tremor when he had handed her the groceries?

"I want the haggling over the house to stop."

"I don't think the appraisal's back."

"Damn the appraisal. It's an older house, Shel, that needs work. Tiffany and I are willing to put in that work. We all need to go on with our lives."

"I sign over the house and you leave me alone?"

"I don't know what you mean."

"Brett recognized you this morning. Forcing him through a red light was dangerous. He's ready to press charges." Probably not much of a lie; Brett had been angry. "And the Peeping Tom act earlier . . . not your best form, Ed."

"Sell us the house. You won't have to deal with me again."

And if she didn't? Would the harassment continue? Could she trust him? Probably worth a chance.

"OK, but I want you to keep your promise."

He merely nodded. Shelly held the door open and stepped aside when he tried to squeeze her arm in passing. He was gone. The house was gone. And she had absolutely no feelings.

She picked up the phone, dialed Stephanie, and left a voicemail. "Stephanie. Shelly Sinclair. I don't want the house sale to drag on any longer. I'm not going to fight Ed for an extra fifty grand. Draw up my acceptance and I'll drop by and sign. Talk soon. Thanks."

There. It was done. There was a finality that felt good—the last remaining tie severed.

Brett didn't call the next day or the next. How could the sex have been off the scale two weekends and then nothing? Didn't how good they were together mean anything to him? On Wednesday she called him.

"Well, hi there, sweet thing."

With one term of endearment, she'd been relegated to Hooters status.

"I sort of missed talking the last couple nights."

"Yeah, you know me. The guys wanted to take off, make use of the nice weather and get some riding in after work."

She bit her tongue and didn't ask if the hitch had been occupied.

"Any chance I'll see you this weekend?"

"Won't know 'til Friday."

"Let me know."

"Will do."

Short and not so sweet. He was distancing himself. She knew it. And there wasn't one thing she could do. Was he afraid of how close they had gotten? How good the sex was? Was Ed scaring him away? There were men, people for that matter, who wouldn't get involved in anything with a hint of violence. Or was this just his MO—a couple good tosses in the hay and he was on the road again? The next woman already weeded from the pack? Who was it who said, "Bad boys just grow up to be bad men?"

The phone was still in her hand when it rang. She glanced at the ID. Ed, again. Should she answer? Hadn't he promised not to bother her? Of course, it could be something about the house.

"Hello, Ed."

"I don't know what your time looks like this afternoon, but I'd like to get together with the boys and at least do a walk-through of the house. I'm glad you accepted my offer. Paul Green will transfer the money to your account—or anywhere else. Just tell him." Jovial—because he felt he'd won? He was so transparent.

"A walk-through should work today. Have Paul contact Stephanie about the money. You've decided to move in before repairs are made?"

"Well, I think Tiffany is just anxious to get this all behind us. With school starting we need to be at a permanent address. Marissa doesn't deserve any more stress. It's really gotten to Tiffany. I think the bickering and nastiness reminded her of her parents. You know she always looked up to you. You were her role model. She's been bitterly disappointed in you, Shelly."

"I'm sure she's adult enough to get past it." Interesting how it had become her fault that Tiffany was stressed. `"Do you know what you want? Anything I can box up ahead of time?"

That was sweet. Maybe things were changing. "Well, yes. If you don't care, I'd like to keep the pictures—the family snapshots—the ones in the garage. Maybe later the four of us could look through them and divide them up. What about you?"

"Just the things from my parents, unless the boys have a particular request."

"As far as artwork I have the only items I want."

"I don't expect to finish today, but it will give us a start. Two o'clock works for me."

"OK. That should be good for me, too. Have you talked with the boys?"

"Yes. They'll both be there."

The old cheery Ed. Happy to be getting his own way? Probably. Or just pleased the love-nest issue seemed resolved? It was a great house to raise children.

Jonathan picked her up at one thirty.

"What did your father have to say?"

"Nothing, really. He asked if I'd thought of things I might want."

"Not a mention of Tiffany or Marissa? I'm assuming she won't be at the house. I can't imagine she'd be there while we're going through things."

"That'd be cozy."

They continued the ride in silence. Shelly hoped she could count on Ed not to make a scene—get all four of them together and use the reunion to rehash his perception of wrongdoing. She had seen so little of Brian over the summer. A few phone calls, lunch at the bungalow that Rachel conveniently couldn't make. Of course, he traveled with his job, but no excuse, really. They were estranged. Simple as that. Another thing she needed to face and decide how she should handle—if at all. Was there ever any guarantee, some fine print on the birth certificate that assured a parent that her child would see life her way? She smiled thinking of possible conversations between Ed and Brian as to his errant mother's ways. But she found herself looking forward to seeing

Brian. Hope springs eternal . . . damn, she had to stop sounding like her mother.

Jonathan braked for a covey of quail. She did miss the wildlife up here—maybe not the occasional bobcat or coyote that would dine on someone's pet, but the flowers and cacti that supported a world of birds and small creatures indigenous to the desert. No, downtown was another world—not necessarily a better one.

"Looks like we beat Brian."

"Brian's not coming."

"What? Your father said he'd contacted both of you—that both of you would be here."

"Actually, Dad didn't contact him. I gave him a call wondering if he wanted to ride with us and he's working in Santa Fe today. Interesting, he told me he'd already taken everything that he wanted. Guess he and Rachel met with Dad and went through the place a couple of different times."

"You're kidding. I'm not losing my mind. I know your father said both of you would be there." Ed never mentioned having already picked things over—leaving her and Jonathan out of the loop. Ed had said something once about his apartment with Tiffany being small. She couldn't imagine Tiffany's place being spacious. But maybe he'd taken a few things. One of the beds or the kitchen set. And if Brian and Rachel got things they wanted, wasn't that just a time-saver? Was it necessary that she know about it? She hadn't been paying attention—and she was the one who walked away. Other than the deceit, it didn't really make a difference.

"Is there anything that you want, Mom?"

"Not really. I told your father that I'd like some of the family pictures. There's nothing else. It's felt good to start over with new furnishings—and leave the memories. It's taken me months to just be able to go back into the house. And it's good that you're with me. Makes things easier." Jonathan reached over and squeezed her hand.

"I guess Dad's not here yet." Jonathan pulled into the driveway. The house looked cavernous and abandoned, curtains drawn, garage door down, no cars in the drive.

"Did you bring your keys?"

"Right here." She'd never taken them out of her purse, but also hadn't used them since she'd left. Odd to be going back after six months. For wanting the house so badly, Ed had done nothing to keep the yard up. Evergreens along the garage's north side were way out of bounds, several of the large Chinese elms had broken branches. He'd been so keen to keep the yard mowed just a few months back, but now the grass was knee-high. But, she thought with a pang, it had been her responsibility. She'd dropped the ball, yet, out of sight, out of mind. Damn. There she went again. She'd grown up with old sayings, but when had her mother's recital become less a commentary on life and more an example of dementia? She had to watch it.

"Wrong keys, Mom. Do you have another set?" Jonathan stepped away from the entrance.

"I'm not going to have keys to fit that lock." Shelly looked over his shoulder and wondered where the brassy-bright Baldwin hardware had gone and whose idea it was to replace it with burnished copper—a much cheaper set.

"He changed the locks?"

"Looks like it."

"I'll go check the back door."

Shelly sat on the bench next to the front door and realized that the five-hundred-dollars-each ceramic urns that had flanked the entry were gone. What else had disappeared? Presumably, to grace the new Sinclair residence, but now would be brought back. Maybe they had been sold. But once again, she reminded herself that she hadn't cared. She allowed this to happen by noninvolvement.

"I'm not sure you're prepared for this." Jonathan held the front door open.

"At least he didn't change the back locks."

"I didn't say that. Everyone's different. I crawled through an open window in the utility room. Mom, Dad's been living here. Did you know that?"

"You're kidding."

"Look for yourself. Oh, and watch where you step, somebody has a new puppy."

The house smelled—that was her first clue. She didn't have to look at the floors to know that someone wasn't picking up after an animal. Luckily, the floors were mostly tile or brick. Pillows from overstuffed furniture were piled in a square on the living room floor. A playhouse for Marissa? There were candy and cookie wrappers everywhere. Empty glasses with scummed milk dried in puddles—both inside and outside the container. At a glance, she didn't think there was one piece of furniture without a stain. Two blinds in the living room had missing slats. And the white plastered hearth had been sloppily painted bright pink and green in large asymmetrical circles. Marissa, no doubt. She had moved from painting the front seat of the Porsche to a larger canvas.

"Does pigsty cover it?" The disgust in Jonathan's voice only echoed her own sentiments. How could anyone live like this?

"It's hard to believe, isn't it? Ed was never much for housework, but filth wasn't in his vocabulary either."

"He could have hired someone. You used to have Iris what's-her-name come help."

"Why would he want to trash this house?"

"Make sure you didn't want it back."

"I told him I'd never come back."

"Then it's some kind of punishment. Ruin something he thinks means a lot to you."

"That kind of meanness makes no sense. Do I have to remind you, Jonathan, your father left me? There is a feeling of punishment, though —a sort of 'I'll show you.' I wonder if Brian and Rachel have seen this. "

"I don't think so or I'd have heard. One thing's for sure, there isn't anything left of value. I wonder where all the artwork went? I didn't want anything, but I guess if I did, I'd be shit out of luck."

"He might want to get at me, but why would he take things from you?"

Shelly looked at bare walls, nail holes and picture-hanging hooks without adornment. A peek in the dining room showed empty cabinets, a buffet with drawers hanging open.

"I don't even want to go upstairs. I'm sure the entire house has been ransacked."

"Let's get out of here if there's nothing else you need to see. I grew up here, but the place is giving me the creeps."

Shelly couldn't agree with Jonathan more—and the pictures in the garage? Some other time. Those could be gone, too. Boxed for her convenience. In a pig's eye. She'd ask Ed to drop them off at Stephanie's. No, she'd have Stephanie tell Ed. She would never come back to this house. And if she could help it, she would not speak to Ed again.

"He wanted us to find the house like this. He did not plan on being here."

Jonathan opened the passenger-side door of his SUV.

"Mom, I think Dad's really sick. Wacko." He made a circular motion at temple level.

"I don't know what to think. That was a shock, but it's his, or their, problem now."

"I'm glad you're done with him—divorced, doing your own thing."

"Me, too."

They were both quiet on the way back. Digesting what they'd seen? Shelly wondered. She'd never forget the destruction—not the way she wanted to remember the past. What could it be like for a child who had never known another house? And what was Ed's point? Some sort of one-sided punishment? Or was she supposed to feel sorry for him?

Jonathan pulled into her driveway and turned off the ignition. "Do you have time to talk?"

"Sure. Coffee or a beer?"

"Coffee if you're having some, too."

They walked across the deck and into the kitchen. He seemed so preoccupied. And serious. Her curiosity was piqued. Even grown, the bickering and nastiness of the divorce had taken a toll. But she knew she couldn't pry. He'd open up when he was ready—he was like his father in that. She gathered up mugs, reached in the fridge for the half-and-half, and carried everything to the dining room table. She made Sumatra, fresh-ground beans, cold water—if she could only hurry the finished product. Finally. "I'll let you doctor your own." She filled a mug and added cream. Jonathan did the same and followed her into the living room.

She sat opposite him on the love seat and waited.

"I've been thinking for a long time about coming forward—not just because of what's happened today. There's been so much hurt from the beginning. I really don't think I recognize my father anymore. I'm shocked by the lies, the duplicity."

She waited and watched him run his tongue over his upper lip, then rub both lips together.

"Mom, Marissa isn't Dad's child."

"What? How do you know?"

"Because I'm her father."

Shelly realized she was staring, but couldn't stop, couldn't even form a comment. Ed had been taken? Throwing everything away over a lie? His fried bologna dollop of mashed potatoes sweetie all a sham? She was startled back to reality by the tickle of laughter that was trying to surface, then swallowed hard when Jonathan's grief-stricken face came into focus.

"Jonathan, I don't understand."

"Tiffany and I had an affair. Well, more like a couple one-night stands. She wanted it to be more and, I think, got pregnant on purpose. And maybe that's unfair; maybe it was an accident. She said she was on the pill. When I wouldn't marry her, she set up Dad. Duped him into believing Marissa was his. Would you believe that I didn't even know he stepped in when I stepped out? Not until you told me Dad had announced he was marrying her."

"Can you prove it?"

"Short of DNA testing? Maybe not. But I have a hell of a lot of cancelled checks that show I've supplemented their income for five years."

"You supported Marissa?"

"Tried to. Tiffany seemed fine with the arrangement. Accepting anyway. Gave me some song and dance about not minding being a single mom. Funny, I never questioned her abrupt about-face. "

"And all the time Tiffany was boffing your father."

"That's what it looks like now."

Earning a salary, receiving child support from two would-be fathers, one not aware of the other . . . not bad. The ultimate scam. Obviously, Shelly had never given her enough credit.

"Why are you telling me?"

"I'm sick and tired of Dad acting like an asshole. I can't believe what Dad's done to you . . . to me. Their staying in our home—trashing our home—reducing you to this. " His arm swept in a half circle taking in the room. "This is a hell of a come down."

"Jonathan, I love this house. This was my choice. I like my life."

"I can't believe that."

"Well, it's true. I'm adjusting—making new friends even. I'm working on a new career. Your father was generous. I don't have to work if I invest carefully—maybe even if I don't."

"That's not the point. You shouldn't have to be doing this. You deserve more. You should be taking cruises with friends . . . you worked your tail off for him, at his office, taking care of us, keeping a home. There should be some reward for that. Dad has his head in the sand."

Shelly took a sip of coffee. "You know the saddest part? Not the lack of a reward for services rendered—I never expected that. But I've been a grandmother for four years."

Four lost years. Funny how she'd always thought things would be so different—the boys would marry, have families, she and Ed would dote on their offspring. Swimming lessons, ballet, soccer, applauding achievements, a sounding board for transgressions. A very important part of her life had just been taken from her. Never to be recaptured, not with Marissa.

"Yeah, I never thought of that."

There was really just one question left to ask—one that she had mixed feelings over the answer. Was she really past being vindictive? Could she really stifle that niggling spark of excitement? That need to utter, "I told you so"?

"What are you going to do with what you just told me? It could be devastating."

"I don't know yet. A part of me wants to tell him—make him see how stupid he's being. Make him pay. Call Tiffany's bluff, I guess."

"But what would you gain?"

"I'd make him realize—"

"Realize what? A lot of things are simply over, Jonathan. It feels right to go forward." She paused. For the first time she realized she was telling the truth. It did feel right. "I have no regrets, only Marissa. I would expect the same from you."

"It's hard to get past the wrong of it all."

Shelly took a deep breath. "You need to let go. I sense that being duped by Tiffany, paying all those years when you worked part-time, really rankles. It would me. Yet, I wouldn't want you to lash out just to get even, cause pain for someone else because you've been taken." He wouldn't meet her eyes. "We all need to move on."

"Don't ask me to forgive."

"I won't. I'm not. Only you know whether you can do that."

"And you? Can you forgive them?"

"Oh, Jonathan, I hope I already have."

She sat for a long time on the sofa. Long after Jonathan had gone. Had she forgiven Ed? Did Tiffany's duplicity make a difference? A woman who had hurt both Shelly's husband and her son? Oddly, she understood. Understood the need of a mother to protect her young, to attain something that she'd never had—the security, the money to provide even the wildest of desires. Begrudging understanding, admiration even mixed with the hurt. No, she honestly couldn't blame her. Try as she might, she simply couldn't hate her. She could only hope that Jonathan would keep the secret to himself.

CHAPTER FOURTEEN

She had not heard from Brett in three weeks. She'd left a couple messages, had expected him to call. But that meant she was expecting normal behavior. She needed to walk away, but when she stopped to realize that she would never sleep with him again, curl into him, feel the warmth and safety of him, be teased, she couldn't hold back the tears. Had she fallen in love with him? Or was it just a reaction to being dumped? How much was ego and how much was heart?

What she needed was a sense of closure. If she called him at five a.m., she'd catch him on the way to a job. So the next morning, coffee in one hand and the phone in the other, she sat on the couch. Should she call? She'd never get it done if she reasoned it to death. She dialed.

"Hey there, sweet thing."

"I've got a problem. I want more than you can give, and I need to give more than you want."

"That some line from a country tune?"

She laughed. "Probably should be."

"Can you just back off, baby? Relax a little. We got a good thing going."

"Sex once a month is a good thing? Never knowing when I'll see you?"

"What do you want me to say? I'll park my ass in a recliner in your living room and never leave you? No can do that."

"And I don't want that. It would just be nice to see you—know when I'll see you. Plan on doing things together."

"My world don't run on a schedule."

"Guess you're just going to have to get used to talking to yourself then."

"Yeah, kinda figured I was gonna get that chance. Hey, Shelly, I hope you find what it is you want."

"Me, too."

She hung up and burst into tears. The temptation to push redial was almost too great. But what for? What would change? What could she say that wouldn't appear demanding and pushy? What could he say that she would want to hear? He wasn't someone you'd live with happily ever after. And that was what she wanted . . . what she knew how to do. She wanted to fall in love, be a companion—have a companion—and walk off into the sunset with this person.

There was no time for moping. The winks had been stacking up in her e-mail, and this was the perfect time to act. If you fall off the horse . . . she wasn't even going to go there. But the online process was fun if you treated it like a numbers game—the more contacts, the quicker you'd find Mr. Right. But it quickly became obvious that Mr. Right was hiding under a rock. Her first date was on a Tuesday. He was on the road until then but called twice. He was a local doctor—nothing like sticking with what she was used to. They decided to meet at the Hilton—drinks and maybe dinner. It was casual and held promise. She had liked him immediately—his attentiveness was a welcome change. He seemed to care about schedules and what she might expect. She found herself rushing home to see if he'd e-mailed and then making sure her cell phone was charged and within earshot.

And he was handsome! As he walked toward her in the hotel lobby, that's all she could think of. He was one good-looking man—graying hair perfectly groomed, expensive slacks and knit shirt.

Conversation came easily and centered around children—his, hers—then turned to former spouses. There had been two in his case. The one who was suing him for five million had been Mrs. Carter for only five years—the "only" was his word. He'd added another one hundred thousand in legal fees to keep her from getting what wasn't hers. "Only five years" . . . what should you be entitled to after "only five years"? It was obvious that he was fixated on not getting taken . . . and, oh yes, she was twenty-three years younger. Was this refrain familiar?

When Shelly first felt his hand snake up between her legs, she didn't believe it. This was a public place; yes, they were at the back of the room in a dark bar, but my God!

"Aren't you afraid the teeth on the chastity belt are going to scar your knuckles? Remove your hand now."

"Shelly, I thought we had an understanding—I'm only interested in sex. God knows I may not have any money left for anything else after Caroline gets through with me."

"I think there was a misunderstanding. I'm not investing this kind of time for just a roll in the hay."

"Whatever. We could go to the car right now and make out for a while. That sounds like fun, doesn't it? Might change your mind."

"No, it does not sound like fun, and no, it will not change my mind. Excuse me." She made it all the way out to the parking lot and into her car without screaming. Why hadn't she picked up on his intentions? Maybe because there hadn't been any warnings. She felt taken and cheap. Were all men like this? Probably a good many. She'd just have to be careful next time. If she even wanted there to be a next time.

But there was. This time, against all warnings after the first coffee date, she invited him to her house for dinner. He was retired military, recently separated from his wife of thirty-one years, and what he might lack in brains, he made up for by being attentive and appreciative and brought her little presents of candles and a china jewelry box. Sweet and thoughtful.

"I've got a surprise for you later, honey. Something you're going to like."

"Tell me now." Some sixth sense said a surprise didn't necessarily mean something good.

"Then it wouldn't be a surprise, now would it?"

She fixed crab cakes with two dips as an appetizer, cilantro mayonnaise and baby dill in sour cream, opened a bottle of good California wine, and checked the shrimp boil. A tossed salad and some peel-your-own shrimp and they'd have a better meal than they could get out. He dozed on the couch until she called him to the table—it would have been nice to have someone to help in the kitchen, but she guessed he just wasn't the type.

Dinner conversation was almost nonexistent. She started several "threads" but there was no pick up. Didn't he ever read a newspaper? She was starting to get just a little peevish when he pushed back from the table.

"You know, I didn't think I'd ever meet my intellectual equal."

"Who was that?" She truly wasn't following him.

"You, of course. Don't sell yourself short, Shelly. You have a good mind. Just because you haven't used it in a while doesn't mean it don't work."

"When was it not in use?"

"Like my wife—raising kids. Let me show you your surprise." He grinned like a fifth grader who was about to do something obnoxious with a horned toad and walked into the bedroom and returned with his jacket. "It was tough keeping this thing under wraps." At which point he brought a calf-length sweat sock out from under the folds and laid it on the table.

"What do you think is in there?" He didn't wait for her to answer but started to peel the ribbed top of the sock back.

Shelly couldn't believe what she was looking at—a molded-from-life twelve-inch penis in transparent red rubber with sparkles. Sparkles? The shaft glowed like a Christmas tree with tiny blinking lights, and when he revved it up a notch, the entire sparkling head rotated.

"Well, if it isn't a cock in a sock."

"You're funny. Does this turn you on, baby?"

"No."

"Oh come on, Shelly. This is one of the best made. It was expensive. Can't you imagine climbing onto Big Red here?"

"So, I go 2.7 seconds on a dildo named Big Red . . . is there a prize? Or do I have to hold out for the entire eight seconds?" She didn't even try to keep the sarcasm out of her voice. How dare he just assume? And the barely veiled reference to lyrics from a popular country song was lost . . . totally lost. She wondered how long it had been since he'd used *his* brain? Forever?

It had been a waste of perfectly good shrimp, not to mention the lump crab. He was gone, but not before he'd asked for his gifts back. And, oh yes, could she wrap the jewelry box? He'd hate to have it get broken. Must have another sweetie just waiting to receive. She put everything in a sack, and not too gently. He probably didn't even know what he'd done. He was still standing on the porch when she'd shut and locked the door.

Then, in quick succession came the pharmacist (ear hair), the owner of five car washes (nose hair), and the vintner (who called his dick "merlot"). In fact, the naming of dicks in general was a colossal turn-off. One man referred to his as "Chuck" when flaccid and "Sir Charles" when (as he put it) it was standing at attention. Another said he liked to call his little guy "Montana." She could see these men spending an evening now and then at the Y with others of like minds, lighting farts, dropping cherry bombs down the porcelain, and trying to trump each other with original dick names. Did men ever get too far past the fifth grade?

Next to dick naming came the men who felt they should state the condition of their tool up front. More than one conversation started something like—"Hi, Shelly, I'm Matthew, nice to meet you. And by the way, I can get it up." Or "Shelly, what a beautiful name. Sure beats Bill, and while we're on the subject of beating Bill . . . ." And one that was repeated far too many times? "How many dates do you think we should have before we go to bed?" Her standard answer was always, "A hundred and seven—and that might be pushing it."

Ugh!

But she could just about handle the explicit sexual references over the nonstop diatribes of high school, post-high school, military, first wife, second wife, politics, children, grandchildren, dead wife, investments, gall bladder operation, ingrown toenail on the left foot, 320,000 miles on the Toyota (can you believe?), Hawaii vacation, Las Vegas vacation, baseball, football . . . She was a captive audience. And jawing was obviously better than sex—needed more. Some McDonald's allowed geezers to keep personalized coffee cups hanging on the wall of their favorite restaurant for those mornings of marathon jawing—the loneliness emblazoned across wrinkled base-ball caps usually sweat-stained at the band.

One man called her and talked absolutely nonstop—he had recently moved to New Mexico and was going to challenge the incumbent in the next Senate race. He was brilliant, math had always been his best subject, he'd never been married, and he'd just tell her now because it was easy to uncover anyway, that he'd had some psychiatric problems but that was a long time ago—at exactly forty minutes in, Shelly said there was someone at the door and hung up.

Some men—the ones that Shelly suspected weighed four hundred pounds—just wanted to e-mail for a while, establish a connection before meeting. Shelly quickly labeled them EBBs—Elizabeth Barrett Brownings—and moved on. If a man didn't want to talk on the phone and meet very soon after, there was something wrong. He was married, not who he said he was, or had something else to hide.

Patrice thought she was being too picky—the guy with ear hair seemed solid and grounded. And didn't pharmacists have money?

"So, what do I do, take tweezers on every date or just a nice, tasteful tube of depilatory?"

"Shelly, it couldn't have been that bad."

"I suppose you find braids coming out of a guy's ears a turn-on? He could have tied them under his chin."

"May I suggest you exaggerate?"

"Not by much."

"And the men who need to talk, can't you just listen? They're only lonely. Maybe once they got over that—. You know, there are services that allow for a series of icebreakers to be exchanged before anything else. You even take a psychological assessment to determine compatibility. Maybe that would be better? You get to know the person. Value him as a person before all this superficial stuff gets in the way."

"Oh yeah, just prolong the ear-hair discovery, the preoccupation with sex, and the verbal diarrhea. Maybe I'll add an ear-hair disclaimer to my profile."

"I really think you're being a little harsh. Give these guys a chance."

"And you think they give us a chance? I can't tell you how many profiles read, 'If you're fat, don't bother.' Or my favorite—'If you wear Birkenstocks and gauze skirts, pass me by. I like my lady to look like one in heels and hose.' Have you ever owned a pair of Birkies?"

"Of course."

"They just made you want to go out and jump other women, didn't they?"

"Shelly, you are so crude. I suppose you liked the guy who sent you a picture of himself holding his penis."

"Maybe, if his fingernails had been clean."

"Something tells me we're back to the nose-hair category."

"Truthfully? I'm getting sick and tired of the stupid, asinine demands of butt-ugly, mental midgets—who just happen to have dicks, and maybe, just maybe, can get them up."

"Well, that's pretty descriptive. But all men aren't that way."

"At this point in my online dating experience, you couldn't prove it by me."

But suddenly things got better. She liked his profile—thought he was honest and was trying not to play games, making a really concerted effort not to play them. He told her he'd call her Friday and did. He was ten years younger but told her that age meant nothing to him—it was only a figment of the mind. If she was going to let it bother her, then it would. But what they had in common and could share far outweighed a simple thing like age.

He had been a massage therapist. She was almost one. He was moving to New Mexico to take a job about two hundred miles from Albuquerque. Once he got the job down, weekends would be free for traveling and, of course, she could always visit him. There was talk of quaint B&Bs, hunting lodges, walks around Santa Fe or Taos. Idyllic. That was the only word she could think of. For all the throw backs, this one was a keeper. And wasn't it a numbers game anyway?

He had been a country singer—opened for some big names in his day—but still wrote songs. Shelly was blown away by how talented he was. He sang his latest over the phone and sent her a CD with ten others. They talked almost every night and made plans to meet. His name was Randy Wright, and the possible meaning of his last name wasn't lost on her. Had she, in fact, found Mr. Right?

Their phone conversations were great—one evening they talked about philosophy until two—Randy drawing her out, listening as she tentatively shared her beliefs. How long had it been? Up half the night trying to solve the world's problems? Explain her place in it all. She was beginning to think a ten-year age spread really didn't mean anything. He had fifteen more years to work but she could follow him as his job moved him around. It wasn't like she was tied to Albuquerque. The boys were here, but that was bittersweet. She would miss Jonathan. She would probably be very good at setting up homes a couple times a year, overseeing moving, getting established in new communities.

Randy planned to retire at sixty-five ... but that would make her seventy-five. How could that work? Would she still enjoy running around the country in her early seventies? How important was a home to her? A place like the bungalow to call her own, plant flowers, visit with the neighbors, have Patrice over?

She didn't see it working, but he just laughed at her that night on the phone. Said again how much he was looking forward to meeting her ... how he treasured their friendship and how he hoped, no, knew it would become more. He couldn't wait to show her his house—a bungalow that sounded much like hers.

And sex . . . how important was it to her? Had she had good experiences? Did she look forward to going to bed with him? What could he do for her to ensure it was good? And then he listened to the answers.

How easily it was to become smitten. She loved his voice—vibrant, young sounding. He laughed easily, a sort of chortle before the guffaw. She found herself trying to make him laugh—find quirky things that she knew would tickle him. He was an important part of her life in a very short time.

They had exchanged pictures—three from her, two just a month old, showing her massage therapy class in the background, and one that Patrice had taken of her standing by the fireplace in the bungalow. His were from the days when he performed, and one from last summer in front of an outdoor grill. They would have been able to recognize each other in a crowd.

He would be in town Friday. Could they meet? Yes, of course. But she wasn't prepared for his thinness. Later she'd wonder about drugs. He made her look fat. In fact, that's the first thing she said to him as he walked up the steps.

"Oh my God, you make me look fat!"

"Shelly, I was just going to say how you don't look sixty, and you have a really cute butt."

"Thanks."

"Hey, opposites attract. You've got a little more padding in places that I don't. I think that's a recipe for comfort, don't you?"

She had to laugh. "I don't think I've ever been called chubby so nicely."

"Am I going to be able to come in or does thin automatically exclude me from making it through the front door?"

"No, of course not. Beer? Wine?"

"I'd take a beer." He reached out and pulled her to him as they entered the living room. The kiss was soft, a little halting and exploratory. Not the bad boy, but nice. And there she went again, using the bad boy as a dipstick measure. She had to stop. New ballgame, new players—actually, totally new ballpark.

"Dos Equis work?"

"My favorite."

"A tour of the house starts in five minutes—and ends in six." She laughed. "It's really tiny. But we can start with the kitchen and get those beers."

"The tile insets behind the sink and stove are great. Tuscany?"

"Yes, the lavender fields."

"The colors are great for accent pieces against the brick-colored tile."

She opened both bottles, squeezed lime into hers, waited for him to do the same, then proceeded to show him the bedroom, hallway, bath, and study. He was more than appreciative of her choices in color—he even made suggestions for contrasting trim.

"The house looks exactly like I thought it would. It looks like you."

"How so?"

"I think of you in colors—the salsa bedroom, for example. Or the pumpkin study. Not everyone could live in a house that had every room a different color. But it echoes your vibrancy—this house is alive. So are you, Shelly." This time the kiss was exciting, teasing with promise. She felt an immediate tingle of wanting and pressed into him, her arms around his neck, and admonished herself not to dwell on the angular sharpness of him. She pushed back words like Auschwitz and Dachau. Wasn't it the person? The inner workings of a mind, the soul, the values of an individual? How could she be so shallow? She was beginning to sound like Patrice—agree with Patrice.

"You don't know how much I hate knowing I have to leave in an hour. But I don't want our first time to be a quickie. Agree?"

"I agree."

He smiled and put his arm around her, and they walked back to the living room. Of course, the hour evaporated. He was thrilled about his job. Counted himself truly fortunate to have it and talked about his future plans. He'd had some hard times recently, lost a business, had to live off of relatives—this was a lifetime's chance to get back on his feet. Plan for the kind of retirement that he wanted. And then to find her on top of it—well, life couldn't really get any better. Then, Pam called.

CHAPTER FIFTEEN

"Oh Shelly, Dad's trying to pass."

"Gas?"

"He's trying to cross over. Leave us. This isn't the time to be a smart ass."

Of course, if Pam had used the term "happy hunting ground" or "the great beyond" or even "his just reward," she would have caught on right away. It was probably uncalled for to be snide, but she wasn't in the mood for another family crisis—no matter how tastefully, euphemistically presented by her darling sister. Shelly shifted the phone to a position that wasn't going to leave a perfect indentation of her earring on her left cheek.

"I didn't realize he was having problems."

"I guess I knew at some level, but I don't think I wanted to see. He was beginning to fall more and now he's pretty much in bed all day. He's not eating."

Shelly could hear the muffled sounds of crying. Should she feel guilty that she wasn't?

"What are the doctors saying?"

"They suggested I call you. They think it could be only a matter of days."

Shelly sighed. One more thing. And just when her love life promised to take off. "How's Mom?"

"Taught the aides how to do the Charleston last week. She's so chipper and cute . . . and crazy."

"I know, as a loon. Does she still repeat that over and over?"

"This month it's been 'Can't the cat look at the queen?'"

"That's an oldie. Should I try to get a flight out tomorrow?"

"If you want to see Dad alive, that probably would be best."

"I'll call you when I get in."

What an interesting time in life. A time to start burying parents, later than other generations but no less challenging. This called for a glass of Rojo Loco—one of her favorite New Mexico wines. She better prepare to be gone a week. Or longer. Had Pam looked into caskets? That tasteful, cheap Costco model? Probably not. At least her father had purchased a crypt in the mausoleum in the Protestant Greenwood cemetery. Not to be confused with the Catholic cemetery some two or three blocks away. Shelly grew up in a time when a "mixed marriage" meant Protestant to Catholic. Did they at least let their dead mingle today?

She'd take a leave from school. Put it on hold until she'd worked through the latest family crisis. Actually, she was learning that there really wasn't a timeframe for things any more—she didn't have to do anything, really, but enjoy what life had to offer, and that included Randy Wright. Her father's death was a reality check, a reminder of ever-fleeting time.

She called the boys. Jonathan offered to cancel the presentation of a paper on solar energy in Portland and come with her. But she didn't see a reason for that. The boys had not been close to their grandfather since grade school. Hopefully, they had some good childhood memories.

She called Brian next. A tough call. She was beginning to feel on her guard with him. Because of Ed? Yes, she guessed so. There always felt like barely concealed finger-pointing. Somehow, something was her fault. And he had apparently been party to emptying the house sans brother and her. The "take the loot and run" posture wasn't becoming.

"Brian, I wanted to let you know that your grandfather is dying. I'm leaving for Kansas tomorrow."

"Are you asking us to cancel our trip to Jamaica?"

"No, of course not. This is just a 'keep you in the loop' sort of call. There won't be any news that won't wait." She idly wondered if there was phone service from wherever they were going to be. Would it be too much to expect him to call her and check? Probably.

"Well, I'll give you a call when we get back." There was a slight pause. "What's he dying of?"

"Probably just plain old age. He's ninety-two. Vascular dementia has hastened his decline. The doctor believes he's had a series of small strokes over the past year."

"Is this something that runs in the family?"

"If you remember, your grandmother had a stroke at seventy-two but fully recovered. I'm not sure I'd say two isolated instances mean it's in the line, at most maybe the proclivity is there. Age was certainly a factor both times. You know, a person has to die of something."

"Rachel will be upset."

Shelly was truly touched. "How sweet. She only met my father once."

"No, I mean if we have children. She's really adamant about not perpetuating any physical or mental weaknesses."

"Yes, of course, how vigilant of her. One can't be too careful." Speaking of careful, Shelly needed to bite her tongue and stop thinking how much he reminded her of Ed. "Have a wonderful trip—it sounds like great fun. My love to Rachel." The prig.

She barely heard his good-bye as she snapped the phone shut. She didn't want to dwell on how callous Brian came across. But he was impossible and had married like kind. Was this child from her womb?

Because she'd get in late afternoon, Pam was going to swing by the motel and pick her up for dinner. It was decided that Shelly would get a motel room and not stay with Pam at the home place. Pam didn't have a second bedroom set up and Shelly nixed the idea of buying an air mattress—too expensive and too uncomfortable to sleep on the floor. But the three voicemails on her phone when the plane landed changed all that.

"He's gone, Shelly. Dad passed away this afternoon at ten minutes past one. Drapers will be making the arrangements and picking up the body. Give me a call when you land and we'll decide where to meet."

The other two messages were also from Pam—what should he wear? She thought a suit. But he usually preferred more casual attire. And what about a tie? His favorite, a wool blend, was full of moth holes. Then a hysterical Pam—they had stolen his dress shoes, his razor, and his walker at the home. No one could find them. What were they going to do about shoes? The funeral home suggested burying him in his socks because his feet would remain covered. But Pam couldn't imagine that. How tacky. No, they had to buy dress shoes.

Shelly smiled to herself, then took a deep breath. Luckily, she had forty minutes of driving before she had to face Pam and become the guiding force in this new stage production of parental burial. And she guessed she kinda agreed—shoes would be a nice touch. But who had stolen his belongings? Inmates? The help? She could just picture some sort of countdown and then at death, the doors to the room would be thrown open and the vultures would descend. Sort of a little bit different take on shopping at Macy's the day after Thanksgiving.

She returned Pam's call and said she'd just meet her at the house. She realized it was still a work in progress, but she was anxious to see what had been done. And she wasn't disappointed. Only Pam could do a kitchen in tones of gray with black appliances and brushed aluminum door pulls, hanging lamps over an island, and a black-and-white tile floor. It was difficult to even remember the everything-yellow and yellowing kitchen of a few short months ago. And the smell was gone. The entire house smelled fresh and absolutely odor free.

"This is terrific. You've done a fabulous job. The kitchen is useable now. And I can breath in here."

"I'm glad you like it. There have been some setbacks. Who would have known there would be so much termite damage? But I'm glad you agreed with my matching the hardwood and then refinishing instead of just doing a quick fix and covering things up with carpet."

"It makes all the difference—preserves the integrity of the house."

"Shelly, I'd like to keep the house, live here and continue the makeover. I could have it appraised and adjust whatever I'll get in inheritance when the time comes. Unless we need to sell it and put the money into the trust to take care of Mom now."

"No, Mom's fine. The trust will take care of her as it stands. It's great to see the house take shape—I do have some good memories of this place." Probably not as many as Pam does, Shelly thought.

"I'm enjoying being home again. Do you remember Lawrence Hofstadt?"

"No, the name's not familiar."

"We were in the same graduating class but never dated. He's a lawyer and came back here to set up practice with his father. Well, we've been seeing each other."

Leave it to Pam. Shelly wouldn't even bet how long it would take Pam to get this one tripped to the floor. How did she do it? Shelly was grinding away online and in a couple short months, Pam was probably headed down the aisle. But it was good to see her happy and see the house that they grew up in take on a new life. And, perhaps, Pam needed this all-consuming focus right now. And a fresh start.

The viewing would be the following evening, the funeral the next day. Her father had requested a service in the mausoleum. Nothing fancy—scripture, two hymns, a short talk by the minister, and one large wreath of flowers provided by the family. One of them needed to see about the engraving of the crypt's granite façade. Shelly would leave that up to Pam. It would just be their parents' names, birth dates, and dates of death.

They found shoes, a new suit, and a new tie—Pam insisted upon folding his favorite tie and tucking it into a pocket. She also insisted on sending him on with his reading glasses, pocket watch, and a clean, carefully folded white handkerchief. Shelly didn't argue. She wasn't sure she saw the necessity of these things. But who knew? Maybe the Egyptians had it right all along—gold plate, jewels, and food. And, not to forget the embalmed Nubians entombed alongside, complete with palm fans and dishes of sugared dates. Should she tuck a package of glazed doughnuts underneath a corner of blue satin?

She idly wondered if she preceded Pam and wasn't going to be cremated, what would have ended up "going" with her? She honestly couldn't think of one thing she'd want to drag into the afterlife. She was getting really good at just leaving things and moving on.

Twenty-two people came to the viewing. Three were fellow classmates, two men and a woman, from his high school class of 1931. People lived such long lives—but if the price for longevity was spending a lifetime in Kansas, Shelly would take her odds elsewhere.

She had discouraged Pam's wanting to bring her mother. No one knew exactly how Nancy would react. If she didn't recognize her husband, that would be easy. But if she did and couldn't understand that he was dead, there might be difficulties beyond Pam and Shelly's expertise.

The home finally had to separate them—put them in adjoining rooms and monitor leaving the door unlocked. On two occasions her mother opened and then proceeded to try and push their father out a large, multipaned window in the dining area. She was taking him home, and of the two, remained agitated over the fact that they weren't in their own "place," as she called it. After first requiring sedation, Charles Walters finally seemed resigned to needing care, and seemed bothered by the visits from his wife. On a number of occasions, he requested that she be removed from his room—she had interrupted his nap. Was this what the end of a seventy-year marriage looked like?

The funeral director, a somewhat effeminate older man that Shelly didn't know, had arranged chairs in an alcove to the right of the viewing room. She and Pam would be able to receive those wishing to express their condolences. The arrangement was comfortable and thoughtful. She was leafing through a high school scrapbook brought by one of her father's classmates when she heard his voice.

"Ed?" The scrapbook slipped to the floor. She had seconds to take a deep breath and compose herself—try, at least, to remain calm. "What are you doing here?"

"We're paying our respects."

It was only then that she saw Tiffany—head to toe in black, including tights with patent sandals. Eclectic. Shelly needed to remember that word when thinking of Tiffany. But she was pissed that she was here. She was an outsider and had no right. So much for never having to see Ed again—be bothered by Ed again once the house was his. Shelly wasn't even going to ask how he knew her father had died. Brian must have told him. She'd given both boys a quick call last evening—left messages, that is.

"I'm just surprised that you were able to get here so quickly. I didn't call the boys until after nine."

"Oh, Pam's kept us up on what's been going on. We made our plans weeks ago."

"Pam? Weeks ago?" No screaming, no screaming, no screaming.

"When Ed called me, I didn't tell you because I didn't want to upset you." Pam was attempting to look contrite.

"We all agree you've been under far too much stress lately. Pam knows how worried I've been."

Conciliatory asshole. Shelly stood and only then realized that Ella or Peg or whatever her name was with the scrapbook was on hands and knees picking up scattered photos. The woman was ninety-one. Shelly quickly bent to help. "I'm so sorry. It was wonderful of you to share these memories." The woman barely nodded and continued to rake the photos in a pile, stuffing them back into the book, looking for all the world like she wanted to bolt. Shelly couldn't blame her; the tension was palpable.

"You know, it's supposed to rain tomorrow. I've ordered a tent for graveside," Ed boomed out. He was not going to be ignored.

"Ed, Dad is being buried in the mausoleum. There's no need for a tent."

"You could at least say thank you. We rushed here to help take care of details." Tiffany had a lump of mascara stuck in the corner of her left eye. When you had lashes like that, why would you use mascara? A reincarnation of a certain Tammy, perhaps? Shelly admonished herself not to be mean. She just needed to turn and walk out the door.

"There's help and then there's the help that's pushed on you when it's not needed."

"Shelly, Ed's being here is moral support. I like a man who's willing to help. Believe me, they're few and far between."

"Good, Pam. You and Ed go over the details. I will see you at the cemetery by three." She walked through the front receiving area, the frosted glass doors to the porch, and down the steps. Mr. Dickerson looked distraught and hurried after her.

"I thought it was a pleasant evening. I mean under the circumstances. And old school chums—who would have thought so many would still be living? You know, my mother is ninety-six come September. Of course, I lost my father when I was a teen. Farm accident. But women live so much longer than men, anyway." He was clasping and unclasping his hands.

Shelly stopped. The man was just rattling on—afraid of what was going to happen if Ed followed her out? Too late. Here he came down the steps two at a time to stop just at her elbow.

"I never did get back after you and Jonathan found the house burgled."

"Burgled?"

"I couldn't believe the mess, and so many things taken."

"Just what kind of burglar brings a dog to shit all over the floor? Or changes the locks on all the doors? Or leaves milk in glasses, or paints the hearth pink? Don't insult my intelligence."

"Well, the cops did say it looked more like squatters."

"Oh, now it's squatters? Ed, you, Marissa of recent Picasso fame, and the little cupcake of a girlfriend have been living there. But, you know what? It's your house. If that's the way you want to live, have at it." She was tired of holding the anger in. And for what reason? Ed didn't play by the rules.

"I realize a lot of this frustration is the result of your not taking care of your investment. If you had just gone back to the house, even once a week, no one would have been able to do what they did." He took her elbow. "Shel, I'm not blaming you. I know the shock and stress of losing your marriage and home has been incredibly painful. And under the circumstances, your selling the house without quibbling over an extra fifty thousand—"

She twisted away and turned to face him. "Trashing the house saved you fifty thousand dollars. Is that what that was all about? Finding a way to keep the appraisal low?"

"I can't believe you'd think I'd stoop—"

"Shut the fuck up. And by the way, where were you when Jonathan and I found the mess?"

"Tiffany and I were able to get in to see Russell Quinlen—last-minute cancellation. When there's a chance to see him, you don't turn it down."

"The fertility doctor?"

"We're exploring our options for a multiple birth."

"Who's the surrogate father this time?" Oh my God, the minute it left her mouth, she regretted it. A sharp intake of breath and Shelly didn't have to look at Tiffany's face to know that Ed didn't have a clue. "I'm sorry, I didn't mean that. I need to be going." She turned but this time felt Ed's fingers bore into her arm.

"No you don't. You have some explaining to do. Or is this just more of your nastiness? Doing anything to hurt us?"

His face was so flushed, Shelly was afraid he'd have a stroke. "I'm not the one who needs to explain." She tried to pull free, but he only pressed harder. "Go ahead, ask her. Marissa is not your child. She's your grandchild." The shove sent her sprawling backwards to scrape both palms against a raised brick border lining the walk.

"You're drunk. And at your father's viewing," Ed bellowed loud enough for Mr. Dickerson and the few people on their way to the parking lot to overhear.

Shelly ignored the drunk statement. "Ask Tiffany. She knows who Marissa's father is." Shelly pushed to a sitting position but decided not to give him any larger target than she needed to. "And if she doesn't tell the truth, I trust you'd believe your son. Or DNA testing. As my mother says, 'There's no fool like an old fool.'" For once, it felt good to use an old adage. Alzheimer's be damned.

She went back to the motel. She didn't answer her cell or the phone in the room. She did not want to hear an apology from Pam for involving Ed or more diatribe from Ed. There was a part of her that wasn't sorry she'd told the pompous asshole he was a grandfather. But she slept fitfully, even after triple locking the door, and woke early. She idly wondered if Ed and Tiffany would come to the funeral, but really didn't care if they did. There was too much to do before the service for "what ifs."

Pam had done a great job of rounding up a pastor, a soloist, and two readers. Shelly shopped for a wreath and had a local florist put together a huge circle of spring and summer flowers. It was bright and cheerful with tulips, jonquils, roses, even a couple dinner-plate sized sunflowers—almost every kind of flower her father had raised at one time. She knew he would have approved.

The day was muggy, but the mausoleum was cool inside the three-foot-thick stone walls. A groundskeeper had set up the chairs and had been there when the wreath was delivered. A late afternoon service had been a good choice; the sun pouring in the stained glass windows on the west wall was radiant. Pam had even thought of pallbearers, and six deacons from the church that their parents had attended years before stood at attention along the stone walk and waited for the hearse.

Because there were just the two of them, Pam and Shelly had opted to meet at the mausoleum and follow the body as it was carried in and not accompany it in the hearse from the mortuary. She was surprised that Pam hadn't asked Ed to join them. But, then, maybe she had. Yet, Ed and Tiffany were conspicuously absent. Thank God.

The service could not have gone smoother. There was a feeling of celebration, not of sadness, and the pastor set the tone by lauding her father's long and productive life. He had spent almost ninety-two years on earth—that in itself an accomplishment. The wreath was removed from its stand and placed on the casket before the service. The casket would not be opened during the service. Both sisters agreed upon that. The vivid flowers were just the right touch and brightened the somber setting. There were several bouquets and two more smaller wreaths that someone had placed around the podium. Shelly would need to get names and send thank-you notes—unless she could push that off onto Pam.

The soloist was accompanied by cathedral-perfect music from a boom box set up in the back of the nave. No one seemed to mind. Had Shelly known of local musicians, perhaps, a live string quartet would have been nice. But there was no reason to make this any more of a production than it had to be. The coffin ended up costing upwards of six thousand, but that included the embalming and renting of the mortuary's chapel for the viewing. Probably a bargain; Shelly had no way of knowing. And it was Pam who had set up these services in advance. Giving her the old home place seemed a small payment for having someone here to oversee—because dare she forget they had another funeral to plan one of these days.

After the service, Pam and Shelly received the condolences of the thirty-odd people who made up the audience—church members who remembered him, the high school pals, several men who had worked with their father, and a few people from the home—and not a hint of Ed. Shelly had prepared envelopes with checks for each person who had taken part in the program and a generous tip for the groundskeeper who helped set up.

Finally, it was over, and Shelly realized how drained she was.

She begged off dinner saying she needed to rest. She wasn't quite up to an evening with Lawrence and Pam. And the, perhaps, endless questions about the paternity of Marissa. Shelly'd start taking care of the myriad of things a death required the living to do first thing in the morning—first meeting with the lawyer to go over the trust and reallocate the money to meet only her mother's needs. She really didn't see a need to prolong her visit more than a couple more days. And she would stop by the home to spend time with her mother—not something Shelly looked forward to.

The highlight of the evening was a call from Randy. How was the service? He'd been thinking of her. He couldn't wait until they could be together. Hurry home. He treasured what they had—never thought he'd find it. Did she believe in dreams coming true?

CHAPTER SIXTEEN

"Hello, Mom." Shelly had planned her visit to coincide with the recreation time after breakfast and found her mother sitting in the lounge.

"Why do you call me that? I'm not your mother."

"I'm your daughter, Shelly."

"I don't know a Shelly."

"Mom, how many children did you have?"

"Well, I had two. Two girls."

"What were their names?"

"Shelly and Pamela."

"Mom, I'm Shelly—your oldest daughter."

"Oh no, Shelly, of course, how could I forget? Oh, what you must think of me. I'm so sorry. You're my baby all grown up. My first baby." Nancy reached out and took Shelly's hand and squeezed. Shelly squeezed back and leaned over to hug her. But as quickly as the veil had lifted, it dropped.

"Now, who are you?" Her mother pulled away.

"Shelly."

"You don't look familiar. Do I know you?"

It was all Shelly could do to keep from crying. The disease was terrible. It robbed the person afflicted and the family, reminding them over and over of their loss—minute by minute.

"Let's take a walk. Would you like that?"

"Oh, I don't know. Aren't they going to feed me?"

"You just finished breakfast. They won't serve lunch for awhile."

"I think they're trying to starve me. It's a great life if you don't weaken."

Maybe if she changed the subject. "Do you still play the piano?" One of the ubiquitous pianos sat in the corner.

"I don't know. I don't know what I know and what I don't know anymore. My mind is just mush."

"Let's go see what kind of sheet music they have."

"I can't go yet. I'm waiting for Harold. Did you see him? He lives here too."

"Your cousin, Harold?"

"Is that what he is? I don't think I ever knew that. Well, I guess what I don't know won't hurt me. There was another man who used to live here but they took him away."

Shelly tensed. Was she talking about her husband?

"Your husband, Charles, passed away recently, but he used to live here."

"Had be been sick?"

"Yes."

"Well, I guess what I don't know won't hurt me."

Shelly kept an eye on the time. A nurse had suggested short visits of no more than ten minutes staggered throughout the day would be less stressful on her mother . . . and Shelly. Her time was almost up. When she said good-bye, her mother didn't seem interested in walking her to the door, but simply turned away. Out of sight, out of mind. Shelly caught herself. She was beginning to sound like an inmate. She'd be hiding those Easter eggs any day now.

CHAPTER SEVENTEEN

Albuquerque had never looked so good—never felt so good. Did a new love interest make the difference? Probably. It was early evening, but a bath and bed were the only things that sounded appealing. She checked her e-mail. Randy had sent a note wishing he could meet the plane. How sweet. He said he had meetings until nine but if she had gotten in on time and felt like staying up awhile, please call him. Shelly quickly e-mailed back— *Home, getting a bite to eat. I'll call at nine.*

Shelly dialed Randy's number at exactly nine, but there was no answer. For some reason, her broadband phone rang only four times and didn't forward to his voicemail. Odd. She hadn't had problems with it in the past. She tried again with the same results. Oh well, he probably went out to dinner with the guys from the office.

When he hadn't called back by ten-thirty, she got

ready for bed. She was exhausted but didn't want him to worry. She tried his number from her cell.

"Hi."

"I'm in a meeting." This in a whisper. "I'll call later."

"I just wanted to say I'm back. Thanks so much for your notes. I've got to get some sleep. Let's talk tomorrow."

She was a little surprised that he had his phone on during the meeting, but how sweet. His wanting to hear from her was genuine and touching. She cracked a window and turned the swamper to low—it was one of those evenings that air-conditioning felt good. And she felt good. No, relieved was a better word. She could go on with her life now—until she would face the same thing with her mother.

And Ed? There was a feeling of closure there, too. She folded the cover back and crawled under the single sheet. Its cool slickness was soothing. She'd barely wadded her pillow under her head and turned on her side before she was asleep.

The shrill jangle of the phone was so startling, she awoke immediately and grabbed it on the second ring. One fifteen. Who—?

"You self-centered, obsessive bitch—how dare you call me three times in an hour? Who do you think you are? You know what this job means to me. I needed to make a good impression. I can't lose this job. I'll have nothing if I lose this chance."

"Randy?"

"Three times," his voice escalated until he was yelling. "I was the laughingstock of the group. They pointed out I'd been in the state less than a month and I had this woman chasing me. Some psychotic, demanding broad. Do you ever think of anyone beside yourself? Maybe you don't have to work, but the rest of the world isn't like you. How dare you wreck my life?" He was drunk and in a rage. She couldn't stop her hand holding the phone from shaking. But where had this person come from?

"Stop it. What are you talking about?"

"It better have been an emergency. That's all I can say. Why would you call three fucking times? On the company phone? You know that's the company cell."

"You told me to. You wanted to know that I was back." It sounded lame when the words left her mouth. This was not a man who cared anything about her—probably never had. She knew without a doubt that if she were standing in front of him, he would punch her. "What kind of idiot leaves his phone on during a meeting?"

He ignored her question. "So, you tell me how you're going to make this right. How are you going to keep this from ever happening again?" She could hear crashing in the background like he was throwing things, kicking furniture.

"Just like this. I'm going to hang up the phone and walk away. Good-bye, Randy." It took two hands to steady the phone and place it back in the cradle. She was stunned. Why did he go off on her? What was his problem? What had really happened that evening?

Fully awake, she sat on the edge of the bed and willed her breathing to quiet. Who was psychotic? She couldn't help but think she'd just dodged a bullet. He had been so perfect. But what was it they said about something that seemed perfect? She would have thought that she couldn't have gone back to sleep, but exhaustion from the day finally won out. When she opened her eyes, the bedside clock said eight. She halfway thought he might have called—some early morning apology a couple cups of black coffee later. But he didn't and again, she was relieved.

"You were so lucky. He could be bipolar or any number of things. Think what could have happened if you had been at his house. I think you're right—with that kind of rage, he would have taken a swing." As always, Patrice offered a listening ear.

"They're out there. I need to remind myself of that."

"I don't know how long I can talk. I think we're supposed to have a meeting in five minutes. I should probably go now. Drinks after work?"

"Sounds good. I just needed to hear a sane voice. Give me a call at lunch." Shelly hung up the phone and put water on for tea, then walked back to the office.

Another disappointment . . . in a long line of disappointments. But she needed to be careful. Not so trusting. Still, she had really lost her appetite for more online dating. Maybe Patrice had been right—a service that cost a little more and did a little more careful matching, didn't allow the individuals to actually interact until they were ready, until they found out more about each other. Would that be better? She guessed she'd try it.

One thing for sure, she'd cancel the service where she'd found Randy. She opened the account, hid her profile, and began dumping her saved "matches." When she came to Randy's, she was shocked. Somewhere in the middle of last night, he'd changed his profile to reflect his move to New Mexico and changed the age group of acceptable dates from the forty-five to sixty category to thirty to forty-five. Talk about a gut-punch. She just sat there and stared. Well, so much for the age difference not meaning anything. Was anything he had said the truth? She guessed not. And the thinness. Prolonged drug use? Cocaine chic? It made sense.

Drinks after work meant the Two Fools on Central. She couldn't help but think she upped the ante to three by just crossing the threshold. She had not shown a lot of gray matter lately. No luck with men and that debacle with Ed. She'd called Jonathan and he reassured her—he was glad the secret was out and sounded genuinely so. But, no, Ed hadn't called. Had she expected him to contact Jonathan? Yes, she guessed she had. Oh, to have been a fly on the wall when he and Tiffany had gotten back to the motel. She would have hated to have been on the receiving end of his anger. A shove was violence enough.

When she gave into it, there was a nagging worry that Ed would "do" something, some irrational, getting-even gesture. But what it might be, she didn't have a clue. There was just some unvoiced need to be on guard. Was it time to get that gun?

Patrice was running late, but looked perfect when she walked in. A black bolero jacket, white cami, and knee-length black-and-white houndstooth skirt—the look was finished by low-heeled, strappy black sandals. The brown cashmere sweater Shelly had thrown on over jeans didn't quite cut it. Oh well. The warm brown did make a nice contrast to her auburn hair, as did the single drop turquoise nugget earrings .She was enjoying not having to be bandbox perfect but being her own person, wearing what was comfortable—and she knew the jeans looked good. But it was time to get rid of the chins. And maybe the tummy. She couldn't always walk around presenting her backside first. No, it was time to rework the front.

"Are you afraid of Ed?"

Good question. Was she? Did needing to be on guard equate to fear? "There's a part of me that is. But I shouldn't base those feelings on a one-time loss of control." She'd just filled Patrice in on the infamous funeral free-for-all. It was nice to get the perspective of someone who wasn't family.

"No excuses. What he did was dangerous and threatening. You couple that with spying on you, belittling you—"

"I know. The bad boy always wanted me to get a gun."

"Not a bad idea. I'd suggest putting in a little time at target practice."

"Patrice, the very idea of arming myself against my children's father seems ludicrous. And even thinking that he might be the ultimate target—well, I can't even go there."

"Thousands of women have said the same thing—some of them are dead. But not to belabor the point . . . what I find really fascinating is that Ed's a grandfather."

"And I'm a grandmother."

"And neither one of you had an inkling."

"The whole thing is pretty bizarre."

"Jerry Springer material, for sure."

"Maybe they'll get past it. Ed will forgive Tiffany, maybe they'll have a child of their own. They'll fix up the house—"

"Do you really see that happening?"

"Doubtful. I see Ed's anger getting in the way. Tough to go from dumpling trophy wife with living proof of your virility to the butt of a bad joke."

"I agree. Ed's ego is going to get in the way of any forgiveness. But what about you? You're finally interviewing docs about a face life?"

"I see Dr. Chen on Friday."

"Do you want me to go with you?"

Shelly smiled. Patrice was always supportive. "No, it's just a consultation."

"Well, I can take the time if you'd like some backup."

"I'm sure this will be straightforward—meet the surgeon, discuss how many chins I hope to dump, and schedule surgery."

"I'm sure you're right. I just hope you like him. I have visions of you shopping all over town for Mr. Right in scrubs."

"Of course, I need to have confidence—"

"Shelly, I'm on your side. This is one time that holding people to certain standards is a good thing. It won't be a showstopper if he has ear hair."

Shelly laughed. "I'm not so sure. That's really a big thing with me. I'll let you know my reaction the minute I leave his office."

"I'll be thinking of you—with more than a little envy."

"You're not sixty yet—you have time."

Dr. Chen assured her she was a perfect candidate for a face-lift. Did he say that to all his patients? She chided him. But in all seriousness, he reminded her that she didn't need to get rid of wrinkles, only excess skin—that little poofiness beneath the eyes and, of course, the chins. Her skin was in great shape, elastic, little discoloration, prime for what he would do. He'd had a cancellation. Would she be ready to go ahead on Monday? Monday? In just two days? A brief feeling of panic . . . but why wouldn't she be ready? If she thought about it for too long, she'd lose her nerve. And if the face went well, would he suggest a tummy tuck to follow? He assured her they would talk, but one thing at a time. He'd see her at the hospital at seven a.m. And, oh yes, have a nice weekend.

A nice weekend? Her palms were already sweaty and sticking to the steering wheel on the way home. She was excited, yet frightened. The unknown—but something she'd chosen to do. And in seventy-two hours it would be over.

She looked around the bungalow. She couldn't just wander aimlessly in twelve hundred square feet for the next two days. She needed to find a diversion. She could go stark raving mad in that time if she didn't. She picked up a novel. *Death Without Company.* Something by a Craig Johnson that Patrice had raved about, said she had to read. The title didn't give her a warm, fuzzy feeling at the moment. But no matter how good the story, Shelly knew she couldn't concentrate. Maybe the new online dating service had miraculously found someone in their database.

Actually, a match had popped up on the new service. A man in Florida. The ball was in her court to open a dialogue by sending questions. She picked out five that were of some interest to her. Ones about having a family or marriage weren't. But do you believe in long-distance romance? How important is chemistry? Those had some potential. This might be interesting.

He fired back answers within thirty minutes. For activities that he hoped his mate would share, he said: "I love to dive, deep-water sail, bike, play chess, and hang out in the hot tub." Hmmmm. She could match one out of five, maybe two if she ever found her mountain bike. But chess? It had been too long. She'd have to take lessons. The other two must be Florida interests—could a Southwest sun worshipper ever become a sea nymph? The nymph part was really pushing it. The most adventurous thing he'd done in the past year? " I placed second in a road race from Dallas to Austin." And his spirituality? "I am a deistic ethical hedonist." Not the usual. Obviously bright.

His questions to her? What's one life event that, in hindsight, you'd handle differently? "I've lived life pretty much without regrets—I've never wanted to wake up one morning and think 'I wish I'd . . . .' The one thing I might have done differently is a little too personal to discuss here . . . maybe later." It was way too soon to even mention having been married thirty-five years and maybe, just maybe, if she'd had it to do over again, she would have bailed earlier.

Her answer to "What are three best traits that you have to offer a partner?": "I could be 'flip' and say I'd never bore you—which would probably be the truth. I have an insatiable interest in learning/experiencing new things. But in short, I know how to be a good partner." She liked her answer. It was the truth. She could have offered more with her answer to his third question— What do you expect in a partner? But after giving it some thought, left it. "I don't want someone to bore me." Did that sound too juvenile? There was more to life. But, in truth, hadn't Ed bored her? And wasn't she looking for more than just the humdrum of mere existence? She didn't need a provider. She wasn't planning a family. She wanted a companion—on the same wavelength. Patrice had been right—this was fun. It made her think . . . and forget.

He made his psychological profile available and she did the same. She studied his at length, and compared it to hers. Intense, forceful, demanding in certain situations, take charge, gets things done—maybe at the expense of others. Was this the kind of personality that she could live with? If you stepped in front of him, would he mow you down? Hers, in contrast, seemed wuss-like, too sweet and caring. Too opposite. Too female? Of course, there would be people who would say that opposites attract. Could her sense of humor and honest caring for people ease some of the sharpness of his personality? Maybe. But it didn't get any better. Under the situation analysis section of the profile, his personality was likely to have to be in control and have the last word. Yuk!

In addition, he valued "being a good citizen" and excelled at "games of competition and skill." He'd find out she'd gotten three speeding tickets in the last five years. Oh God, he'd put her in stocks or a pillory in the front yard—her head and two hands hanging through—the neighbors laughing . . . throwing things.

OK, this had to get better. But no. She was respectful, win-win oriented, enthusiastic, sharing, a planner . . . stack that up against reality-grounded, initiator, goal-driven, detail-oriented, forceful take charge, someone who could put feelings aside to reach his goal. This looked hopeless. Especially when the profile concluded that what she must have at all costs was equality and a friendly, social environment free of all hostility. And what did he have to have? Someone as bright and goal-oriented and driven as he. No way! This was a recipe for disaster.

It wouldn't work. Wasn't this really just semantic nose hair? Could she live with such an anal . . . Republican? There it was. Maybe the worst thing she could accuse him of. And she knew he was one . . . had to be. Hadn't "bleeding heart" been a part of her vocabulary at one time? Maybe, still was?

They reached the status of "open" communication and he e-mailed to say that she might have heard that they were having some hurricanes in Florida and it would be a few days before he could call. Phone service was spotty and he was pretty busy protecting property and removing downed trees from the storm last month. She e-mailed back that the time frame was perfect. She was entering the hospital and wouldn't be home until afternoon. Monday. And then wouldn't be able to talk for a couple days. Was it a procedure that she had to have done? Or elective? Absolutely perfectly elective, she answered. He excused himself from being snoopy but had been a medical researcher for many years. Did she feel comfortable sharing the type of surgery? Facelift. Had she done her research? Interviewed more than one doc? Talked with several of his patients? Looked at fifty before and after pictures? Yes, yes, yes, and then, yes. Did she have support? Family? Friends? Yes.

He was really looking forward to talking with her. He gave her his phone numbers—a cell and one at home. He'd wait to hear from her. She was to take her time. And even then there was no guarantee that she'd get through. They'd been hit pretty hard by the storms—they were lucky to have an e-mail connection. Had she had a chance to compare their profiles? Yes. What did she think? Either a clear case of opposites attract or there's absolutely no hope. He agreed, but added, "Won't it be fun to see which?"

CHAPTER EIGHTEEN

Monday morning. Patrice picked her up at six a.m. Albuquerque Regional Medical Center was less than five minutes away. The ten-floor hospital had been St. Joseph's, for years run by sturdy, knowledgeable, caring nuns who wore even sturdier oxfords. A recent merger had made it the city's largest health conglomerate. The nuns were gone: no soft padding of rubberized soles through the corridors with the occasional squeak around corners. No holding hands in prayer with families in sorrow. No rosaries swinging from habits. The new corporate owners pledged patient satisfaction and the highest level of patient care. Call her a cynic, but Shelly never believed corporate mission statements. Especially not those prominently displayed in every hallway.

The admitting clerk was having a bad morning. But who wouldn't at six a.m.? Dr. Chen, it seemed, was running late, and the clerk didn't know where to put her. And her records showed that Shelly hadn't paid the anesthesiologist. But there wasn't one, Shelly reminded her. For a facelift, Dr. Chen would administer the anesthetic.

Grumpy humphed a couple times and told her to take a seat in the waiting area.

Patrice had secured two side-by-side chairs in the corner and offered her a section of the day's newspaper, but Shelly waved it aside. Reading demanded a little too much concentration. Maybe if she just people-watched. Monday was certainly the day of choice for surgical procedures. The place was packed. A nurse with a clipboard got off the elevator and called out five names. Actually, she called out four names, looked up, and then walked over to an elderly Chinese woman sitting with someone who could be her daughter. After a spirited give and take with the younger woman, the nurse stood to one side while the younger bent over the older. Slowly, the mother started to remove her jewelry—a ring, earrings, two bracelets. The earrings, two drops of jade, were the first to be handed to her daughter. Then, carefully, the others. Finally, the two clasped hands and the younger supported the older as she rose. Entwined, an arm around the shoulders, an arm around the waist, they walked slowly to the elevator. What would it be like to not speak the language and need hospitalization?

The others around her didn't seem quite so interesting. A young man in the corner, stocking cap pulled low, almost covering his eyes, wore all the trappings of a gang member—lots of tattoos like the ones to be gotten in the state pen, baggy pants, chains hanging from a low-riding waistband. But if he looked like one, was he one? Not necessarily. He seemed to be by himself. She felt rather than saw his eyes watching her. A middle-aged couple, the woman clasping the man's hand, all the while smoothing the material of her skirt with the other. Nervous gestures belying fear from uncertainty? Of course. She wondered what tics she was displaying.

Shelly just wanted this over with. She had to admit that she was spending time thinking of the guy in Florida. Actually, he had a name—Ron Meyers. She could kick herself, but once again she was impressed by the caring—but hadn't she been there before? And rather recently? This was different. But how? She just had a feeling. Nothing she could explain, but something to hold onto. Did the two thousand miles separating them make the situation hopeless from the start? Perhaps. But she was such a Pollyanna she believed that true love could overcome distance. But wasn't she getting ahead of herself? True love shouldn't even be in the picture . . . yet.

She wasn't in the first group being ushered to the elevator and she wasn't in the second. Patrice glanced up with a reassuring smile. She had had a number of procedures—sinus, two hip replacements, a knee. It was old hat to her, but not to Shelly. She'd gone into convulsions with amoebic dysentery—Ed had insisted on hiring a native cook that summer in Ecuador who had no understanding of washing after restroom use. And Shelly had given birth to two children. That was it. End of hospital stays. She should count herself incredibly lucky or healthy. She was down two teeth but still had her tonsils and her appendix.

Of course, being the wife of a pathologist had offered more than a few clues about surgical procedures. But it wasn't like she had kept up on new surgical techniques. She had made certain that everyone knew she was allergic to codeine, which ruled out all of the Percocet, Percodan group.

Finally, it was her turn. Patrice would be called later. Someone would come for her after Shelly was checked in. It was already forty-five minutes past six. She wished it was forty-five minutes past six Tuesday morning or Wednesday. She slipped into a well-worn cotton wraparound with ties everywhere, yet the gown was guaranteed to flap open in all the wrong places at all the wrong times. Had it really had blue checks once upon a time? What kind of washing could suck the pattern off a piece of yard goods? The mesh footies with rubber strips on the bottom were another fashion statement. The food-server's hair protector finished "the look."

She knew she'd be in surgery for two and a half hours and after a brief recovery, Patrice would drive her home. And she'd have a new face—not the pretty, finished product. The bruising would be brutal but wouldn't last long. And there would be no chins. Would she look younger? Probably. But she only wanted to look refreshed, a youthful color to her skin and rested. Too much to ask? She hoped not.

CHAPTER NINETEEN

It was lunchtime when Patrice pulled her SUV under the emergency canopy. Other than her Gucci sunglasses not fitting over the bandages, Shelly felt pretty good. Considering. It was always a good sign to be hungry, and she was famished. Because all sustenance had to be delivered through a straw, a chocolate malt was the answer. And there was only one old-time soda fountain that could deliver the goods—the Model Drugstore. Even Patrice stooped to having a strawberry milkshake. Patrice ran in and got both to go. No reason to excite the populace by parading her bandaged head—now the size of a basketball. And the eyes . . . did those cinder-black holes in her face really belong to her?

Shelly downed a Motrin the minute they got to the bungalow, assured Patrice that she would be fine, and settled in to read her e-mail and nurse the chocolate malt as long as she could—then go to bed. The bungalow was cozy; the world seemed a long way away. If one had to mend, this was the place to do it.

Amazing how e-mail could pile up in barely a day.

But she was looking for a special one and then she saw it. The message was short—"I know you won't be home for a couple more hours but I wanted you to know how much I'm thinking of you. I hope all has gone well and look forward to your call." Thoughtful. And she was looking forward to talking with him. She appreciated his support.

She walked back into the bedroom. Getting out of the confining jeans felt great. A T and underpants were fast becoming a staple. Suddenly, she had no energy—a nap would be perfect. Her bed was pure heaven. She pulled up the light blanket, fluffed the pillows, propping two more behind her to keep herself semi-upright, and sank back—but was absolutely wide awake. Tossing and turning was out of the question; she was still praying that she wouldn't sneeze. Gingerly, she sat up and felt the ball of gauze that was her head. Maybe a glass of wine would be that something to help her unwind.

She found a merlot that she liked—was surprised that there was still a bottle of Rojo Loco in the cabinet—and carried goblet, bottle, and straw out to the deck. Which was it you weren't supposed to drink through a straw, wine or beer? She didn't remember but guessed she'd find out.

Late August and an afternoon monsoon downpour had left a touch of coolness in the air. Would it be an early fall? Winter was just a short three months away. Suddenly she felt very alone. What hadn't happened in the last six months? Was she ready to forge ahead? The holidays . . . how very different from last year. This time around without a father, without a husband, and in all probability without her oldest son. Would she even decorate? A tree suddenly seemed like a burden.

She dragged a folded lounge chair away from the wall, took a deep breath, set it up, and then lowered herself into it, keeping her head upright and steady. The wine was delicious, the air invigorating. Just the right combination to fuel her thoughtfulness. She relaxed into the swayed, striped canvas with three bright turquoise pillows supporting her neck and head.

So, she'd looked into the mirror and had seen this Muslim woman with an egg-shaped head in white headdress. And the puffiness obliterating eyebrows, making her nose seem an afterthought in its smallness—like a head shot of a Pillsbury Doughgirl. Not pretty, but promising. And it was over. One more cutting to go—if she decided on the tummy tuck.

The sun lulled her senses. Her life seemed suspended in time with not one thing important enough to change course for. She was at the rudder. Wasn't that the big difference? She was trying on her life like a much-cherished coat and found it warm and inviting—comforting. Something that had been stored away and had all this time needed airing. Maybe a new set of buttons or a bright scarf.

Would the parameters placed on a late-in-life romance seem constraining? Take away the comfort of this newfound life? Would she, yet again, give up things that she might want? Put feelings and needs on hold? What were the rules of the game at sixty? She'd be so disappointed if it was all about old patterns. Old expectations.

The shrill ring of the phone startled her. Who knew she was home besides Patrice? And she thought Shelly'd be napping. She should have brought her cell out to the porch, but the phone in the kitchen was only a matter of steps away.

"Hello." Was that her voice? It was tough to talk through bandages.

"Shelly? Ron Meyers. I didn't expect you to answer. I was just getting ready to leave a message."

She immediately liked his voice—the energy was contagious. "I could always hang up—I'd hate to ruin your expectations."

He laughed. "Nope. I'm not going to trade in the real thing now that I have it. Do you feel like talking? Maybe I should ask, can you talk? The bandaging's got to be pretty restrictive."

"I'd love to for awhile—no promises on how long I can hold out."

"Just let me know. This can be a short one, but we have lots of catching up to do."

"So, where do we start?"

"With whatever you want to know. I'll answer anything—I'm not even going to qualify that. I want so much for us to start off on the right foot."

"Me, too. I had almost given up on online dating. Have you had good luck?"

"Not before now. Oh, a few dates, but I never felt a bond. I have to say I've appreciated your honesty. I've known what was going on in your life from the start. A lot of women would lie about cosmetic surgery."

"Probably. I'm not having things done to look like a sixty-year-old Barbie, though."

Laughter, then, "I'm fifty-eight and definitely not Ken material. Maybe, never was. And a sixty-year-old Barbie is pretty frightening."

"So, what are you looking for?"

"Companion, someone to challenge me, not roll over and play dead, but have well thought out arguments as to why I might be all wet."

"Does that happen often?"

"What?"

"The all wet part."

"Is this a sneaky way of finding out if I'm incontinent?"

Now it was her turn to laugh and realize how very sore her face was. "I was thinking of your profile. That's some scary stuff."

"How so?"

"The need for control. Even down to curtailing daydreaming. I like to live in never-never land once in awhile. I think I solve most of my day-to-day problems by running them through a 'what if' scenario accompanied by a second cup of coffee in the morning."

"Well, your first mistake is believing everything you read. Results of psychological profiles have respectable margins of error or of generally missing the mark altogether. I think 'open to interpretation' is the phrase most often used."

"Doesn't negate the fact that you're a pretty high octane engine."

"If that means I can get a lot done in a short period of time, yeah, I'll agree. Do you see this as a problem?"

"I'm not sure I could keep up."

"You don't think opposites attract? You don't think that a more laid-back approach to the world's problems wouldn't look good to me?"

"I wasn't thinking of it that way."

"The key is my being open to seeing things differently than I have in the past—be willing to try new methods of solving problems."

"Doesn't that sort of beg the 'old dogs, new tricks' question?"

"You know what? I love this. You asked me what I'm looking for? First and foremost, intelligence. And I've found it."

"Another guy referred to me as his intellectual equal but he was an idiot."

"Hey, who said anything about 'equal'? And I could probably get references about the idiot part."

They both laughed. She wished she wasn't getting so tired. Beyond tired, actually. She'd rest her jaw on her hand if she could find her jaw. The day's excitement was catching up.

"Could I call you tomorrow?"

"I'd be disappointed if you didn't. Anytime after seven my time would work."

This time her head barely hit the pillow before she was sound asleep.

Patrice stopped by on her way to work with a skillet breakfast from Flying Star.

"You need to keep your strength up. Remember, I'll be back at one."

Shelly was getting the bandages off. She didn't know whether to be thrilled or apprehensive. She felt like the movie heroine being handed a mirror after the operation to change her disfigurement. What if she still had chins?

But she didn't. She could tell already that other than some swelling and skin that had a distinct green hue, the excess chins were absent! Hurrah!! Dr. Chen oohed and aahed and was obviously pleased with his work. And didn't she feel more comfortable with a doc who got ego involved? And hadn't she chosen him because he referred to his work as artistry? And, yes, she was going to go ahead with the tummy tuck. In two weeks. But she was stopping there. The boobs were just going to have to battle gravity for a while—maybe forever.

Looking in the mirror this time was exciting—if she could overlook the bruising that spread to her chest and circled her ears. But she already looked one bar-fight away from beautiful. Well . . . that was an exaggeration, but she was pleased. A fall storm with the weatherman's dire prediction of "gale-force canyon winds" was going to keep her inside—not that even with a bottle of cover up she'd be tempted to go out.

By midafternoon she was feeling pretty isolated. The day was black-gray and the promised winds had split her thirty-year-old apple tree in half—depositing half in the street and the other through the wooden fence bordering the deck. What a mess. She left a message for Patrice at the office; her firm had a contract with a landscaping company—did she think they would be able to remove a tree and maybe patch the fence? Then it was light a fire and relax until six before placing the call to Florida.

The knock on the door startled her. There was still a light rain, and the darkness of late afternoon made her shiver and reach for a sweater. She didn't recognize the man standing under the eaves, but the insignia on his jacket read North Valley Landscaping. Could be the guy about the tree. She pulled the door open.

"The other guy's in the hospital, right?" She laughed. Old joke, but probably appropriate. "Actually, Patrice said you were recuperating and needed a hand with a tree."

"That was fast. Come in." She shut the door and held out her hand, "Shelly Sinclair."

"Um, sorry, Derek Thompson, North Valley Landscaping." He shook her hand. "Let me assess the damage and I'll get some of my guys on it in the morning."

"That would be great. I can't believe you came right over."

"Your friend is pretty persuasive. Thought you'd try to move the tree yourself." He grinned. "You're on my way home. The storm didn't do the downtown any favors. Lots of cleanup to do. This is minor, but annoying." He turned to look at the apple tree in two pieces. "I'll move the big stuff out of the street and put out some markers. That should cover you until tomorrow."

She watched him work. Nice guy. Cute. Tall with a head full of soft brown curls. She vaguely remembered Patrice mentioning him—Shelly thought he was the one that Patrice liked to watch work with his shirt off. That could be. He'd left his jacket on the porch and the T-shirt outlined a great upper torso. And he had to be within ten years of her age. But the accent was great. English, her favorite.

A cup of tea suddenly sounded good—the perfect warm-up for a dreary fall day. How impressionable, but maybe he'd like one, too. She put the kettle on, waited for it to boil, then leaned out the back door.

"I was about to make a cup of tea. Would you like one?"

"Sounds good. Thanks."

"Judging from the accent, you probably know more about making this brew than I do."

"Been in the states too long. The accent is about the only thing British left."

"Sugar? Milk?"

"No, this is fine." A sly smile. "It's criminal to ruin good tea. If you have a moment, let me show you something."

She followed him around the corner of the deck. A limb from the apple tree had crashed through two strips of planking and it was apparent that the wood was rotted.

"Oh, no. This looks awful."

"Hopefully, worse than it really is. I won't know how extensive the damage is until I get under there, but I'd prepare to replace the entire deck. Doesn't make sense that it's rotted in only this one spot. I'm booked about three to four weeks out, but could put you on the list for the first week in October unless you have someone who does maintenance for you."

"No, I don't. That would be great."

"It's a deal then. I'll have my guys trim back the apple. It needs to be removed, though. It'll be a good time of year to plant in another month or so. Do you want me to replace the tree when I take this one out?"

"Yes, but I don't want another apple. Too messy. What would you suggest?"

"I'm partial to ash—an Arizona or mountain might be nice, and I'd go with a pretty good-sized one for starters. That way you won't miss the shade of the apple for too long."

"I guess I need to go look at trees." Another thing she hadn't planned on but now needed to be done.

"Try Plants of the Southwest. If you find something you like, have them hold it for me. I'll use my discount and pick it up."

"Great. I'll let you know what I find."

"The tea is good. What kind is it?" He set his empty cup on the deck railing.

"Buckingham Palace Garden Party."

"Never heard of it."

"Only fortifies my belief that Americans fall for anything imported—if it sounds foreign, then it must be good."

"Probably so." He laughed. "Hope that applies to me."

Cute. But she couldn't help but laugh, too. "I guess we'll see."

"Well, this isn't getting the truck loaded. Thanks again for the tea. Call if you need anything. I look forward to getting this deck fixed for you. In the meantime, be careful where you step." He handed her his card and took off down the steps.

It was tough to wait until after six. Curiosity and that cat thing was for real. But Ron answered on the first ring. Eager? It would seem so. Shelly knew she was—eager to find out more, see where this might lead.

"So . . . bandages off?"

"Yes. I have working parts again—and I can talk. You know I have about a hundred questions . . . things to ask you—about you."

"Such as?"

"All the personal stuff—have you been married, do you have children, where do you work, how long have you lived in Florida—that sort of thing."

He didn't mind sharing the particulars. His mother died when he was ten and his father, not being able to cope, sent him to boarding school. There were solicitous aunts and a much younger sister, but growing up—if he honestly were pressed to answer—he'd probably never felt loved. And remedying that hadn't gone smoothly.

There had been a first marriage—a relationship during college that lasted two years and instead of breaking up, they got married. Big mistake. Marriage number two was later in life, lasted for twelve years; he'd been divorced for not quite two and had a twelve-year-old daughter—the light of his life.

A daughter? Did she live with him? No, but it would be a deciding factor in decisions such as where he might end up living—at least, for the next six years. He would never risk the chance of being out of touch. How did she feel about having a child in her life? Fine. Actually, the possibility was exciting.

As to work, education and future plans . . . an engineer by education, master's level, but was currently the CEO of a healthcare firm; he had several patents in the medical field and planned on law school by the end of the year, specializing in patent law. Florida was home—some twenty-five years' worth—after an upbringing in the Midwest. Her turn.

She heard herself rattle on about a childhood in Kansas, a conservative mother and father with a no-frills approach to life. She moved on to the thirty-five-year marriage with two children. He stopped her with a couple of questions about Ed and seemed genuinely shocked that he'd run off with the receptionist. Was that too much information? Shelly wondered.

A college degree in English Literature seemed lame but she mentioned it. She debated whether to add the almost-completed license in massage therapy and decided against it. She didn't know him, and it might put her into more of a "woo-woo" light than she'd prefer. Massage therapists often had New Age written all over them. And that wasn't really her MO. But she wanted him to know everything, and found herself going back to Tiffany and Jonathan and Marissa—describing in detail the triangle of people who changed her life forever.

She'd lived in one place—even one house—all her married life; he'd lived in Europe, Japan, and Australia. A specialty seemed to be start-up companies—get the funding, get them off the ground, and then move on. Life in comparison to hers had been lived to the fullest. He wasn't tired of travel, in fact, just the opposite. In retirement, as he handled his half-dozen patent cases a month and had lots of time off, he wanted to travel extensively. Did she like caviar? The best in the world was to be had at Stockholm's Opera House restaurant—next to the Grand Hotel. They should go there.

She found him exciting; their conversation never stalled out for lack of interest or comment. By the end of the weekend, they had racked up over twenty hours of talking. They had settled on a ritual of talking every night at ten. Monday was no exception. She got ready for bed, poured a glass of wine, fluffed up the pillows, leaned against the headboard, and waited for the phone to ring.

"You know, in a very short period of time, I can't imagine life without you. I don't want to scare you away, but I'm going to spend the rest of my life with you."

"You can't know that—not in one week."

"Haven't you ever felt, actually known, that a special something existed between you and another individual? Something that defied time? And knew it almost from the first word the person uttered?"

Thirty-seven years ago . . . had she felt that for Ed? She thought she had. But she was young. The world itself was promise. And then she was choosing a man to have children with—establish a home with. This seemed so reckless in comparison. On one hand, it seemed harmless to take a chance—ride along on a whim. Nothing ventured, nothing gained (there was one for her mother). But didn't she risk being hurt? Badly hurt? Was there such a thing as an upscale bad boy?

"Shelly? Are you there? I've upset you, haven't I?"

"No, not upset. I'm just trying to remember if I've ever felt that way—could be so certain, so soon. It's almost love at first sight. And 'sight' isn't even an option. Do you think there's such a thing as electronic pheromones?"

"Why not? Are you saying you don't feel the same way?"

She did feel the same way, but was reluctant to tell him. Hadn't she made some questionable decisions in the not-so-distant past? Obviously the Badboy, not to mention Randy, the screamer. How many times had she reminded herself—if it seemed too good to be true, it probably was?

"I just don't want this to go poof."

"How could it go poof?"

"By going too fast. Planning a future before we even meet."

"I think you need to have faith."

"You're probably right."

He was on the road between Tampa and Orlando and didn't stop their conversation for a drive-through fast food fix. He longed to leave the high-carb road food and be more settled—maybe even home-cooked meals. Did she like to cook? Yes, but didn't often take the time anymore.

"You know we need to set a time to meet. Do you still want to come this way?"

"Yes." The idea of getting away was appealing. The possibility of Ed popping up in the bedroom window again needed to be avoided.

"Let's make a real vacation out of it. You can even bring your toys. I need to know what turns you on."

"Toys? Oh, right. Sorry, not into them, or vice versa." She flashed on Big Red.

"It's the unusual woman today who doesn't have a toy or two."

This stopped her. That seemed to be the consensus of popular opinion. What was she supposed to have done? Divorce Ed and run out and replace him with something in latex? Fact was, she wouldn't have wanted to replace him . . . but the bad boy, that was a different story. Surely there were better, different, more realistic ones than Big Red.

"I'm sure I must seem odd. But I don't own a toy. I couldn't stand to go into those stores."

"Shop online. Google some addresses and take a look. Better yet, find a store that appeals to you, let me know, and we'll go shopping together. Not that I'll be any help—I just think it would be hysterical to do together. Worth a laugh or two, wouldn't you think?"

She had to agree. And it was a good idea; certainly one she would admit to having been tempted with before. Hadn't Patrice mentioned a girls' afternoon of discreet shopping? Yeah, right, slip into the News Stand with a bag over her head. Toys. Imagining Ed and dildos made her laugh out loud. He would have been appalled. She was amazed at how easy it was to talk with Ron. No subject was out of bounds—they were both comfortable discussing intimate issues. Was this something that came with being sixty? The number of intimate issues that could crop up? Lubricant, for example, was just not a topic of discussion in your twenties or thirties or forties—unless you were doing something creative with whipped cream. Being sixty changed the language of the bedroom—for both parties. The purple pill was an unknown just a few years ago. But before hanging up, she promised to look, at least that, and report the next night on her finds.

Ron sent a couple of URLs and she found a couple more and was blown away by the sheer number of devices. What toadstool had she been living under? There was a whole new world out there that she'd never seen.

"So, what do you think?" He was at home and sounded relaxed.

"Do you know how out of it I've been? I had no idea that dildos came with remote controls."

He laughed. "Did you see the ones modeled after the appendages of various porn stars?"

"Do people really buy those?"

"My guess is they do. Law of supply and demand, and they offer a lot of them."

"Should I ask what has made you an expert in this field?"

More laughter. "Good question. I'm going to disappoint you, though, if you expect an expert. I've been in a store one time—coming up with a gag gift for a friend's birthday. And I admit to checking a couple online stores just out of curiosity."

"Still a lot more experience than I have—how discreet are they? Can I count on whatever I order arriving in a plain brown paper wrapper? Or whatever the equivalent is today?"

"Believe me, the plain brown paper wrapper is the mainstay of their business. Did you see anything that you liked?"

"I think I got stalled out reading about flavored gels versus tingling gels—not to mention scented gels, gels that need to be warmed, gels that require water. The peanut-butter flavored gel caught my attention."

"Sort of mind-boggling, isn't it?"

"Yeah, but the penile colors threw me. Why bright blue or space-age silver with stripes? Couldn't there be a standard penis color with a few choices based on ethnicity? Such as nude or toast or cinnamon? And sparkles and lights . . . who's going to be down there to enjoy a Christmas display? Uh, don't answer that."

"You know, I think you're really getting into this."

"Enough to know I should get into toy penis design. I was really put off by the ones in glass."

"What?"

"Yeah, Pyrex or CorningWare. I've forgotten which."

"Glass dildos?"

"Supposed to be the best."

"I warned you I wasn't an expert, and glass . . . the very thought is scary."

"I agree. Even if the latex ones are an obnoxious color or shape, they would be better than glass."

"So, should we take a look?"

"Ron, I'm not sure I'd be comfortable shopping with you . . . not yet, anyway."

"I want you to be comfortable. You have to be comfortable—I know I'm not a pervert, you don't."

"If I get something, I'll bring it with me."

"That's a deal. And I won't be surprised or disappointed if you don't. You have to be comfortable with all this."

He easily changed the subject to a restaurant in St. Augustine that they absolutely had to try someday. A friend had just dined there and said the wine list was outstanding. And wasn't the tummy tuck scheduled for Tuesday? If she felt like it, she was to call him when she got home, but he wouldn't expect it—those things could really lay a person up. She needed to start healing—face and tummy just two weeks apart; even Superwoman would be reeling. He was sending her a couple articles on a new salve that diminished scarring. Good stuff. She needed to take a look.

"Tell me again, you were looking at what?" She'd called Patrice after she'd said good night to Ron.

"I think you heard me. Ron suggested it. I'm not a

toy person—you know that. I wouldn't even go shopping with you."

"I remember. Should I worry that this man seems to be awfully familiar?"

"It's comfortable. I can't believe the things we talk about. The minute I said that I'd rather pick out a toy on my own—that I wasn't comfortable shopping together—he moved right on. Not a problem."

"Shelly, I think you need to go slowly. I know you're blown away by his caring and his ability to seemingly have all the answers, but it's way too premature to fall in love."

"I was too shocked by what happened with the screamer. If anything, I'm waiting for this to fall apart."

"Well, don't forget I'm picking you up in the morning. Tuck time."

How could Shelly forget? But this time there were no jitters. Her face was perfect. Exactly what she wanted. And a tummy, or less thereof? Well, for one thing, a bobble wouldn't be in plain sight. But she had total confidence in Dr. Chen. It would be perfect, too.

She insisted Patrice take her car—getting in and out of the Beemer would be a far sight better than straining new stitches trying to climb into an SUV. She certainly wasn't going to be needing the car for three or four days. She had a lot of mending to do. The three-hour operation under general anesthetic wasn't fun. She couldn't stand up straight. The Velcro-tight bandage around her midsection prohibited even taking deep breaths. Patrice was staying the night just as a precaution and for some help in sitting and standing.

"I'm going to get you home, tuck you in, and then get some lunch. Anything sound good?"

"Lotta Burger?"

"Oh, good grief, I was thinking soup. But guess that's evidence you're going to live."

Patrice helped her lower her very bruised torso onto the couch, fluffed pillows behind her head, and was out the door, but not before handing Shelly the phone.

"Short and sweet—no marathon calls. You need rest."

"Yes, Mom."

"I'll be back in half an hour."

Shelly reached Ron's voicemail and suggested he wait to call her until morning. She had visions of wolfing down the burger and then going into a coma for twelve hours. She was beyond tired and too full of drugs to stay awake. And far, far too ouchy to move.

The burger was perfect. Eating like the condemned had become a habit lately. Luckily this was the last scheduled surgery—any more malts and burgers and there would be need of another tuck. But she didn't pass up the fries—it was just difficult doubling over and eating. But there was no way she could have sat at the table.

"Damn." Patrice sounded exasperated.

"What?"

"I left my overnight by the door at home. I can't believe I forgot it. Guess I was in too much of a hurry. After I clean up here, I'm going to leave you in bed, phone on the nightstand, TV remote beside it, glass of water, a Motrin just in case—"

"You won't be gone that long. I can't think that I'll need anything. And just leave these dishes—do them later."

"You talked me into it. And I won't be gone long. Later, gorgeous woman-to-be."

"Yeah, right." At the moment, discomfort was overriding any excitement about the finished product.

"I'm going to close the door and pull the shades. You need rest." Patrice bustled around the bedroom, opened the window farthest from her a couple inches, and pulled the shades, pushing them against the casement at the bottom. "No light is going to sneak in here. And don't forget your pulley. If you need to sit or stand, use it. No strain on those tummy muscles." Patrice gave a test tug on the bungee cord that looped around the solid four-poster foot of the bed.

What tummy muscles? Other than being acutely aware of a very tight, very wide Ace bandage circling her torso, all else was numb. But she nodded in agreement.

"I'll be here by two thirty—depending on traffic. I don't want to hear a peep out of you when I get back. Sleep is the order of the day." A kiss more or less blown in Shelly's direction and Patrice was off.

Shelly wasn't sure how long she'd slept, but she jolted awake knowing how really badly she had to pee.

"Patrice?"

No answer. Maybe she was on the deck. Oh well, she could test the pulley. Slow going and a lot of maneuvering and finally her feet touched the floor. The exertion had been so great, she sat on the side of the bed and took a half-dozen deep breaths. Better. But standing put a whole lot of pressure in a dozen new places. She winced, caught her breath, and willed her feet to move forward. She clung to every piece of furniture going out the bedroom door— the nightstand, the dresser, the door itself.

The bathroom was a gargantuan challenge. Getting up and down on anything was almost impossible. And no Patrice. She'd forgotten to check the clock on the nightstand, but it was getting dark out. It must be late afternoon. Hadn't Patrice said she'd be back at two thirty? Oh well, she'd probably run by work and got caught up in something that had to be done.

The bathroom counter was close enough to leverage her way upward and then, standing, she knew what she had to do. Check Dr. Chen's handiwork. Positioning herself in front of the mirror, she carefully rolled the full-cut gauzy top upward, tied its hem in a loose knot, and went to work on the Velcro strip on the torso bandage. Inch by inch it separated. And then, with an ear-splitting finale, it fell away. Not pretty. A happy face with a grimace. She fought a temptation to find a magic marker and add two large oval eyes on each side of her belly button . . . belly button? Oh my God, it wasn't there. Could it still be lying in a stainless steel tray beside the operating table? They save the original and simply sew it back as a last step. Stranger things had happened in surgery. Even perfect Dr. Chen could have forgotten.

She continued to roll the fabric upward, fighting panic. Finally. There it was . . . between her boobs. Well, maybe that was a slight exaggeration, but it was greatly out of place. She would never be able to wear slacks "at the waist" without looking like a nerd—slacks in place at the ribcage. Was it an error or would the errant button reposition itself after the swelling abated? She guessed she'd have to wait and see. Probably not worth worrying about.

Shelly flipped on the TV on her way back to bed. The clock on the nightstand said six. Odd that Patrice hadn't called—but then she'd assume Shelly was asleep. The announcer was saying something about being live at the scene of the rollover earlier that afternoon at I-25 and Montgomery. Shelly glanced at the screen and caught her breath, then gripped the bedpost with both hands. Upside down or not, that was her car. That was the BMW. Patrice, my God . . . what had happened? She felt sick and very, very helpless.

Onlookers described a black pickup side-swiping and forcing the car onto the median, causing it to flip. The driver of the BMW, tentatively identified as Shelly Walters Sinclair, had been rushed to Lovelace Medical in yet-to-be-determined condition. So much for notifying next of kin first before a name was released—but maybe that was only in case of a fatality.

Shelly reached for the phone and steadied herself. The receptionist at Lovelace Medical was unable to put Ms. Sinclair through to Ms. Sinclair because she wasn't a relative. If she was a sister or the mother, then there wouldn't be a problem. Why wasn't she family if she had the same name? But then wasn't it funny to have really the same name—two Shellys? Shelly idly wondered if the young woman was blond, then explained the situation . . . again. She was the owner of the car, not the driver. The injured party was Patrice Caplan—how did she know that? Good question. Yes, it could have been a carjacking. Yes, it could be a man in recovery; she had no way of knowing. A man named Shelly Sinclair. Shelly hung up in frustration. She felt like she'd just gone through a slightly different rendition of "who's on first?" If she even allowed herself a derogatory thought about twentysomethings' reasoning capabilities, she'd sound like her father. She'd just call the police.

But the banging on the front door kept her from doing anything but start the treacherous trek to open it. It would take her forever to get there. She flipped on the hall light. At least whoever it was would know someone was home. The living room was an obstacle course and every step was painful, but she could see the two officers through the narrow-paned glass on the sun porch.

"Mrs. Sinclair?"

"I saw the news. The driver—I've been trying to find out how she is. Is she all right? " Shelly pulled the door fully open.

"Ms. Caplan is going to be fine. Well, that may be relative. Dislocated shoulder, possible broken collarbone, and a concussion. She'll be held overnight for observation. I'm Officer Barker and this is Officer Miller. May we come in?" Shelly unlocked the screen and gingerly stepped to the side.

"Thank God, from the look of the car it could have been far worse." Shelly paused by the French doors into the living room. "I've just had surgery. The going is a little slow."

"Miss Caplan told us. She's beside herself that she's not here." Officer Miller, a trim young woman who looked good in a uniform, stepped up beside her. "Is there someone else who could stay with you? I would be glad to make a call."

"Thanks. I'll get in touch with my son later." Shelly had no intention of calling Jonathan, but maybe she should give it some thought. She stepped over the threshold to the living room and lowered herself onto the loveseat. "I loaned my car to Patrice, who picked me up after surgery today. It was easier for me to slide into my car than her SUV." Shelly waited while Officer Barker checked his notes. Both chose to sit opposite her on the sofa.

"Ms. Sinclair, are you or have you been threatened recently?" She could feel Officer Barker's eyes watching her for any reaction.

"Threatened? Why would you ask that?"

"A number of eyewitnesses have given statements that Ms. Caplan was being followed—tailgated—for a mile along the freeway before being struck from the rear. This corroborates her story. She's adamant that she did nothing to provoke the incident."

"I can't imagine Patrice being confrontational. I'm the one who's pretty loose with the sign language, never Patrice."

"If this was not just a random example of road rage, then we need to explore the possibility of intention— someone believing it was you and deliberately striking your vehicle to cause you harm."

"Did anyone get a license number?" Patrice was beginning to feel numb and not just from surgery.

"Covered with mud." Officer Miller offered.

"A description of the driver?" She braced herself. Shelly didn't think she could stand it if Officer Barker described Ed.

"Illegal tint on the windows. No one could get a good look."

Shelly almost sighed in relief. But would Ed be capable of such a thing? No. She could never believe it.

Officer Miller referred to her notes. "Ms. Caplan shared with us that you're going through a divorce."

"Well, I'd like to think the 'going through' part is over. But, yes, I'm recently divorced."

"Amicably?" This from Officer Barker.

"There are those who would say amicable divorce is an oxymoron."

"So, we can assume that there have been problems?" He wrote something in his notebook.

"Not problems, exactly." Shelly paused and realized that they would probably wait for as long as it took to get an answer. She didn't look up, but felt two pairs of eyes. A deep breath and an exhale. "My husband was involved with—planned to marry—a much younger woman, in her twenties, and thought that he'd fathered her child, but it turns out . . . " She halted; it was difficult to go on. Maybe if she thought of it like sharing an old episode of *As the World Turns,* it would be easier. "My youngest son is the father. I don't know, but I can imagine the news has put a damper on things. In short, my former husband has been under a lot of stress."

"Ms. Caplan mentioned stalking, striking you, forcing his way into your house. This seems a little bit more problematic than just a reaction to stress."

Why was she so reluctant to be more open about the extent of Ed's . . . intrusion? Because she'd been married for so long? Because she thought she knew the man? Knew he didn't have a mean bone . . . .

"I don't want to make excuses for him. There have been some ugly moments. I just don't think he could be capable of—"

"You'd be surprised. Sometimes it's the quiet ones that just go off." Officer Miller seemed to know what she was talking about. "We need Dr. Sinclair's address."

Funny. Shelly realized that she didn't know exactly. She had the old work PO Box and, of course, their former house—maybe Ed had routed the squatters and really was living there now. Like he hadn't been before. Yeah, right. Officer Barker handed her a sheet of paper and she wrote down what she knew, including Ed's cell phone number and the name and number of his lawyer.

"We need to get you back to bed." Officer Miller stood.

"I can manage if you'll lock the door behind you."

"Shelly!" The door banged open. Well, speak of the devil. "What are you doing out of the hospital? You don't belong here. They said you were in surgery."

"Ed, this is Officer Barker . . . Officer Miller. I haven't been in an accident. Patrice was driving."

"Patrice? How seriously injured is she?"

"Bruising, broken collarbone maybe, a concussion, but she'll mend. I've had some elective surgery, that's all."

"Dr. Sinclair? We'd like to speak with you. And I think Ms. Sinclair needs to rest." Officer Barker was good at taking control. And Shelly really wanted Ed gone.

"I think it's pretty obvious that I need to take care of my wife."

"Former wife, I believe. And I don't think she wants to be disturbed."

"I don't think she needs anyone to speak for her; she usually does pretty well on her own. I can only imagine what she's been telling you. You know, you've got the drama queen here. Another Oscar performance, eh, Shel?"

"Why would you say that, sir? What could she tell us that you wouldn't want us to know?" This from Officer Miller. Were they trained together? Probably, Shelly decided.

"Look, I have nothing to say to you. I saw the news, recognized my wife's car, and got over here as quickly as I could."

"Why didn't you go to the hospital? I believe the news mentioned which one the driver was taken to."

"I called Lovelace Medical and like I said earlier, they said she was in surgery."

"So, why come here?" Officer Miller asked the very question that Shelly was wondering.

"To take care of things. Pack what I thought she might need and take it to her."

"Do you have a key to Ms. Sinclair's house?"

"No, but she always forgets to lock something. And I considered this an emergency."

"And that warrants breaking and entering?" Officer Miller was giving him no slack.

"You people are being ludicrous. We've been married thirty-five years. I know this woman. I know what she needs. I had every reason to believe that she'd been seriously injured. Since when has trying to help been a crime?"

"Breaking in is the crime. Because of what witnesses have reported, we are working on the assumption the hit and run was intentional."

"Officer Miller? It was Miller, wasn't it?" Ed acknowledged her nod, then continued. "I can think of no one on earth who would want to do harm to this woman. Absolutely no one."

"And that includes you?"

"I'm not even going to grace that with an answer. I'm the father of her children."

"But not the father of the young woman's child? The young woman you were going to marry? I believe left Ms. Sinclair to marry? And this has led to some anger on your part?" Officer Barker was reading from his notes.

"Well, it looks like you've been here long enough for the family laundry to be displayed." Before anyone could react, Ed leaned over Shelly and grabbed her by the chin. "Look at me, you stupid bitch." Both officers grabbed an arm, pulled Ed upright, and dragged him backwards. "I'm sick and tired of you maligning my reputation—"

"That'll be enough of that. You'll be coming along with us and I suggest you call your lawyer." Officer Barker quickly cuffed him.

Shelly's cry of pain was lost in the shouting. She'd reacted by pulling back and then feeling a searing spike below her ribs. It took her breath away.

"Are you all right?" Officer Miller knelt beside her, but Shelly didn't trust her voice to answer. Finally, she managed to nod. "I want to call your son or take you back to a hospital. I don't like leaving you here alone."

"She won't be alone." All heads turned toward the door. "Patrice asked me to take Ms. Sinclair to the doctor in the morning, then pick her up. I believe her SUV is here. I think it would be a good idea if I just stay the night." He held out his hand first to one cop and then the other. "Derek Thompson, a friend of Ms. Caplan and Ms. Sinclair."

"Is this all right with you?" Officer Miller checked.

"Of course, it's all right with her. This is what she's used to—a parade of men. How many tattoos does this one have, slut?"

"Get him out of here." Officer Barker nodded at Shelly and propelled Ed forward.

"Call if you need anything. And, take care." Officer Miller followed.

"Nice guy. I'm glad I had the evening free. I can see why Patrice was concerned."

"Listen, you don't have to babysit." Shelly ignored the 'nice guy' comment. She didn't want to discuss Ed with a stranger.

"No? Patrice read me the riot act. Take care of this woman. Don't let her out of your sight."

"I don't think you have to worry. A foot race is out of the question."

"That's a relief. I was hoping for a quiet night—a beer in the fridge, a TV somewhere. Feel like watching a movie? I brought *The English Patient*. Have you seen it?"

"One of my all-time favorites."

"Best adaptation from a novel."

"I agree. The novel's a little tedious, but the movie is great. Would you think me antisocial, though, if I passed?"

"Not at all. But I think you'd be more comfortable lying down."

He offered both hands, pulled her upright, and then put one hand under her elbow. The trip to the bedroom was at her pace—two steps forward, stop, start again. He didn't seem to mind.

"Bathroom?"

"I'm fine."

"Well, looks like this is it. Covers back. Pillows fluffed. In you go."

"Thanks." Bed. Shelly thought nothing had ever felt this good.

Four days later, she was up and around and sorely missing her wheels. The Beemer was totaled, her insurance reluctant to cover a secondary driver. More phone calls and more hassles. Finally, a check to BMW for almost original cost. Minus, of course, depreciation and normal wear. What had it been now? Two months? And a whopping one thousand miles? Oh well, she was to pick up the new car on Friday. This time black instead of silver metallic. But none of this mattered. Patrice was going to be fine. An arm in a sling and lots of soreness, but fine.

Ron wanted her to "buy American." Their first fight? Almost. He finally gave up trying to interest her in a Lincoln. My God, a Lincoln? Visions of Mame Sinclair driving the wrong way . . . and wasn't the Mustang sporty and fast? And cheap? He had no right to tell her how to spend her money, but frugality had virtues. But didn't get her heart racing. Mustang Shelly. She thought the song had been done already—or something close to it. So, she won if it could be called a contest. Maybe one of wills. Hadn't his profile warned her? Overall, it had been amicable—a spirited discussion, not an argument. Yes, she could live with this man.

On day five she went with Derek to look at trees and chose a beautiful maple and a mountain ash. It was like running around with Johnny Appleseed—he was the tree guy. He could even spout the Latin names—genus and species. He finished the deck and it looked fantastic with new railing. He'd made it bigger and wrapped it around the house. A horseshoe of decking. The extended seating area included a half-circle bench around the new ash. Their nursery forays always ended with a beer at the Two Fools. It felt so good to be out and running around—standing upright. And, if she were to be honest, getting some attention from someone who seemed to think she had a brain in her head.

It became necessary to fight the narcissistic tendency of looking in every plate-glass window as she walked by. No more bruising around her face, and the tummy was gloriously not there. Never to be seen again. She was pleased and felt like life was taking off. A love, good friends, a new car—and she hadn't heard from Ed. Follow-up on the accident was a dead end. For so many witnesses, no one had come up with a clue about the driver of the black pickup.

A month went by, then two. Nightly conversations centered around a visit. She was putting it off as long as she could—she wanted to be completely healed with a scar that wasn't still flashing neon. Yes, she wanted to go to Florida. Nothing sounded so good as long morning walks on the beach, intimate dinners at specialty cafés, making love on sun-warmed sand. He wanted her to stay at least a month. She didn't know, didn't want to commit—but a couple weeks would work. She couldn't stop the scenario of "what if" from running through her head—what if he was short and bald, what if he wasn't who he said he was, what if he thought she was too fat, too thin, too loud, too whatever? And what if he had ear hair?

Ron was so positive that they were meant to be that his excitement came out in planning. They'd take a few days and drive up to St. Augustine. He knew a B&B that she'd adore. And there was that restaurant that they had to try. Or maybe he'd try to snag the time-share at Daytona from his former wife. Would she like to stay on the beach? And, oh yes, a restaurant in New Smyrna Beach served the best grouper known to man—did she like grouper?

But he wasn't sure they'd get out of the airport. What would she think if he got a room at the airport Hyatt? They could spend the first night on neutral ground, then go on into Orlando in the morning. He wanted to make love to her between room service (maybe lobster thermidor?) and messengers delivering flowers and champagne and chocolates.

"If I see Avis in your eyes, I'll walk on by." It had become a joke between them.

"Darling, you're not going to see Avis and I won't either. Shelly, I'm in love with you. I meant it when I said I'm spending the rest of my life with you. I know it's difficult to believe now, but you'll see."

She marveled at how close they were. How much she physically wanted him. And the feelings were not one-sided.

"I think we need to have sex—try it out anyway, see if we're compatible. That last is a joke, Shelly, there's no doubt in my mind that we're compatible."

"We'll know in another two weeks." She'd booked a flight to Orlando for November 10.

"Why not phone sex in the meantime?"

"I've never had phone sex before."

"Does that mean you don't want to?"

"No, just unsure how we begin."

"For starters, you have to be touching yourself."

"I got that part."

"Now, just listen to me and follow with your imagination. OK? Tell me what you want to do to my cock . . . Shelly?"

"I'm still here. I'm not sure I can tell you."

"Do you want me inside you?"

"Yes."

"Could you be a little more descriptive?"

"I don't think so."

"Maybe if you wrote down what you wanted to say—"

"And just read it?"

"It's a place to start."

"That would be terrible."

"I'm just trying to make this easy for you."

"I think it's a problem because we've never met."

"Just give me a body in your imagination. I'll never know."

"Doesn't really seem fair."

"OK. Just describe the last time you got laid."

"I couldn't do that."

"Why not? I'm not threatened."

"It was the best sex of my life . . . Oh my God, I'm so sorry, I didn't mean to say that. It was a loser relationship—went nowhere. I walked away. Good sex isn't everything—I want, no, need a lot more."

"I know that. But I'd like to know what he did that made it so great."

"Ron, this isn't working. I don't believe in talking about past relationships. I've already said far too much."

"I'm not like other men, Shelly."

"I don't know that."

"I'm so looking forward to our spending time together—planning our future together. We leave ourselves open to too many missteps now. I think we've outgrown phone conversations."

"That will be remedied in thirteen more days."

CHAPTER TWENTY

She called him from the Albuquerque airport that morning to kiddingly assure him that she was at the gate and boarding. She knew she'd over-packed but had no idea what they'd do—she was prepared for anything. Clothes-wise. But otherwise? Was there a chance that she wouldn't find him attractive? And what if she was a disappointment? Did adults, under the circumstances, shake hands, wish each other well, and walk away? Simply get right back on the plane? How easy would that be after all the promises? The suspense? The hopes. Not very, she guessed.

Patrice had wanted her to take the stun gun. Her ever-practical, caring friend. But what would Shelly say if it accidentally fell out of her luggage—just Jack the Ripper protection? Just in case. That would instill confidence.

And thinking positively—where did she want the relationship to go? What if it was everything she thought it could be? Was she ready to commit? Was she ready to move to Florida? She had a sense of self now, maybe for the first time ever. Would she have to give that up? Because she just didn't see how she could. She liked this person, the one inside her skin, the one who could face down demons and survive, maybe even flourish, coming out stronger and more at ease with her world.

But most importantly, the one thing Ron gave to her was hope, a peek at a future filled with laughter and love and caring and discovering. There was a sweetness and beauty to this hope.

She could not believe how nervous she was when the plane landed. Walking to the connecting shuttle trains that would take her to the baggage claim area forced her to keep up with the crowd, not hang back for fear of being trampled by dozens of Disney-intent families with small children. He was meeting her just outside the carousels at the base of the escalators. She quickly ducked into the last restroom in sight. A quick once-over—hair, makeup, clothes. Would she pass? A spritz of hairspray, lip gloss. Had her choice of casual attire been the right one? Clogs, jeans, and a pullover sweater in a blue-gray that matched her eyes? Could a mail-order bride from some Slavic country be any more nervous?

Finally, she couldn't stall any longer. A few deep breaths and she was back on the concourse and on the escalator. She willed her eyes to scan the crowd. She had pictures, but that wasn't the real thing. What if she didn't recognize him? But she did. He was standing to her right and his grin was engaging. Dark hair, straight and styled without even a hint of gray, and eyes so deeply brown they reflected light. High cheekbones, great tan, and those sparkling, laughing eyes. Sunglasses, something expensive in tortoiseshell and black wire, were folded and tucked in the front of a tan, collarless pullover. He hadn't lied about his height—six feet even—and he looked great in a black poplin jacket over jeans. And not a trace of ear hair.

"Hi Sweetie, you look terrific." He took her hand and drew her to him. "I can't believe you're here." The kiss was tender. "Let's get your bags. There'll be more of that later."

She pointed out her bags and he retrieved them. She called Patrice and left a message—"no need for stun gun." He overheard and she had to explain. He laughed and said Patrice must be a really good friend. They made small talk on the elevator—the weather, this was the best time to visit Florida. What was the best month for Albuquerque? Did she have a good flight? She felt shy and drawn to him all at the same time. But not once did she lose sight of the fact that from this moment on her life would be different . . . very different. She knew that she would be spending the rest of her life with this man. And loving him.

He'd reserved a room and set it up before he met her plane—baked Brie, grapes, cracker-bread, two pounds of Belgian chocolates, and champagne. One bottle chilling in a bucket bedside and two more in the suite's fridge, she discovered later. The view from the tenth floor was of a green lushness that made Albuquerque look dirty and barren in comparison. Palm trees. Could she get used to seeing them every day? Maybe. Yet, there weren't any mountains, just a certain flatness—sort of a "frondy" Kansas.

He stood behind her and slowly turned her to face him. "I can't believe you're finally here." His kiss was passionate, but not pushy. He followed her lead. She stepped into his embrace and put her arms around his neck. With her lips slightly parted, she felt his tongue trace the edge of her top lip and then the bottom before gently pushing into her mouth. He was playful, leaning into her, holding her in a kiss, then backing away ever so slightly, making her come to him, and she felt the urgency rise in her, starting between her legs and in tiny electric shocks skip upward.

He led her to the edge of the bed and, standing in front of her, undid her jeans and helped her pull the sweater over her head. She undid his belt, unbuttoned, then unzipped his jeans, and running a finger around the waistband, began to inch them downward. He had flipped off the room lights, leaving the bathroom door ajar. A light above the sink pushed tentacles of pale amber across the carpet. The room was softly gray with smudged edges. He kicked his jeans off, filled two champagne flutes, and set both on the nearest nightstand.

"May I?" He reached around her, unhooked her bra, and slipped it down her arms. She willed herself not to move, pull away. He stepped back and studied her.

"You're beautiful." She caught her breath as he took each breast and gently kissed a nipple, then turned and handed her a glass of champagne.

"To us, Shelly, and the start of a new life."

When she would look back on that first twenty-four hours, nothing had before and nothing ever would again equal the simple beauty of physically and verbally making a commitment. They didn't prick their fingers and press them together, but the bond was no less intense nor less loaded with promise. When they weren't making love, he was holding her, talking about all the things they would do together.

He ran a finger over the scar, then bent over and kissed it. "Hell of a happy face."

"I'll be glad when it's faded."

"Patience, Shelly. It's disappearing already."

When they slept—what little they did—he was touching her. A hand, a foot, or his entire body snugged up against her back. Sometimes she curled into him. And the last words she heard when drifting off, "I love you, Shelly." If she could define happiness, this was it. Hadn't she waited a lifetime for it?

CHAPTER TWENTY ONE

She watched him sleep and was awake when orange light sought entry around the edges of the drapery. She made coffee and carried the mug to an alcove sitting area. The room's air-conditioning was icy cold and gave her goose bumps. She would have traded the tee and panties for a parka in a heartbeat. This was not swamper country, and humidity and refrigerated air were staples—like it or not. But pulling the shades up flooded the area with warmth, and what the sun didn't accomplish, the coffee did. By the time Ron joined her, she was toasty.

"I thought I'd been abandoned." He bent and kissed her. "Any more coffee?"

"Coming up."

"Stay there. I'll get a pot started. Want to do room service or get breakfast on the road?"

"I sense a need to get going . . . make a move, anyway."

"Not saying that I couldn't take you right back into that bedroom and ravish your body . . . again. But there's a whole world out there. Let's go check out the sights."

The sights started with two brown bags of fish-and-chips to go. Long strips of king salmon deep fried in a dark beer batter with tangy tartar sauce and extra lemon wedges. The perfect brunch! They ate as they drove, Shelly breaking off pieces of fish, slathering on the tartar sauce, and trying to keep from dripping as she popped a bite in his mouth.

"I'd like to show you the house. Janey and Elizabeth are in Miami for a few days." The house in question was some six thousand-plus square feet on a lake two hours outside Orlando. He had designed it—put heart and soul into the forest green marble accents on a wraparound kitchen counter and fireplace mantel, the twenty-eight-foot-high beamed ceilings, the Olympic-sized swimming pool in a twenty-eight hundred square foot enclosure that also housed a hot tub and barbeque.

The house was everything he said it was. Huge. Gorgeous—but very occupant friendly. The three acres of "grounds" were immaculate. He walked her down to the dock that stretched out into the lake.

"Come with me." He opened the gate and led her up the four wooden steps. "When I'd travel I'd think of being back here—on this dock. I used to spend a lot of time out here when I was home. It's a great place to think or bird-watch or both. Helped me get through some problems over the years."

"It's beautiful. Where would you go to find the same serenity?" The calls of several birds echoed across the water. The marshland along the edge teemed with wildlife. Cattails and scrub brush rose up six feet or more some twenty feet out into the water.

"Nice thing is, it will never change. The lake can't be developed and no motor craft ever launched. Do you mind if we sit? Better yet, look at it from this perspective." He sat, then leaned back, lying flat, staring up at the sky. "Try it."

Shelly quickly stretched out beside him. The November air was comfortable—a perfect temperature of seventy-eight degrees with a cooling breeze that skimmed the lake. She had thrown on a black pullover and matching cardigan over jeans, and it'd been the right choice. More than once she'd caught an admiring glance.

The sound of lapping water underneath her was soothing. "I see what you mean. I love it here." She watched a very small cloud, an orphan, move across her view. Then several birds crisscrossed too high above her to identify.

"In a world of our own." He propped himself up on an elbow. "I wish we lived here. I wish I'd met you earlier in life. I hate to think of how our time together might be limited. No, not because of any immediate illness—yours or mine—but just the limitation of our ages. I want this to go on forever." He smiled. So did she.

"We have twenty years, I bet." Shelly offered.

"We should." He continued to gaze at the water. "So, tell me, could you live in Florida?"

I could live here, Shelly thought, but knew that was out of the question. The house belonged to the former wife, and she and the daughter would live in it until Elizabeth started college. And wasn't Shelly through with big houses? Meaningless, cavernous space for two people. But could she live in Florida? Both of them liked the ocean—walking the beach.

"Are you ducking the question?"

"No. That is, I don't want to duck it. I know this is home for you. It's just very different. Coming from the high, dry—it would be a shock to my system."

"Then we'll have to have two homes. Are you willing to hang onto the bungalow? Maybe rent it?"

"I'd hate to rent it. Jonathan might want to live in it, though. I'd miss Christmas in New Mexico; that would be the time of year that I'd want to go back."

"Arranged. I have no problem with that. We might have Elizabeth with us sometimes."

"That would be great. She'd enjoy the holidays there."

They were both quiet then. Shelly slipped her hand into his. She was at peace—certainly for the first time in a long time, maybe ever. He turned on his side and slipped a hand underneath her sweater.

"Isn't this a little public?"

"Look around you. The marsh is pretty good camouflage."

And it was. She turned toward him and lifted her head. "I think this place is tailor made for lovemaking." She closed her eyes and felt his lips meet hers. The kisses were rhythmic, teasing, long, and caressing. His cologne floated around her, carried on the breeze. Finally, she sat up and slipped off the cardigan and pullover, her bra, and jeans. He watched. There were no words and none needed. She propped up on one elbow to watch him undress, then, naked, they moved to lie full length, her breasts pushed into his chest, his leg between hers. It was clouding over and the breeze felt distinctly cool, but there was a fine mist of sweat across his shoulders. It was warm being held this way, snuggled against him, feeling his breath in her hair.

She reached down and slipped her hand around his hard-on and heard his quick intake of breath. Then, wiggling out of his grasp, she knelt between his legs and put her mouth over the head of his penis. Cupping his balls, she ran her tongue up the shaft and around the head, all the while listening for sounds that would assure her she was doing the right thing. She didn't have to wait.

A throaty, "Yes," was all the encouragement needed. When she knew he was close, he pulled her up beside him and, leaning over her, ran his tongue over one nipple, then the other, all the while exploring between her legs.

Had she ever wanted anyone so much? She let her body float on a tingling that escalated until she wanted to scream. She pulled him down on top of her, but he sat back and pushed to his knees to lean above her, placing her legs around his neck. Somewhere in this altered state, she was meeting his excitement with her own. And then, just as she was on the edge, he dropped to all fours and, with her legs around his waist, finished her by rocking forward and allowing her to pull against him. With a burst of acceleration, he rode with her to climax himself, leaning down to nuzzle and suck one nipple, then the other. He slumped across her and she turned her head to taste the sweat on his chest. He pushed to an elbow, cradled her face, and kissed her eyes, her nose, and her lips.

"Wow. Is that an OK word to use?"

She laughed. "As good as any."

"I never want you to leave. I want to hold you like this forever." She couldn't stop smiling and snuggled into him. The afternoon had slipped away, and it was easy to doze in the last of the sun's rays adrift on feelings of satiation. Her even breathing finally matched his.

The splatter of raindrops was a shock. Cold and stinging, they pelted their naked bodies. Laughing and scrambling upright, they hurriedly grabbed for clothing. How long had they slept? Dusk was an orange-pink smear that met the water in the distance. Suddenly the shower intensified; sheets of rain bounced against the wooden planking of the dock and spattered their ankles. No matter how fast they could dress, they were already drenched.

SUSAN SLATER

"Glad no one has a camera."

This after he'd put both legs in one leg opening of his shorts. They had to shout above the storm's intensity. "Just grab your clothes, don't worry about dressing. We can ride this one out in the hot tub." He grabbed her hand and ran.

Her teeth were chattering by the time she'd run the length of the dock and across the lawn to the screened-in pool area. He pulled the cover off the tub and turned it to full jet force.

"That'll get your circulation going. I'll throw our clothes in the dryer and grab a couple towels. More champagne? I could probably scare up a bottle."

"Will your neighbors report us for streaking?"

"Never have before."

"Oh? So this is normal Meyers activity?"

He was laughing. "Not that I know of—not on my part, at least. Be back in a sec."

She settled into the swirling water up to her neck and let the heat thaw stiffened limbs. The nap on the wooden dock reminded her that she just might not be thirty anymore. The rain had subsided somewhat but a fine, cool mist drifted through the screened panels to her back. The temperature opposites—mist on her face and her body in swirling heat—were invigorating. But it was the first sip of icy champagne that zapped her senses when it hit the roof of her mouth.

"And a chocolate for madam?" He held out a box of truffles dusted with cocoa powder, each circled in foil.

She laughed. "Just exactly what I don't need." But she took one. What was it about dark chocolate and champagne? They were made for each other.

"Why don't we spend the night here and take off for St. Augustine in the morning?"

They talked until two, with Shelly sitting cross-legged on the king-sized bed in the guest bedroom and Ron propped up against the headboard. He shared his plans for law school—an investment of four years that would serve them well for the rest of their lives. What did she want to do? Ah, there it was again, the dreaded "to do." But this time she had an answer.

"I want to be your wife if it's a full-time position."

He held out his hand and she crawled up to snuggle next to him. He tilted her chin back and looked into smiling eyes.

"Yeah, it's full time. And it just so happens there's a vacancy."

He kissed her, pulled her close, and held her. Then, mischievously, asked, "What if I burned every T- shirt you own and bought you lingerie?"

"I'd just buy more T-shirts."

"I was afraid of that. OK, let me ask differently . . . would you wear lingerie once in a while?"

"Yes."

"OK, it's a deal. Why do I like women who know their own minds?"

Shelly laughed but wondered if there had been a time, somewhat recently even, that she wouldn't have been quite so forthright. The Shelly of a short nine months ago didn't exist anymore. And she was comfortable in her new world.

A rain-kissed Florida morning, even in November, added a dose of mugginess to the brightness of a perfect day. Shelly slipped on a long-sleeved gauzy top and a clean pair of jeans. She brushed her hair straight back behind her ears and pulled the brim of a baseball cap down low. Gold bangle earrings and she was ready.

"Can I say something rather personal?"

"Of course."

"There's no way you're sixty. Shelly, I mean that. You have fantastic skin, no wrinkles—you really look terrific."

"You don't have to say that—you're going to get laid anyway."

"I better. But I mean it—you're beautiful. I'm the luckiest man alive."

"I love you."

The days in St. Augustine were idyllic. Great restaurants—there wasn't a wine on a list anywhere that he couldn't describe. They had Cuban food one evening and went back for lunch the next day just to have specialty sandwiches—ham and cheese on bread with a crispy brown crust but soft white insides.

Their room at the B&B was the top of a carriage house behind the main dwelling. Vibrant stained glass filled the loft openings to the outside where they used to pitchfork hay to the floor below. The proprietor set out a decent sherry and decanter of port every evening in the Victorian parlor. It was a perfect ending to their days.

They walked everywhere. Whether it was only to one of the neighborhood bars or the dining room of one of the area's elegant hotels, strolling hand in hand had its own element of romance. Even amid the press of tourists, the world was outside their consciousness. They made their own environment, always touching, a quick kiss now and then . . . .

But it was the beach and the long afternoons blending into evenings, watching the sun slip behind the edge of water, that held the most magic. Here the world was dunes and sea oats and a straggly grass groundcover that Shelly couldn't name. She collected shells, silly nondescript ones of dubious value to anyone but her. They would be reminders placed in her bathroom, maybe glued above the double sinks—a collage of sea memories. Ones to look at every single day and smell the salt air, feel the breeze that skips along the waterline, watch the frothy edging of the surf dissipate in the sand, often a truly ignoble ending to a mighty wave.

Late one evening—almost midnight—they built a fire in the sand and sat huddled until the fire caught and warmed them. Thanksgiving was just a week away, but it was difficult to think of turkey and all the trimmings with the surf pounding behind her. Every time the world tried to push back into her consciousness, she resisted. They made love, toes to the fire, struggling to get it right underneath a light blanket. Laughing when fighting with fabric overrode passion.

If she'd wanted to ease back into the real world, she wouldn't get that chance. A tearful Pam called at five a.m. Their mother had fallen and the doctors wanted to make certain that the "do not resuscitate" clause was still viable. They had described the situation as "touch and go." Inner cranial bleeding, possible concussion, several broken bones in the face. A distraught Pam begged her to reconsider. They couldn't kill their mother. She would have no one. With a little prying, it seemed that Lawrence had moved on, but not before he proved himself a falling-down drunk—an alcoholic who had, perhaps, totally missed the wagon as it pulled through, let alone fell off of it.

Shelly did a quick assessment of time. It was November twenty-first. She would leave in the morning and fly directly to Wichita. And, yes, she would take whatever time was needed to help. Shelly wasn't sure with what. Their mother was in the hands of the doctors. But soothing Pam was her first priority. At this point she wouldn't book a return flight into Albuquerque until she knew what was happening. If there was to be a funeral, then that would take time, and a holiday would slow down getting final paperwork done on the trust. It would be fun to have Thanksgiving dinner in the old homestead—Pam's new homestead. Two weeks wasn't out of the question. Could Pam pick her up? Shelly would call her with details once she secured a flight.

"What do you want to do your last twenty-four hours?"

"I bet you can guess." Ron had gotten up when Pam called and was making coffee in the tiny kitchen off the bedroom/sitting room.

"The ocean?"

"You're getting to know me."

"Another fire—"

"Less blanket this time. I think we're past needing a bundling board."

"But no less champagne?"

"That would be perfect."

She made plane reservations, called Pam, and left a message. Now the day was hers. She refused to let it become bittersweet. They would see each other soon. They hadn't solidified plans, but maybe would today. They had been sidestepping the issue of what next—who would go where and how soon.

Breakfast was on the main drag—blocks of shopping that even at eight in the morning attracted hordes of tourists. The breakfast burrito with packaged hot sauce was not the quality she was used to. Good Mexican food and margaritas were tough to duplicate. Funny, but she'd miss New Mexico's food—there'd be no breakfasts of eggs over easy, papas and frijoles, smothered in cheese, Christmas (red and green chili) with two homemade tortillas—no Garcia's Kitchen, that is. Was she getting cold feet? Trying to trump up reasons not to move to Florida? The step was a big one, but she'd never felt so certain about the person in her life. This was meant to be. And shouldn't she be willing to follow him anywhere? Hmmmm. Shades of the old Shelly—white chargers, happily ever after, glass slippers . . . rose-colored glasses.

They shopped. A designer rip-off bag for Patrice and one for her. A can of caramel corn made with maple syrup and toasted pecans for Jonathan shipped to his apartment. Two pieces of stained glass for the bungalow, again, shipped home. She'd have to tell Jonathan to expect them. The galleries were fun, with great art in a wide variety of pieces—glass, oils, watercolors, jewelry. Their tastes was not unlike. She might have given a bright floral oil higher points, but otherwise, they agreed.

"I'm going to drop you off at the room while I fill up the car. One less thing we'll need to do in the morning."

The B&B provided a beach basket and Shelly packed a bottle of champagne, some packaged nibbles from the room, and a thermos of iced coffee. She slipped a bathing suit on under shorts and tee and changed to sandals. The ubiquitous baseball cap and she was ready.

They stopped on the way to get two Cuban sandwiches to go and fill the ice chest at a convenience store.

"I found an old beach umbrella in the trunk. We're going to be in the lap of luxury today."

They found a spot to set up camp at the edge of the last row of dunes but not far from the water. Perfect.

"Hungry yet?"

"Not quite. Let's walk for awhile." Shelly was beginning to fight the sadness that comes from separation . . . and not knowing.

"As long as we're going for a walk, you might want to wear this." He reached in his pocket and pulled out a gold starfish about the size of a silver dollar, only this one had a 3/4 caret cabochon emerald in the center and 1/4 caret diamonds on each point. It was beautiful, and the chain was twisted gold elegance.

"Oh my God, it's exquisite. You didn't just get gas in the car. I remember seeing this pendant in the very first gallery we looked in."

"Yes. Local artist. I've always liked her work, but more than that it's a reminder of how much I love you, of our time together, of all this." His gesture took in the ocean and beach. "We'll never duplicate this. There will be wonderful times, but never with the freshness of a new beginning." He kissed her lightly on the lips.

"When will I see you again?"

"Let's talk about that." He slipped the chain and pendant around her neck and an arm around her waist. "Want to sit closer to the water? I'll bring the umbrella down."

She nodded and walked ahead to the water's edge, slipped off her sandals, and waded to ankle depth. The water was beautiful, calm and green, but cold. She sat down and dug her toes into damp sand. He set up the umbrella, then went back for the cooler. Finally, he stretched out beside her.

"I've been thinking. I really do have options for law school. I'm not tied to Florida. My daughter's here and that's an important reason to be close by, but you have a house and a couple sons. It would be easier for me to close down an apartment here and move to Albuquerque. I could fly back once a month for a weekend with Elizabeth. I definitely want to be with you for Christmas unless you've made plans. Janey is taking Elizabeth on a six-week holiday tour of Europe. I'm supposed to house-sit, but I can arrange for someone to do that. I thought we might like to tour California's wine country, spend some time in San Francisco. Depending on when school starts, we could celebrate the Chinese New Year in Chinatown."

"Yes, a thousand times yes to everything you've said, but what are the options for school?"

"I could apply to the University of New Mexico but start online until I can get in. I'll be spending Thanksgiving with Elizabeth and her mother but could be in Albuquerque by December fifteenth. I'll keep my apartment here until I know something for sure. My last day with Healthstar is December first. It should all fall into place."

"If UNM doesn't work out for whatever reason, what then?"

"Then, a school in Florida. But that's a ways off. If there's room for two in that bungalow, then that's my first choice."

The fact that he'd be with her in twenty-four days made parting bearable. Barely. He came inside the terminal with her while she checked her bags and then they got a cup of coffee. When she needed to get in line to go through security, he reluctantly dropped her hand but reminded her to just count the days. After this, they'd never be apart again. She couldn't shake the feeling of sadness and stood looking at the exit long after he'd gone. She had never felt so alone. And she knew dealing with Pam and her mother wouldn't brighten her mood. She still had an hour before takeoff. A newsstand was nearby, but the prominently displayed magazines hawking the mindless antics of underaged starlets couldn't break her mood. She was feeling a sadness far outweighing the situation. They would be together soon—less than a month. Why was she being so silly?

Pam was on time but looked like she hadn't slept. Their mother was in ICU and the prognosis was still "wait and see." Pam barely reached the outskirts of Wichita before she burst into tears. The last month had been terrible. Shelly assumed she was talking about Lawrence, not their mother. And she was sorry, but she'd gone ahead and checked Shelly into a motel. She just hadn't had time or money to fix up the second bedroom. Shelly quietly counted to ten. She should have gotten a car; well, she'd do it in the morning. She felt as exhausted as Pam sounded. They rode in silence most of the trip home.

It was decided that they'd go to the hospital in the morning. It was already eight in the evening—there would be nothing for them to do there now. They agreed that it would be best to check with the attending physician before seeing Nancy. Pam didn't seem interested in talking about her problems and Shelly didn't pry. And frankly, some alone time sounded good. She'd call Ron before going to bed and hopefully catch him at the apartment. She vaguely remembered that he had a meeting in Tampa but didn't remember when he said he'd go down. Pam helped her carry her bags into the room and then left after a quick hug.

Shelly turned her cell phone on to check messages and smiled at the first one.

"Hi Sweetie, I just wanted the first voice that you heard once you landed to be mine. Can't begin to tell you what the time together meant. It's a dream come true. So, hug your starfish and give me a call later. Love you, darlin'."

She'd walk across the street to Newell's and grab a late dinner. But the moment she stepped outside, she reconsidered. The November Kansas night was brisk. Clearly, Florida clothing missed the mark. She had jeans, running shoes, and two pullovers—one a turtleneck and the one with a matching cardigan. She went back inside and pulled on the turtleneck, socks, and running shoes.

She kicked herself, but ordered a slice of banana cream pie and coffee. It tasted as good as it looked in the glassed case. Maybe if she jogged back . . . . She was beginning to feel incredibly alone—isolated, even. Her world—either one of them—was hundreds of miles away. She needed to get on with her own life. Get closure on this one and move forward.

She didn't realize how tired she was until she called Ron and then couldn't stay awake long enough to talk more than thirty minutes. But how wonderful to know that she was wanted, that someone didn't want to live without her, missed her, and was counting the days until they could be together.

Snow! The gray dawn matched her mood. She remembered awakening when the heater came on around two a.m. and wondered then if the temperature had plummeted. She had a rental delivered to the motel but didn't relish driving in the freezing temperatures, slick roads, and low visibility. She flipped on the weather channel; supposedly, the white stuff would taper off by late morning. Hadn't she walked on the beach yesterday? It seemed like a lifetime away.

A quick call to Pam. Should Shelly pick her up? Or just meet at the hospital? Pam would prefer a ride but didn't mind waiting until the snow let up some. Shelly would call before she started over, but ten thirty would probably work. Calls to Jonathan and Patrice and a quick message left for Ron. She missed him and would call later to report on her day. He would be in meetings all morning but there was comfort in just hearing his voicemail message.

Pam had a heavy sweater she could borrow and could even loan her a down jacket if she preferred. Shelly knew the jacket would be snug and opted for the sweater. How cold could she get walking from the car to the hospital front door?

Very cold, she found out. The snow had stopped, but the temperature had dropped another ten degrees with a fifteen-degree wind chill. Kansas in winter. The accumulation of snow was just enough to totally obscure the parking lot stripes and gently drift into the corners of the electronic sliding doors so that a flurry of white escorted them into the lobby.

Dr. Sylvan had left a note at the information desk. Their mother would be in testing for most of the morning, but buzz her office when they got there and they should have a few minutes to talk.

"I'm putting her on my radar screen for hospice. I don't think we'll lose her in the next few days, but the next month or so will be telling. I simply want you to be prepared. She had stabilized for what was, perhaps, years, and now we're seeing a quick downward spiral not uncommon in Alzheimer's patients. Her speech has deteriorated and I doubt if she'll recognize either of you. I know this sounds brutal—it's a brutal disease. It's been a few months since you've seen her, hasn't it?" Dr. Sylvan turned as Shelly nodded. "I don't want the change to shock you."

A sniffling sound from Pam and Shelly realized she was crying. She reached out and took her sister's hand. Would Dr. Sylvan think it was odd that Shelly remained dry-eyed? Sorrow was not a blanket emotion that affected everyone the same way, and there had been just too many tears recently. Shelly felt drained.

"Do you know what the home plans to do about restraints?" Shelly had hoped her mother's fall had scared them into doing something. A little proactive thinking would have been nice and much easier on all concerned.

"I've ordered an electronic monitor—twenty-four hours. And they'll be putting her in a low bed with railings with a three-foot wide pad that encircles it. She may have to be confined to a wheelchair during the day. I think she's too confused to use a walker."

Quality of life or lack thereof came to mind. Shelly was finding these necessities heart wrenching. Would it have come to this so quickly if her parents had continued to live in their home? She quickly stopped that way of thinking. There had been no way that her father could have cared for her mother. They did the only thing possible.

"Can she have visitors?" This from a barely composed Pam.

"I'd like you to hold visits to ten minutes or less. I honestly don't know if she'll become agitated, but if she does, ring for a nurse."

Again, their mother was in a room by herself. The biggest difference that Shelly noticed was in her expression—there was none. Her mother looked at them absolutely blankly. No smile, no quizzical glance, and no greeting. The fall had ravaged her face—blood had pooled under the skin below her left eye, and the lid drooped to more than cover her eye halfway. A cut, its ragged edges taped together, ran from above her left ear to her chin in one unbroken semicircle. It didn't help that in removing the carcinoma, the surgeon had taken a tuck in one nostril, pulling the tip of her nose to the side. She and Pam agreed that there should be no plastic surgery—not at ninety-one, and not under the circumstances. Still, the result was bizarre. The focal point of her face was pointing toward her ear.

"Mom, how are you feeling?" Pam took Nancy's hand only to have her mother pull away.

"Would you like some juice?" Shelly picked up the straw lying next to a serving-sized carton and poked it into the indentation in the top of the small box. She held it out, but her mother only stared up at her—totally uncomprehending.

"Go to the bank now."

"What, Mother? I didn't catch what you said."

"Something about the bank," Pam offered.

But whatever was important about going to the bank would go unknown. There was simply nothing more. Her mother appeared to be in a stupor. Drugs? The concussion? Shelly caught Pam's attention and pointed toward the door. Pam nodded, kissed Nancy on the forehead, and followed Shelly out.

"I couldn't have stayed longer." Shelly knew she'd have a picture, perhaps her last, of her mother looking like she'd gone ten rounds before she lost the fight and became comatose.

"Me, either."

"I think I'll stay the week and make certain that there isn't a drastic change before I head back to Albuquerque. Is there anything I need to take care of before I go, anything you need?"

A sigh, then, "I've been thinking of moving back to Tulsa."

"Before Mom dies?"

"I've had an offer on the house and I'm considering accepting. Since Mom doesn't need the money, I'd use it to make a new start. My old boss called and offered me a half interest in the dress shop. I told him I'd take it."

Shelly was speechless. But, of course, this was the old Pam—her world on her time and someone else's money. No wonder she hadn't furnished the guest room. She had planned to leave. Shelly was quiet and knew Pam was watching her.

"It's been great to have you here when the folks needed someone."

"I'm glad I could help."

But apparently that was the end of it. Attention span of a sparrow. But Shelly suspected she knew one of the reasons—Pam simply could not see her mother die. She needed to distance herself. Pam had always been fragile, or had lived life making those around her believe it. And now that she thought about it, would Daddy's little girl have stayed around once Daddy was gone? Not likely. And what could she say? She wasn't able to come back, live at home in order to see her mother five to ten minutes a day—and watch her die. And if she were being fair, the Lawrence debacle was probably an embarrassment. Small towns never got bigger. Not in attitude, anyway.

"What's the offer on the house?" A sixty-five-year-old house in a small town with outdated wiring, a suspect roof . . . would Pam's cosmetic touches give them a decent price?

"One hundred fifty thousand."

"That's great! Much better than I would have thought. Have you said yes?"

"Tentatively. I wanted to discuss it with you first."

"I think you need to grab it."

"Oh, Shelly, I knew you'd understand. I just have to do this. My life is evaporating—there's not a lot of time left to do everything I want to do."

"What's the timeframe?"

"Lauren and Michael—you remember them, don't you? They're principal owners of the shop. Well, they've offered to fly up, rent a U-Haul, and drive me back to Tulsa. They are the sweetest people."

Pam always had good friends. Thank God, because she always seemed to need them. The kind that went the extra mile. Her life had never followed the axiom "The shortest distance between two points is a straight line."

"Great. How quickly are you doing this?"

"Actually, this weekend."

Pam must have been pretty certain that she wouldn't stand in her way, Shelly thought. She pushed words like conniving, cunning, and opportunist out of her mind.

"Sounds good."

Shelly was vaguely ticked. She wasn't going to hang around and get roped into packing; maybe she'd leave in the morning. One of the things Pam had supposedly done was pack up the house and put everything into storage—but if she hadn't, she'd be called upon to help sort. And there really wasn't anything that Shelly wanted. Whatever Pam didn't take, Shelly would deal with when they buried their mother. Another trip back and maybe soon.

Had she flown back this time to assure her younger sister that she wouldn't stand in her way? Probably. So much for Thanksgiving dinner with Pam in the newly renovated home place. The house that her father had built was soon going to be owned by someone else. Again, she begged off dinner and went back to the motel to pack and arrange a flight out.

CHAPTER TWENTY TWO

If Thanksgiving plan "A" was out of the question, what was the backup? Dinner at a hotel with Jonathan? But, of course, he'd made other plans—there were even hints of a girlfriend—and Brian didn't return her calls. Probably out of town and not checking voicemail. She must remember to get his new cell number. Both boys had assumed she'd still be in Kansas—so had she. The day dawned clear, if a bit nippy, perfect day for a fire, a hot toddy, and not getting out of sweats. Turkey with all the trimmings was looking more and more like a Marie Callender's potpie. Even Patrice was going home to family. Shelly had known this day would come, but she didn't think her first holiday without key players would mean she'd be totally alone.

But as Ron had said last night, this would be the last holiday they'd be separated. Ever. She smiled. He'd called that morning just to wish her a happy Thanksgiving, but she was in the shower. He said he'd call at ten p.m. her time—that gave him until midnight to eat, clean up afterwards, and chat with Janey's parents and brother. He wasn't looking forward to the perfunctory family stuff alone—he wanted her beside him. But soon, they'd be together. Eighteen days to be exact. He was moving a few things over from his apartment to prepare for the house-sitting, so not to worry if he was running late. He was looking forward to hearing her voice. She was his world. "His world." How comforting and what promise.

Should she have been surprised that Ed showed up? Probably not.

"Let's go to dinner. Your choice, but I hear the Hyatt downtown really puts on a spread." She stood in the door-way, then grabbed a sweater off a hook and stepped out, pulling the door closed behind her. He was not coming in the house.

"I've eaten."

"Come on, Shel. 'Tis the season to overeat—I bet you have room for some pumpkin pie."

What was this half-ass attempt at levity? The last time they had had any interaction was over two months ago, and he'd called her a slut and had been led away. She was on guard and stood with her hand on the doorknob.

"Shouldn't you be home with your family?"

"You're my family, Shel. My only family. I've been a fool."

"I'm not your family. You made a choice." She turned to go in.

"No, wait. Hear me out. Tiffany left me. You were right; we had the testing done and Jonathan is Marissa's father. I won't live with duplicity." He reached out to take her hand.

She pulled back. "Good-bye, Ed. We have nothing more to say to each other." Shelly pushed the door open behind her.

"No, wait. I want us to start over. Shel, I'm having the house fixed up—our house. We'll be happy there again."

"*We* don't exist anymore. There is no Dr. and Mrs. Sinclair. Go on with your life. I've gone on with mine."

"I can't live without you, Shel. You're everything to me."

"I can't help but feel this realization is coming a little late." With that, she turned, went inside, and locked the door behind her. She had no idea how long he'd stood on the porch. But she found herself straining to hear—footsteps, a tap at the window . . . breaking glass. She reached for the phone and dialed 911. No, she wasn't being threatened, per se . . . it was a feeling. There had been an incident about two months ago and he was forcibly taken from her house by two officers. No, she didn't have a restraining order. Yes, she'd get one. Yes, she'd stay inside and make certain all windows and doors were locked. She had put in an alarm. There was nothing that could be done—not until he made a move, threatened her in some way. Not very comforting, but wouldn't she be out of all this very soon?

The evening moved along at a snail's pace. She'd rented *The Piano* and *The English Patient* and watched them both. Two old favorites. Funny how Derek had chosen one of her favorites to share—without even knowing her.

Ten o'clock came and went. Moving must have hit some snags. She made a cup of coffee, then decided a dollop of Bushmills and whipped cream would be yummy. She stoked the fire, checked the clock—eleven on the dot—and sat down to read. It appeared that Ed had gone, but she wasn't quite ready to go to bed. How often did she really get a chance to enjoy a book?

The stillness of the room jerked her awake. The fire had gone out and a chill had settled around her. What time was it? She must have fallen asleep. She got up, carried the half-drunk glass of Irish coffee to the kitchen, and checked the clock. Three a.m. Should she be worried? Should she call him? He was probably so exhausted after the day of relatives and moving that he'd fallen asleep. No, he'd give her a call in the morning.

But he didn't. There was no call to wake her. She picked up her cell, checked for a voicemail, and dialed his cell. No answer. She tried the house. Janey and Elizabeth would be on their way to Miami to begin the holiday cruise-tour of Europe, but Ron should be there. Again, no answer. A couple months back he'd given her the number to his private cell—the one that linked him to Elizabeth and others who would always be able to get in touch if they needed to reach him. She rummaged in the nightstand drawer, but couldn't find the slip of paper. Had she left it in the office?

She slipped on sheepskin slippers and her robe, then padded to the computer. It was where she'd left it—pinned to her bulletin board. Could it already be eleven his time? She dialed and waited; no answer. Somewhere, alarm was beginning to surface. But why? She ran back over the past two days. She'd talked to him the day before Thanksgiving and he'd left a message yesterday morning saying he'd call last night. She knew he was moving . . . so, why worry? Because this was the very first day in almost four months that they hadn't talked. They had spoken every single day until now. If something wasn't wrong, then something was very different. Two people in love and planning a future wanted to talk every day—needed to, even.

Five o'clock meant early dusk. The darkness was bringing panic. A day had gone by—another day of not knowing. She tried his phone numbers hourly. Too much? She'd only left messages a few times. Where could he be? What could be going on? By eight o'clock she decided to call the Orlando and Tampa hospitals. Nothing. No Ron Meyers had been admitted.

She couldn't sleep. Every noise was magnified—was that a ring? She'd picked up the receiver at least four times to hear a dial tone. Patrice wasn't coming back until Sunday—surely all this would be over in two more days.

But Sunday came and she hadn't heard. She cried herself to sleep and cried herself awake. She checked the obituary notices online for Florida and found that a Ron Meyers had died in 1997 in Eustis. Wrong year, wrong place. Patrice called her in the afternoon.

"Everything points to something catastrophic—unless he just got cold feet."

"That would be catastrophic. No, we set plans in motion. A lifetime of plans."

"Doesn't mean that he couldn't change his mind."

"There was no indication of anything like that—any holding back. He was the one so certain early on that we'd spend our lives together."

"I don't want to say this to be hurtful, but is there any way that you could have been hoodwinked? Maybe led astray—led to believe that things were different than they really were?"

"I suppose. Anything's possible. But why? He took me to his house. It was exactly like he said it would be. It was obvious that his former wife and daughter lived there. They were real—he hadn't lied. He spent a lot of money on us in the ten days—the B&B, meals, wine, champagne. Nothing threw up a flag, nothing."

"Is there any possibility that he would have decided at the last minute to go on the cruise with his family? Maybe his daughter begged him to go and he was able to get an extra spot at the last minute. He could have thought it would be the last time he'd have with his daughter for awhile and he took advantage of the opportunity."

"That's interesting—maybe even in the realm of possibility—but why no call?"

"Maybe he thought he had left a message. I know nothing about ship-to-shore calls, but it isn't too far-fetched to assume that he tried. Or maybe he was reluctant to disappoint you and plans to call later."

"He would have e-mailed, at least. He wouldn't hurt me." But he was—already had. She absently fingered the starfish around her neck. A couple-thousand-dollar piece of jewelry—didn't that mean something?

"Oh, Shelly, I hate this. I'm so sorry this has turned out this way. I wish I had answers."

By the end of the following week, Shelly was numb. She had called the police, but was more or less dismissed. Just because someone hadn't called was no reason to suspect foul play. The moment Shelly inadvertently let it slip that she'd met Ron on the internet, she knew she'd lost credibility.

Should she go to Florida? Try to retrace his steps? Perhaps hire a private investigator? She still periodically checked hospitals. How could someone disappear without a trace? Had there been foul play? Had he really gotten cold feet? She couldn't believe the latter. No. This was a man who had sworn to love her, support her for the rest of their lives. She felt dizzy from lack of sleep and far too much coffee. She couldn't think straight. Surely there was a simple explanation—something right under her nose that she hadn't thought of. But the facts remained—it would soon be ten days since they had talked. He was supposed to be here in seven more.

She kept busy by getting a packet of information from UNM School of Law. Should she send it? But to where? She tried each of the three numbers once a day, sometimes crying so hard she couldn't leave a message. Interesting, the mailboxes attached to each line were never over limit. There had been several work-related calls when they were together. She couldn't be the only one calling. Was that a part of his particular phone service? They automatically dumped into a holding box. Or was someone taking the messages off each day? That thought chilled her—that he would be listening to her and not returning the calls. Could he be someone who got his jollies from promising the moon, only to jilt the intended? She hadn't heard of it before, but why couldn't he set up women, promise to marry them, get their hopes up, and then simply disappear? She was certain that stranger things had happened—stranger people existed with far stranger fetishes.

She finished her Christmas shopping. It had been three weeks. She stopped wearing the starfish and did not buy him a gift. But could not stop thinking of him every waking minute. She cleaned out the garage, telling herself that it needed to be done, but knew that in case, just in case, he did show up tomorrow, there would be space to get his car off the street.

She half-convinced herself that he would come. He could want to surprise her. Something had happened, but then he'd come to his senses, realized how much he loved her, and would rush to her side. She purchased shrimp and steaks and busied herself with shopping and menus. Then she shopped for new sheets and comforter—black silk sheets were decadent, but perfect. And chocolates—A box of Godiva dark nougat and two bottles of champagne, Louis Roederer Brut Premier. She finished off the afternoon by buying fresh flowers—every room of the bungalow looked spring-like and inviting. She completed the garage by dragging two bulging, heavy-duty garbage bags to the curb. There, done. Room for a Lincoln.

And she waited. Garage cleaning was a wasted effort if she had really thought he'd be there. She hung around, cell phone never out of reach, but it was just one more frustrating day. By nine o'clock she was exhausted from anticipation. And crying. How could he just blow off their date to begin a life together? The holidays loomed bleak and unrelenting in their forced cheerfulness jingling back at her from TV screen and radio. Maybe, he would come for Christmas . . . but, maybe, she had to stop thinking that way. Stop the torture of every ring of the phone making her heart skip a beat. She had to look beyond, gather herself up and start . . . again. Hadn't she learned that she could be alone—stand on her own two feet?

Resolve. She wished it came in pill form. But at whatever cost, she needed to "swallow" it, maintain it, and go on. Jonathan was spending the holidays with friends back East. Brian and Rachel were in Baja. Patrice offered to change her plans, but Shelly insisted she see her family and gave her a ride to the airport. Christmas in one more day.

She called the nursing home and asked that a nurse hold the phone to her mother's ear. Shelly's wishes of a Merry Christmas were met with silence. The nurse, however, assured her that her mother had stabilized and had not fought the restraints, in fact was doing rather well in them. "Well" was relative, Shelly thought. She planned to fly back out the end of January.

But in the meantime it was Christmas Eve. Shelly idly thought of stocking up on potpies . . . one for Christmas and one for New Year's. Instead, she ordered dinner from a local restaurant and started a fire. A New Mexico Christmas always meant tamales and posole and biscochitos for dessert. She made coffee and flavored it with cinnamon. Could broiled grouper have ever replaced this? She thought not.

Funny, but she no longer panicked if she forgot her cell. She wasn't tethered. But she couldn't swallow hard enough or throw up long enough to dislodge the leaden weight at her core. Something precious, a gift not given before, had been squashed and left to rot. How would she ever purge herself of that? But she still cared. Still knew there was an explanation—something plausible. She periodically checked hospitals, but finally ruled out a catastrophic accident or death. And the phone messages continued to be deleted—they never overflowed even when she left twenty plus just to see what would happen.

He was playing games. Slowly, anger and love and wanting and needing and worry blended together. A volatile mix. What would her reaction be if he called now—some five weeks since they'd been together? Just what would she accept as reason enough for the pain? Unless the former wife and daughter prolonged their trip, they should be back by the first week of the new year. And then she would know. Definitive answers were ten days away. But was she ready? Hadn't she passed on hiring a PI simply because she didn't want to look stupid if the PI or she found Ron in bed with someone else? Yes. A few months of phone conversations and a few days together did not add up to knowing someone—the kind of knowing where you'd bet your life on what he would or would not do. So, she waited. Not patiently and not without tears. What if the wife didn't know who she was? Wouldn't give her information? Guess she'd deal with that when it happened.

She went online and ordered the Miami, Orlando, and Tampa papers—and combed through them every day. Nothing. Vanished without a trace. How could that happen? How could she have misread the situation? But had she? Maybe she had wanted so badly for something to be true that she hadn't made allowances for something as simple as his changing his mind. Starting a new life was not for the faint of heart. There were money issues—something they hadn't really talked about. She had more of the stuff—would that have been a problem? In the calmness of retrospect, without being blinded by love, there would have been problems. Maybe ones that drove him away.

She talked to Pam on Christmas Day. Their mother continued to mend, but there was no difference in her cognitive skills. Pam planned a trip back up to spend a few days the week after New Year's. She had bought a charming cottage in Tulsa and was busy fixing it up—it was perfect for her; everyone said it looked just like her. The same old Pam. But Shelly thought she seemed happy again. "Again" being the key word here, and Shelly vowed silently not to ever let her life become so dependent as to lean on someone else for happiness—need someone else to define her existence. In fact, in all the searching for, the longing for the white charger and that perfect rider, hadn't she learned it was up to her, with two feet on the ground, to be stronger and much better prepared to meet whatever would be thrown her way? Alone or together. Hadn't she learned to be a survivor? But why was there constant testing? She could do without that.

New Year's Eve was no less painful. A night when she had fully expected to be curled up on the couch with someone toasting a new, exciting life instead was filled with tears and sadness. She went to bed early. She was simply sleepwalking through her life, one day at a time. She couldn't become interested in anything; good books were put aside unread. She knew her life couldn't continue this way, but wasn't certain what it would take to shake her out of the stupor. Of course, if she were to hear . . . .

And then one morning, the "you've got mail" ding from the computer shattered the silence. She put down her cup of coffee. She was sitting at the dining room table watching snow swirl across the new deck. How did she know? She just did—she had felt it coming. The message waiting for her in the next room was from Ron. Any cocoon of safety around her unraveled in a nanosecond to expose her core. The beating of her heart told her of the danger. But she couldn't keep hope from flooding through her very being, enveloping her.

CHAPTER TWENTY THREE

My darling Shelly—

I'm a coward—I'm sure you're calling me far worse. But I couldn't face hearing your voice or seeing you once again. If I had, I'd never be able to do what I have to do. I never set out to hurt you but you'll find that hard to believe. I want you to know I didn't lie. I believed the things I said to you. I thought it was time to search for a mate—that I needed a mate—wanted someone to complete my life. You were that person. I fell in love with you—wanted you at all cost. I couldn't believe my good fortune. But, in reality, that cost turned out to be too high.

I shared my good fortune of finding you with my daughter and she was devastated. She equated our loving one another as a denial of my love for her. She felt the distancing that I was, no doubt, doing since I met you. You rocked my foundation but I'm fifty-eight, not eighteen. I have responsibilities. I cannot shirk them. My daughter needs me now and will need me for some time to come. I cannot establish our life at a possible cost of depriving my daughter's needs both physical and monetary.

Don't begrudge me my sense of duty. I have a strong sense of right from wrong. I could never start a life with you under a shadow. I could never start a life with you and end up hating my hastiness, my dereliction of duty, which would eventually cheat you of all you deserve. I can't think of a time in my life I've made promises that I couldn't keep. Nor a time when I've intentionally hurt my daughter.

Janey and Elizabeth both asked me to go on the cruise with them. It would be a time of celebration of family. I saw how necessary it was to get away; side-step the intensity of us so that I could think straight and make the right decisions. In the face of losing me, Janey has begged me to reconsider my relationship with her. She would like us to complete the job (Elizabeth) we started and make a home for our child. I agree with her. I was hasty in walking away two years ago. I would not have seen this if I hadn't faced a chance at a new life with you.

Now that you've had some time to put things into perspective, I know you'll understand my sacrifice. I love you, Shelly. There's a part of me that always will. Do I wish that I'd never found you? Sometimes. Only because I'm acutely aware of the enormity of my loss. But 'tis better to have loved and lost than never to have loved at all.' Ha. There's one for the English major!

I know you. You will move on. You will find what you are looking for—what you deserve. Believe me when I say that in all the conflicting emotions on my part, I want that for you.

And what will you learn from this? You will know that you are beautiful, you defy age, what you have to offer is not readily found—at any stage in life. It is still valid, still precious and will be treasured by the right person. Years mean nothing. You will know that if you so choose to find a mate— that companion, lover, husband that now you think you need.

But examine that need—if it is still borne out of habit,

out of expectation, out of a false sense of things made easier—
move on, invest in you and draw upon all that strength that
makes you, you. If you find that other person and can honestly
say to yourself that he will enrich you, open your eyes to the
world—let him move into your heart accepting and melding
his strength with yours—then enjoy! Let me quote Shelly
Sinclair, "It was meant to be." Always, always a friend in
absentia—Ron

She moved the cursor to Delete but let it pause there
and didn't click. How self-righteous. Unfeeling. Pompous.
Where in all that diatribe did her feelings come into play?
When had she been consulted? If most relationships were
60/40 then this one was one hundred to zip. Was the
whole idea of dating a ruse to get Janey back? Consciously
or unconsciously? She'd never know. She was "his world."
How could he have said all those things? Asked her to
marry him and not be man enough to pick up a phone
when "duty called" to tell her—immediately, to her face—
that he'd changed his mind. Had gotten cold feet. Felt it
best to renew his past commitment. As her mother would
say, "Isn't it always better the devil you know?"

Was she angry? Pissed that he really hadn't said he
was sorry for the pain, the lie of not answering the phone?
Were the tears for love lost or feeling taken? Disgusted
was more like it. Wasted emotion, wasted time. Maybe
he'd waited this long to contact her because he knew she'd
already be getting over him—letting the anger and disgust
override any feelings. How could she have so wanted to be
Cinderella? Again.

But wasn't there more than a little disgust with
herself? What had being sixty really changed? The search
for the golden penis—did it go on forever? Was she simply
programmed to want a companion? This mate that would
make her life complete? Yeah, she probably was. Wasn't

it in the human DNA? And didn't those with mates live longer? If you didn't go to hell first for being boy-crazy. And there didn't seem to be an age limit on that.

But this was it. No more online, no more living, sleeping, eating with a cell phone next to her. No more searching, wondering, "Was this it? Could he be the one? The prince?" In all likelihood, sans armor and horse . . . wouldn't it be nice to just not care about ear hair? Finally, resolution: A man would not define her life. At least, a new mantra.

She forwarded the e-mail to Patrice. Always good to get a second opinion.

"I think you dodged another bullet." Patrice had suggested meeting at Zinc's for lunch—hoping a Brie tart would cheer her up, no doubt.

"I've lost faith in my judgment."

"I don't think you have to go that far. Obviously, there are some duds out there."

"And every one of them has my name."

"But there are good men, too. It's a numbers game— eventually you hit the jackpot."

"No. I've thought this through. The search ends now—no more online, no more dating. At least, for a while. I'm going to finish the massage therapy license— take the test and maybe hang a shingle. One of the girls from class called. She's taken a job with a cruise line and wants me to interview, too."

"Couldn't that be construed as running away?"

"I don't think so. It'd be a nice breather. Certainly new scenery."

"As long as you're sure."

"Stephanie called. Ed put the house on the market. At a fire-sale price. She wondered if I wanted to pick it up . . . make some money on it." Shelly signaled the waitress for another breadbasket.

"And?"

"Absolutely no way. I don't even want to go near it. But before someone snaps it up, I would like some of the bulbs and iris that I've planted over the years. Remember all those along the drive? Lots of award-winners that might not be appreciated by a new owner. I wonder if I could just go and dig a few up?"

"I wouldn't see why not. Thinning wouldn't hurt. Take Derek with you. He'd be glad to help."

January had rushed by in a blur of cramming and putting in extra time at the clinic. Even beautifying the bungalow was put on hold. The license was now in sight. She passed the exam the second week of February and decided against working the high seas but accepted an offer to join one of her instructors in her clinic. It felt right. A year or two of experience and then plenty of time to be adventuresome. And be around when she lost her mother. An overnight visit home had made that apparent—she was going to lose her; there was not a lot of time left. Her mother had no speech and little comprehension of what went on around her. She slept eighteen out of twenty-four hours each day. This visit Shelly had sat quietly with her mother and said her good-byes. Yet another ending.

And there had been no dating. She'd canceled every online service. She hadn't heard from Ron and didn't expect to. She didn't think she could handle a "but let's be friends, anyway" kind of proposal. Let bygones be bygones. Now, she just smiled when she heard echoes of her mother.

Surprisingly, there had been no word from Ed. The house was under contract and if Shelly wanted those bulbs she needed to get a move on. She had asked Stephanie to let Paul Green know that she would be "thinning" the bulbs in the two garden strips along the driveway. He could let Ed know or not, she didn't care. Saturday was looking like a good day to get it done.

And then on a whim, she called Derek. Yes, he'd enjoy helping. One o'clock? He might be running late—he'd been standing in for one of his men whose wife had just had a baby—and probably couldn't get away before three. That would be fine. She gave him directions. She knew it would take longer than that to dig up everything she wanted. And she'd be labeling as well as dividing. At least the weather was warm for late February. Early spring warmth that coaxed trees to blossom before zapping them with a killer frost in March. Just typical New Mexico.

Saturday morning she rounded up everything she'd need. But couldn't find the rake. Hopefully, Derek would bring one. She wanted to leave the area if not manicured, at least neat and trim. Putting a shovel in the BMW made her instantly wish for the station wagon back—or Patrice's SUV. But she wrapped plastic bags around sharp edges and put hand tools in the trunk. She had boxes and already-labeled storage bags. She might try to force some of her hyacinths. So they would go in the fridge. And she could only hope the crocus hadn't already come up.

She found herself humming. It would feel good to work in the ground again. And she promised that this spring, her garden at the bungalow would be even better. Make her home a showplace. Derek would be a great help. She'd already decided on where she'd like two more trees. Fruit trees, but away from the deck. She'd ask him. It was fun to share planting with someone. There was a native plant symposium on Thursday at the Garden Center— maybe he'd like to go.

She dressed in layers, knowing by two o'clock she'd be down to shirtsleeves and was even tempted to put the Beemer's top down. Maybe on the way home. It was so easy to succumb to spring fever. And there was such a feeling of promise. She'd be sixty-one next month—what a difference a year had made. She reveled in a feeling of strength and independence. Hadn't she proved that she could handle just about anything? The lessons had not been learned without pain. But she had no regrets.

She parked in the driveway. No reason to stay in the street with the house empty. She unpacked the car and carried all the tools to the flowerbed, then lined up her labeled bags. She hadn't been thinking. Probably there was still a rake in the garage unless Ed had moved everything out. It would be easier to get the mulch off the beds if she had one.

She walked back to the Beemer and got the garage door opener out of the glove box; Jonathan had asked her to give it to Stephanie. She was glad now that she'd forgotten. It worked smoothly; the code hadn't been changed. And, no, Ed hadn't moved anything. Box upon box leaned against the sides and back of the garage . . . still. A plethora of garden implements was clustered next to the kitchen door, including two rakes. The propane grill—that hadn't been used in years—was pushed against them. Three mini-blinds in forest green mixed in—from when they redecorated Brian's room? That had been twelve years ago, at least. Junk. Everywhere junk. Born of a man who couldn't throw anything away. Two oversized stalls and only one place to park a car. And then she caught her breath.

There was a truck in the one empty stall—a black pickup. Oklahoma plates. And if it was the truck she thought it might be, there was no mud to obscure the license this time. She ignored the voice in her head urging her to get out, go back to the car, and call the police. No, she needed to be certain—beyond a doubt. She was tired of being told there was nothing that could be done unless she knew—knew for a fact that there was a dent on the passenger-side bumper.

She turned sideways and inched back against boxes, toward the front of the truck, and leaned down. There it was. A nasty gash still lined with metallic silver—no mistake where that had come from.

"Satisfied?"

A scream escaped her and she banged her head on the side mirror, jerking upright. She started to inch backwards but the whir of the garage door being lowered stopped her. Trapped. Think and stay calm. Talk to him.

"I didn't know you owned a truck, Ed. Where's the station wagon?"

"Tiffany has the wagon; the truck belongs to her brother. He needed a place to store it when he went home."

"The truck used to try and kill me? He needed a place to hide it."

"That's a little melodramatic. I'm sure he only meant to scare you. A shame you weren't driving."

Had she heard correctly? Just a scare? A shame intent was thwarted? She looked closely at the man in front of her. Ed could always look scruffy on weekends—chores before a shower and shave—but now he looked derelict. Soiled T-shirt, what looked to be food stains on his sweat-pants, and at least a week's growth of beard. Always a first hint of depression when personal hygiene is ignored.

"I can't believe you would do such a thing."

"I didn't. Tiffany put him up to it. She's more than a little upset about how you've handled things—just blurted out the question of Marissa's paternity in front of everyone at the viewing. Knowing that it would be a shock for me. For her. She thinks you planned it to break us up."

"And totaling a seventy-thousand-dollar car was vindication?"

"You know, an eye for an eye—"

"It didn't dawn on the two of you that a little honesty could have prevented an awful lot of pain? For an awful lot of people?"

Ed shrugged. "She's a fighter. Can't help but admire that. And there was some question about which of us really was the father. She didn't actually lie."

"She was boffing the two of you at the same time?"

"How crude, Shelly. There might have been some bit of overlap before she chose to establish her life with an older man."

"Overlap? Your son refused to marry her. That seemed to help her make a decision. At least your son did the right thing and supported his baby."

"That's what he's told you. I'm under the impression that that didn't really happen. Oh, a token buck here and there, but nothing that would come close to 'support.'"

"I've seen the receipts. Your son was meticulous with record keeping." A bit of a lie, but she knew Jonathan—if he said he'd supported Marissa, then he had.

"Anything can be fabricated."

"Even a marriage."

"It wouldn't have happened if you'd been more aware. More into my needs. You seemed to give up on building a life together—continuing to build."

"That's a cop out. The only way it wouldn't have happened is if I could have turned the clock back thirty years. I could not have met your need for youth. But, perhaps, you couldn't help it. Frontal lobe changes in older men can have disastrous results." Too much of a dig? A little bit of a low blow, but she wasn't taking on blame for the situation. It was not her fault.

"What do you mean by that?"

"I think it's safer to blame your straying on something chemical than my inattention to your needs."

"Of course, you would say that."

"All right. I'd like to hear how you were attentive to my needs. In fact, in the last five years, what were my needs? What did I want? Was I happy? Did I enjoy our lovemaking? Our travels? Just how tuned in were you?"

"This is ridiculous."

"No, it's not. I'm tired of the finger-pointing. We're two people who lost touch. Stopped loving one another. Stopped being interested in the other's needs. In hindsight you're right, I'm as much to blame. I needed to go on with my life—try new things, new challenges. I needed to grow, Ed, in ways that the marriage didn't let me. I just didn't know it."

"That is just so much bullshit. You needed to be my wife—and act like it."

"Well, this isn't getting the bulbs dug." Shelly reached in her pocket for the garage door opener.

"I'll take that. This should have been turned over to Stephanie." Ed twisted the opener roughly from her hand.

"Open the door, Ed. I'm walking out of here. You have no right to stop me."

"I don't think you're going anywhere."

"And why not?"

"We need to talk."

"What have we been doing? At least attempting. What's left to say?"

"I have to make you see—"

"I 'see' fine. Ed, this is about making choices. I've said this before. You chose to dissolve our marriage and start a new life. You need to accept any consequences of that decision and move on, and I need to thank you."

"I need to get even." Was the voice a little petulant?

"Get even? With whom? I don't understand, Ed."

"You did not have the right to ruin my life."

"I did not ruin your life."

"You made me the laughingstock. Told all our friends what a fool I had been. Cuckolded by my own son. But then, you always pandered to him. He could do anything and you'd excuse him. Nothing was too good for Jonathan."

"I have seen very few of our former friends in the last year. No one that I would share intimate details of my life with. As far as the boys go, I don't think either one of us showed favoritism when they were growing up."

"Jonathan hardly speaks to me."

"It takes two, Ed. Have you called him? Asked to get together for a talk?"

"He wouldn't listen."

"You don't know that."

The sobbing startled her. Suddenly Ed slumped against the front of the truck, struggling for breath between wracking sobs.

"I've ruined everything. Lost everything I ever cared about. This isn't the way I'd planned it."

"Life can be surprising. There are no guarantees. Just ask me; I think I've become an expert."

"Callous bitch. Get in the house. You first."

He stood facing her, then motioned her ahead of him with the gun in his hand. A gun. She felt her hands go ice cold.

"What's the gun for, Ed?"

"To be honest? I don't really know."

"Then leave it here."

"No. I can't do that. I'm glad to see it makes you nervous. Makes you pay attention, doesn't it?" His laugh sounded absolutely crazed. If she'd wondered about his mental stability before, her questions were answered now.

"I don't want to be harmed and I don't want you to harm yourself."

"Oh, you don't, do you? You're not the one holding the gun—do I have to remind you of that? I think decision-making is pretty much on my side."

"I don't see what this is going to gain you."

"Everything, Shelly, and then again, maybe nothing."

He wasn't making sense. But keep him talking. What else could she do? It was still two hours before Derek would show up. Not that she wanted to involve someone else in this debacle—still, it would offer a diversion. How else could she get the gun? Could she even get it if he were off guard? Think. What do they tell you to do in these situations? Run? Fight?

"I can see those wheels turning, Shel. Thinking how to get out of this mess?"

"Thinking how I could get you the help you need."

"Oh, so now I need help?"

"You've said so yourself in so many words. You think you've ruined your life—"

"I think *you* ruined my life."

This wasn't going anywhere—they were beginning to talk in a circle. She walked up the three steps to the utility room and pushed the door open. The room was empty.

"Looks like you've sold some things."

"Actually, Tiffany needed a washer/dryer."

"Generous of you." Shelly stepped into the kitchen. "Ah, and the kitchen appliances, too." She walked to the sink and then turned to survey the room. "Just what is she going to do with a Wolf range? Two Wolf ranges?"

"Stop being so condescending. She has as much right to nice things as you do."

"I was thinking more in terms of dragging them around. Not easy things to move."

The sound of the doorbell shocked them both. Then someone trying the latch, the door opening, steps in the hall. "Shelly? Are you in here? I was able to get away early."

"Derek, don't come—." But he could not have heard her above the deafening explosion of the 9mm. She hadn't seen Ed put the barrel in his mouth, but when she turned, the fragments of flesh and brains and bone literally covered the pantry door. Quivered there, some particles slipping down the paneling to pool on the floor. And Ed, the back of his head gone, slumped against the edge of the island.

"No, no, no, no, no." She couldn't stop screaming. Even when strong arms enveloped her and turned her away. Made her stop looking.

"Shelly, look at me. You're all right. I want you to sit here while I call the police. Can I get you a glass of water?"

She must have said yes because now she had a tumbler of cold water in her hand to press against her forehead. How had this happened? Was this an ending that she could even have imagined? So final. So desperately final.

CHAPTER TWENTY FOUR

The funeral was Friday. It wasn't written down anywhere, but Brian was adamant—Ed wanted an in-ground burial with a service at graveside. Cremation had not been addressed. That had always been their plan—urns in the mausoleum with appropriate plaques. Shelly wasn't certain when Ed had changed his mind, but she didn't care. He would be buried to the right of his mother. Together for eternity. Mame would be pleased.

The day was gray and overcast and chilly—threatening rain at any moment. The black sheath with crocheted bolero wasn't really warm enough when the sun wasn't out. And her feet ached. She was reminded how seldom she wore nylons anymore, or heels. Not part of the usual dress of a massage therapist.

There had been a viewing the evening before, but Shelly didn't attend. She just wasn't up to the solicitous pats and hugs from well-meaning friends who were there more out of curiosity than anything else—to see how the family was reacting. Rumors were probably already circulating about who was and wasn't in the will. She was still numb, still trying to figure out if she'd seen the signs—no, the signs were there; she just didn't believe them. But could she have been able to change anything? Something she'd always wonder. But as for the viewing, she stayed home and indulged in a couple glasses of wine instead.

Pam called. No, she wouldn't be able to get away for the funeral. She was recovering from a slight operation. No, no, nothing serious . . . more reconstructive, but nonetheless uncomfortable. Shelly idly wondered what a "slight" operation entailed. But it was sweet of her to call. Pam was well—back on her feet, in her words. No, she hadn't been able to get away to see their mother, but soon. She'd stay in touch.

Brian and Rachel were handling the arrangements. Shelly's interaction with the two of them had been brief to the point of being curt. She and Jonathan were being totally excluded. Was she being blamed because she had not been willing to "try" again? Had been more interested in establishing a life of her own? And Jonathan? Did Brian know the true story of Marissa? It would seem so. Brian almost seemed relieved to be severing ties with his family. Would time heal wounds? She wasn't counting on it.

Shelly had thought that Tiffany and Marissa might have come to the service, but they were conspicuously absent. She wasn't the only one who glanced up every time a car pulled to the curb. There were over two hundred people—hoping to see some spectacle of family strife played out in front of an audience? Yeah. She idly wondered if the Tiffany and Marissa story had gotten outside the boundaries of family. According to Ed it had.

The *Albuquerque Journal* had quoted an unnamed source as saying the doctor had been despondent over the dissolution of his thirty-year marriage—thirty-five, Shelly automatically corrected—and a failed attempt at reconciliation. Did that point a tiny finger of blame at her? Probably. But people would read in what they wanted. She couldn't stop them. It sounded like Ed's propaganda shared with a supposed friend had turned into one of those spotlight seeking, "I don't want my name used, but . . ." situations. It was as good an explanation as any—wounded ego, depression, aging didn't offer acceptable reasons.

She tried not to squirm. It would feel so good to slip out of her heels and just stand stocking-footed on the bare earth. Cold as it was. Instead, she slipped an arm through Jonathan's and smiled. She wished she could lighten his mood. He was struggling with the enormity of his father's actions. Perhaps, time would be the best healer. She gave her attention to the minister extolling Ed's virtues. And then it was over—words spoken by several colleagues and Brian, a soloist sang two songs accompanied by a string quartet protected by a tarp that had been quickly erected, and the casket was lowered into the ground. Rachel stepped forward and threw two single long-stemmed flowers on top. Orchids? Roses? Shelly couldn't see what they were; it seemed more theatrical than sentimental. Brian dabbed his eyes and studiously ignored his mother and brother.

Those hoping to offer their sympathies to the family had to cross to opposite sides of the plot to do so. The women from the office were kind and she felt their condolences heartfelt. Paul Green's comments seemed perfunctory and forced, and the others just became a blur, her murmured "thank yous" all but lost as people hurried past after a moment's squeeze of her hand or an "air hug," not even beginning to embrace her but going through some ritual dance, bowing and nodding like large birds in shades of gray and black. Only Patrice truly hugged her and promised to call later.

And Derek. She'd looked up to see this really handsome man in a black jacket, black turtleneck, and gray slacks walking toward her. Wow. Had he always been this good looking, or hadn't she been paying attention?

"You look great."

"I clean up pretty good." He laughed and easily slipped an arm around her shoulders. "Hey, you're freezing. Here, wear this to the car." He slipped his jacket around her. "I'm assuming you're free to go?"

"The sooner, the better." A quick kiss for Jonathan. No, she wouldn't be needing a ride, but she'd call later.

"Where are we going?"

"Wherever you'd like. I was thinking drinks and dinner?"

"Sounds perfect."

He chose a Thai restaurant in the heart of downtown—one that Shelly didn't even know existed. She instantly loved the décor, a wonderful blend of Eastern and Western. But the aroma of simmering curry was an exotic perfume. She knew exactly what she would order—Punjab beef and soup, the one with coconut milk and mushrooms. Suddenly she was ravenous.

They were seated by the window overlooking Gold Avenue—a great place for people watching. And they both indulged, without speaking—just watching shoppers rush by, hugging coats, holding hats or scarves snugly on heads. The restaurant was warm and the hot tea that Derek ordered was relaxing. Was anything quite as good as a cup of hot tea to make the world right?

He lifted his cup and held it out. "A toast."

She followed suit and waited.

"To new horizons."

"I'll drink to that."

"You know, Shelly, I think you need a diversion."

"I agree, as long as it has an accent."

She got the chuckle she wanted and liked the warmth of his eyes. Why was it when you weren't looking, opportunities could pop up right in front of you?

DEDICATION

I dedicate this book to:

Murr—For being my "mom on call" for those times I've needed a relative with Real class!

Bron and the Boys—Mothers and grandmothers don't always come in cookie-cutter exact, off-the-shelf, perfect packages. Life is nothing if not a learning experience. Believe me, there was nothing in the fine print to guide me.

Robert—Tough, but you just can't choose your family. I'd change the players—all but you. You're a keeper.

Patrice—This one's for you. Here's your moment of immortality.

Newton, KS—Thanks for the memories.

Husbands, lovers . . . near misses—Remember, "this book is a work of fiction. Names, characters, places, and incidents are products of the author's imagination or are used fictitiously. Any resemblance to actual events or locales or persons, living or dead, is entirely coincidental." Yeah, right.

Air Park Crew—The Diva loves you one and all . . . even Terry.